OVERNIGHT SENSATION

RICHARD TYLER JORDAN

OLIVERHEBERBOOKS

Published by Oliver-Heber Books

Please note: This title was previously published as Tricks of the Trade

0 9 8 7 6 5 4 3 2 1

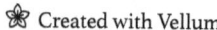 Created with Vellum

For David
(Again. Always.)

"Hollywood. They take your soul, give you indigestion, ruin everything you ever create, and what do you get? Nothing but a lousy fortune."

—Academy-winning screenwriter Frances Marion

1

"Warning: She's in a mood. Her Prozac suppositories have gone rogue," hissed Mitch Wood, personal assistant to the executive VP of publicity and resident tyrant of Sterling Studios.

Mitch, who fancied himself the love child of Oscar Wilde and Joan Rivers, was giving copywriter Bart Caine a red flag and cast a sympathetic look before sending him into the lion's den. Bart's palms began to sweat. With a deep breath and a middle-finger salute to Mitch, he steeled himself for the confrontation that awaited just beyond his boss's door. He felt like he was entering the Coliseum, but instead of battling lions and gladiators, he would be facing the most ferocious beast of all—Stephanie Hough.

Stephanie Hough was the kind of person who would make even Satan himself take a step back and say, "Damn, girl, you're cold." She was a walking, talking caricature of a Hollywood executive—all sharp edges—and was often compared to a snake in a power suit slithering her way through the cutthroat world of motion pictures with a forked tongue and a heart made of ice. Her office was a perfect representation of her soul too—cold and sterile. It had been designed to make people feel like they were being punished for some unknown sin. It was where joy went to die a slow and painful death and seemed less like a movie studio executive's place of business and more like a post-apocalyptic bunker: polished concrete floor, exposed infrastructure and air ducts and a wet bar. An enormous flat-screen television played classic Hollywood movies nonstop, which seemed to be the only thing Stephanie cared more about than crushing her underlings.

As Bart gingerly took a seat on one of the two Barcelona chairs facing Stephanie's glass-top desk, he tried to pretend that he was oblivious to his boss's phone conversation. But that was impossible. "Fuck you, Hutton," Stephanie whispered playfully into the mic of her telephone wireless headset like a Bond villain plotting world domination, and simultaneously shot Bart a withering look. Bart supposed that Stephanie could actually be a cyborg sent from the future to make his life a living hell. After all, she had the dead eyes of a T-1000.

With all the confidence of a Chihuahua in the presence of a Rottweiler, Bart sat in silence, clutching the pages of a press release he'd written (and rewritten three times). If he didn't get Stephanie's approval this time, he didn't know what the hell he was going to do. The press release announced a new romantic comedy that Sterling Studios would be shooting with Hutton Brawley, the studio's biggest star, to whom Stephanie was at this very moment speaking.

Like all hyperbolic Hollywood press releases that issue from the studios' spin zones, Bart's work was like a cheap wig at a drag show—fake, flashy, and completely over the top. He knew his writing had less integrity than a politician's promise, and even the monkeys in the LA Zoo could probably do his job as well. But hey, he was working at a prestigious film studio, and that counted for a lot.

The new film had an all-star cast, including the infamous British actress Mare Dickerson, also known as *Nightmare* Dickerson. Mare had made a name for herself playing busty virgins in period costume dramas. But things had taken a turn for the worse when she let slip in an interview that she was sleeping with the author of *The French Sickroom*, a best-selling novel that made *Fifty Shades of Grey* look like a children's book. The movie adaptation had been a flop, and Mare's career went down the toilet faster than a penguin on an ice slide. Now she was trying to make a comeback, by ditching the indie flicks about anorexic prostitutes and hoping for a role that wouldn't require her to take her clothes off—for once.

For Bart, working for Sterling Studios was like being trapped in a never-ending episode of *The Traitors*—exhausting, frustrating, and with little hope of winning the grand prize. He had bigger dreams than just being a cog in the Hollywood machine. He was a closet novelist, which was like being a unicorn in a petting zoo—no one believed you existed until they saw the proof. Unlike his friends and colleagues, who had more screenplays than brain cells, Bart was a prose purist. He dreamed of the day when he became the next Jackie Collins and could tell his boss to shove it. As he waited for Stephanie's attention, Bart nervously scanned his latest draft, praying that God would strike him with lightning if he found a typo or a misplaced modifier.

Draft Number 3

<u>*FOR IMMEDIATE RELEASE*</u>

Legendary Academy Award®-winning director/writer/actor Hutton Brawley and BAFTA-nominated Mare Dickerson are set to star in Sterling Studios' new romantic comedy *I'm No Angel*, directed by Gus Girard from an original screenplay by Lowell

Pierce and Rachel Gladstone, it was announced today (insert date), by Stephanie Hough, executive vice president of marketing at Sterling Studios. Brawley will also serve as producer. The film, scheduled for summer release, will shoot on locations in Manhattan and London.

In this modern-day folk tale, comedy and chaos collide when handsome Jarred Lange (Brawley), a quirky New York publishing executive, refuses a court order to surrender his beloved Central Park West penthouse apartment to his ex-wife, Erin (Dickerson), and their six ethnically diverse adopted children. Complications arise after Erin decides to take revenge and hires legal eagle Max Skylar (Terrance Lamb) to arbitrate. However, Erin's less-than-virtuous past catches up with her and plays havoc with her battle for control of the multimillion-dollar residence—and the couple's sublimated, yet undeniable, love.

Blah, blah, blah.

Somehow, Stephanie's complete lack of self-awareness made her think she was a genius. She was like a toddler playing with a calculator—sure, she was pressing buttons, but she had no idea what the hell she was doing. Her secret talent was making snap decisions. Unfortunately, those decisions were usually as inappropriate as wearing a bikini to a funeral. It was like watching a train wreck in slow motion, except the train was Stephanie's career, and the wreckage was everyone else's sanity.

Case in point: the time when a group of animal rights activists picketed outside Sterling Studios because Stephanie had been caught on camera kicking a stray dog in Beverly Hills Park. When questioned by reporters, Stephanie shrugged it off, saying, "It was just a dumb animal. Who cares?" Her callousness earned her the nickname "Stephanie the Tinseltown Tyrant" among animal lovers, and her reputation as a heartless monster only grew from there.

Any sane person would have apologized and promised to court her better angel. But not Stephanie Hough. Oh no. She doubled down. Stephanie's response to the animal cruelty accusations was just as callous. Instead of expressing remorse, she blamed the dog for being in the wrong place at the wrong time. "It's not my fault that the stupid thing didn't get out of my way fast enough," she said with a shrug, as if the pain of an innocent creature meant nothing to her. But Stephanie was an equal opportunity offender. She didn't discriminate based on race, gender, or sexual orientation—she offended everyone equally. It was like she was trying to set a world record for being the most hated person at Sterling Studios... and in Hollywood.

Stephanie Hough's reputation for being a sneaky little weasel was almost as legendary as her bad taste in pantsuits. One time, she secretly recorded a meeting with a hot-headed producer of brainless action movies. The meeting quickly turned into a verbal sparring match, with the beady-eyed producer blaming Stephanie and the marketing team for his latest bomb of a movie starring Jake Hunter. According to sources, the producer had threatened to "shove that marketing plan up your (bleep) and light it on fire."

But Stephanie was always one step ahead. After the meeting, she sent the audio to Valerie Langston at the *Hollywood Reporter*. And boy, did Valerie deliver. Her article was like a heat-seeking missile aimed directly at the producer's ego, and it was all thanks to Stephanie's secret voice memo. She proved that in Hollywood, sometimes the best weapon is a willingness to stoop lower than a limbo champion.

Stephanie Hough's sneaky, backstabbing ways might have made her a pariah in most social circles, but in the cutthroat world of Hollywood, it was practically a job requirement. And no one understood this better than Cy Lupiano, the buck-toothed Napoleon who ran the feature film division at Sterling

Studios. Cy loved Stephanie's no-holds-barred approach to wooing and coddling talent. He saw her as a kindred spirit, a fellow sociopath with a taste for blood and a talent for making A-listers cry. Stephanie had a real talent for reducing even the biggest stars to quivering, cross-eyed messes. One minute, Keanu Reeves would be the cool, collected action hero, and the next minute, he'd be hyperventilating and wondering how he could have ever signed on to work with this crazy lady.

But Stephanie didn't care. She had a distorted sense of self-value that was based entirely on how many people she could verbally eviscerate. And when a movie flopped at the box office, she was quick to throw it back in the face of the stars who dared to question her marketing abilities. "If you'd made a better movie, maybe people would have actually wanted to see it," she'd snark, her tongue sharper than a sushi knife.

In short, Stephanie was a force to be reckoned with. And if you crossed her, you'd better watch out. Because she had the power to make your life a living hell, and she wasn't afraid to use it.

Now, as Stephanie continued her phone conversation—which consisted of a lot of nonverbal sounds and low-decibel snorts—she leaned back in her black leather executive desk chair and pretended to ignore Bart, the cornered mouse cowering before a ravenous cat. Her phone conversation was all grunts and snorts, like a caveman trying to communicate with a smart phone.

Of course, there were rumors around Hollywood that Stephanie was more than just a powerful executive—she was also a powerful seductress. Everyone knew she was sleeping with Hutton Brawley. And if the gossip was to be believed, she was also busy with the agency's chairman. Her life was like a soap opera, only with fewer evil twins and more backstabbing.

Now, looking at her wristwatch and tittering in a confidential tone into the telephone, Stephanie leaned forward and snapped her fingers at Bart with an impatient "gimmie, gimmie, and make it quick" gesture to hand over the press release for her review and approval.

For a moment, Stephanie divided her attention between listening to Hutton and reading the press release. Then she raised her green eyes to Bart with a look of exasperation, picked up a black Sharpie marker, and scrawled *NO!* in large, bold, block letters across the page. She tore the papers in two and flipped them back across her desk. "Hold a sec," she said to Hutton.

Stephanie glared at Bart like a lioness about to pounce on a wounded antelope. "'Sublimate'? Seriously? Do you think our audience is a bunch of Ivy League professors? This is a press release about rom-com, not a damn dissertation on postmodernism! If you can't write in layman's terms, I'll find someone who can. And there are plenty!"

Bart, looking shattered, tried to maintain his composure. "I just thought adding a little intellectual flavor might elevate the press release."

But Stephanie wasn't having it. She leaned in closer, her eyes blazing with frustration. "Intellectual flavor? Bart, you're no Shakespeare."

"This is the third rewrite, Stephanie. I need a little more guidance," Bart pleaded. "What am I saying or not saying here that you want changed? I need feedback."

"Feedback? How about this: make it less shitty! I don't have all day to hold your hand."

Outside Stephanie's office door, Mitch couldn't help eavesdropping and loudly chuckling at Bart's response. Stephanie picked up a half-full plastic bottle of Evian water from her desk and threw it out the door at her assistant, where it crashed and then bounced off the framed poster for *Double Indemnity,* starring Barbara Stanwyck, which was Stephanie's favorite old movie and star.

"Don't get smart with me, you skinny-assed shit!" Stephanie sniped. "No! Not *you*, Hutton, for Christ's sake!

"The stuff you write around here stinks on ice," she continued ranting at Bart. "That's gotta change, mister. I'm warning you. You owe me, and the studio, your undivided attention."

"I'm doing the best I can, I promise."

"I advise you not to tangle with me, mister.

"No. Not *you*, Hutton! Outta here, you little cocksucker. I want that press release!"

As Bart exited to the outer office, he shot a look of misery at Mitch, who, in solidarity, pretended to choke himself in a silent scream. Mitch then grabbed a nearby stress ball and chucked it into Stephanie's office. "Oops, missed the trash can." He shrugged.

Sotto voce, Bart said to Mitch, "How can her throat stand the strain of all that screaming?"

"Let's just say her tonsils get lubed regularly." Mitch smirked.

"All I want is enough 'fuck you' money to jam those damned suppositories up her fat behind before I leave this dump," Bart said, while close to tears.

Mitch, who, like Bart, did not suffer fools easily (and was known to scream as loudly at Stephanie as Stephanie screamed at him), said he'd happily help with the suppositories but that they'd be packed with plutonium. Mitch, in his own way, was a very sweet-natured man. His life was devoted to planning his weekends at clothing-optional resorts in Palm Springs and luring Federal Express delivery guys into the supply room for coffee-break blowjobs. He smiled at Bart, batting his thick eyelashes. "You need a man to take your mind off your crappy job. That always works for me."

"Are you auditioning to be my intimacy coordinator?" Bart joked. "Anyway, I don't have the time for dating. Plus, I'm a hopeless romantic. I can't do quickies the way you do. I'll just have to settle for being Jamie Dornan's stalker."

Affecting a Yiddish accent, Mitch said, "I think I've got a guy for you! I know you're not his usual type—you being an *Anglo*—but he does know Jamie Dornan. He needs a new companion, and you're just slightly butch enough to maybe pull it off. You have no objections to dating someone rich and who used to be famous, do you?" Mitch cajoled.

"Oh, please! Not an actor!"

"Not anymore. See today's *Variety*? Hint: His initials are Peter Jacks."

"*The Grass Is Always Greener* Peter Jacks? It's all over the news, his sex video, I mean. Brian, over in Research, gave me a copy last week! My grandmother practically peed her pants when I played it for her. She loved it!" Bart thought for a moment. "Peter's too scary. Plus, isn't he straight or bi?" he asked.

"Gender fluid is the new socially responsible term, sweetums. I just think that you need to get out and consort with a different crowd. Whatever you're doing now doesn't seem to be working."

Bart made a face that suggested he actually agreed with Mitch, sad thought that may be.

"Truth be told, he does prefer men," Mitch conceded. "*Young* men. Young *Hispanic* men. Young Hispanic men who spend all their free time in the *gym*. Young—"

"I get it." Bart put an end to Mitch's commentary on Peter Jacks's sexual preferences. "How do you even know Peter?"

"I play in a very *wide* circle, my dear."

"Why don't *you* date him?" Bart pressed.

Mitch smiled coyly. "Who says I haven't? But you know me. 'I Never Do Anything Twice' is my theme song."

2

To be an *old* star in Hollywood, all you have to do is *not* appear in a feature film, sitcom, or made-for-streaming movie for a couple of seasons. The public quickly forgets.

Peter Jacks was about to be an old star. At age forty-five.

Five years ago, his hit TV show, *The Grass Is Always Greener,* premiered and made an overnight star of the stand-up comic from Washita County, Oklahoma. On Peter's weekly program, which was an instant hit, he played a goofball high school science teacher with a perky wife and two Neanderthal preteen sons. The lovable but ancient Sally Sunshine had been thrown into the cast as the kindly grandmother to the boys, and to give the show an air of geriatric dignity, elevating it slightly above typical sitcom fare of *Setup. Joke. Setup. Joke. Setup. Joke.* The canned laugh track didn't seem to irritate the millions who immediately made the show #1.

This massive success had happened after only a couple of weeks appearing onstage at the Comedy Cure on Sunset Boulevard. Peter had been "discovered," and he was suddenly thrust to the top of the "Hollywood Hot Heap." During the very first season of *The Grass is Always Greener*, Peter won a People's Choice Award for Favorite New Male Star and an Emmy as Best Actor in a Comedy or Variety Series.

Peter liked being famous. But once the television tabloid show *Totally Hollywood* got hold of the skeleton in what Peter thought was a hermetically sealed closet, the Middle America audience who loved him on prime-time Sunday evenings, loathed him this Monday morning, as bold headlines in the entertainment sections of newspapers across the country all proclaimed variations on: Ass Is Grass for Green Star!

Peter's television persona was that of the virile, all-American male, complete with beer gut, nose hair, on-screen farting, and promoting NRA gun-ownership ideology. In actual fact, he was a hick from Oklahoma who happened to have a comedy gimmick that endeared him to all but the most inflexible PBS-watching demographics.

His now-revealed secret? Peter Jacks, the kindly *Father Knows Best* for the twenty-first century, had a propensity for kinky sex. Strip his clothes off, lash him to a St. Andrew's Cross in the wine cellar turned dungeon of his Hollywood Hills mansion, and he was a happy camper. Peter also liked to digitally capture all the action for posterity on an elaborate video monitoring system. Which was a really stupid idea. Peter was so naive he didn't believe the tabloid media kept sex workers on retainer to ferret out just this sort of dish for their scandalous headlines. Thus, when "a source close to the star" leaked one of Peter's self-made videos, the habitually nervous network suits and sponsors of *The Grass Is Always Greener* couldn't keep a straight face. But they also knew they couldn't keep Peter on the air. They used the morals clause in his contract to get him off the show. It was only a matter of time before the tape went viral, like a Kardashian sex tape. And it did.

The video that had been stolen from Peter's home showcased a particularly innovative scene of sadomasochism. But the amateur lighting was so poor, it was hard to say for sure that the person having all the fun was actually the beloved television star caught like an idiot on *Stupid Human Tricks*. Only his distinctive voice as he begged for mercy from the excruciating ecstasy of electrical jolts provided by a posse of thugs was left undistorted. Although Peter's publicist tried to claim it was a forgery, the video made the rounds at every party in Hollywood, thus sealing his fate.

If only Peter had been videoed begging for electrical prods from a wife or girlfriend, he could possibly have pulled a Hugh Grant. Late night chat show hosts would have leaped to book him as the opening guest, and Peter could have acted sheepish and apologetic and laughed at himself amid all the jokes. Heterosexual America would have adored him more for being a *man*.

But then there was the country's puritanical God Squad of hypocritical evangelicals who were the self-appointed arbiters of the world's morals, many of whom had invited Peter into their living rooms and laughed at his silly on-camera muggings. They were no longer laughing. Peter instantly became the new poster child for the virulent disease known as *Hollywood*. The public at large couldn't risk subjecting their innocent, gun-toting children to the possibility of subliminal masochistic messages encoded in the program's weekly scenarios.

Peter's weekly comedy routines would have been misconstrued. Test tubes in his character's school laboratory would have been interpreted as phallic images. Locker-room and shower-room jokes and what weekly guest stars did and said would all appear to have sexual connotations. If the script called for him to change a fuse while puttering around the house on a weekend, audiences would have squealed uncomfortably as they imagined Peter's delight at being the recipient of something high voltage.

So middle-aged Peter Jacks was washed up in show business, without any marketable, real-world work skills. He wasn't even bright enough to earn a real estate agent license, which many a failed actor in town got as a backup job.

Still, he was determined to make a comeback. Whatever he had to do and whomever he had to use to achieve his aim was fair play. "As God is my witness!" he said, imagining himself as a starving Scarlett O'Hara holding a rotting sweet potato. But making a comeback in Hollywood is much more difficult than starting out. Ask Kevin Spacey. Today the talent bookers for late night TV want only the hottest stars from the latest blockbuster movies or television shows. Peter Jacks feared that his name was soon to be merely a footnote in *The Comprehensive Guide to TV Throughout the Ages.* He would be all but forgotten, like Dana Plato from *Diff'rent Strokes,* who'd had to get a job in a Las Vegas dry-cleaning store before eventually OD'ing herself completely off the planet.

In the meantime, Lydia, the beard in Peter's life—the woman he'd palmed off as his "spousal unit"—wasn't above filing for palimony, which she had been secretly planning ever since the first season of *Grass* when *People* magazine profiled the couple in a Valentine's week issue entitled "Happy Hollywood Honeys."

The grass was getting browner by the minute.

∼

"Holy Christ!" shouted Michael Stone, Peter Jacks's agent at Actors and Others Agency, as he grabbed *Daily Variety* from his assistant, Troy Everett, who'd just brought in the trades and rags bearing the news of Peter's excommunication from his own hit show. "Why didn't I know about this before?" he screamed at

Troy, who was merely the messenger. "I'm his goddamn agent, for Christ's sake! Why do I have to read this in the papers! Nobody tells me anything!" he ranted.

"They're telling you now," Troy said.

"Ah! Scratch the surface of any actor and you'll find an actress." Michael swacked the paper with a backhand. Michael looked up at Troy. "That just came to me. 'Scratch the surface...' It's pretty good. Is it original or a famous line?"

"Got me," Troy said. "Although it sounds like Dorothy Parker. Or Oscar Wilde." Troy knew his boss was basically an idiot who had probably never heard of Dorothy Parker and more than likely thought Oscar Wilde was a hot dog. *I think that you're an Oscar Wilde weenie*, Troy sang to himself to the tune of an old Oscar Mayer TV commercial.

"Find out if that's a real quote," Michael ordered. "I want it to be attributed to me. It's a good line, don't you think? Don't just stand there looking at me, for Christ's sake!"

Troy nodded, winked, and walked away. He knew his boss was a wuss. No amount of screaming and bitching could ruffle Troy, who saw through Michael the way that Haley Joel Osment saw dead people.

Michael Stone was not an Actors and Others Agency hotshot power player, although he desperately wanted to be one. He had thought that with Peter in his stable (like common barnyard animals, actors are often referred to as being in a *stable*), he was on his way to full acceptance. He had discovered Peter at the Comedy Cure in LA. After a couple of blows of coke and a long night of convincing Peter to sign a contract for personal representation, Michael had hooked him. And within days of Peter signing his agency contract, from out of the blue NBC dropped the no-name comic into a pilot called *The Grass Is Always Greener*. The show went to series, replacing the low-rated comedy *Mrs. C. and the Chimpanzee,* and it became an instant hit.

Now, this dreary Monday morning, faster than a zap from a cattle prod, Michael and Peter were both in *career interruptus*. Michael's client roster was mostly a disaster: old has-beens who couldn't get a job regardless of their once famous celebrity names. Now the milk from his only cash cow, Peter Jacks, had dried up—literally overnight.

Michael, seated behind his desk, swiveled his chair around to face the tall smoked-glass windows overlooking the murky, leaden January skies above Beverly Hills. "Am I to be agent to the Fossil Freaks my entire career?" he cried to himself. "Peter, you son of a bitch! I'm extremely disappointed in you. You've fallen into the same stinking cesspool as my other clients. Is it me? Am I a jinx?"

Michael could barely get his other so-called stars a little work here and there. Mostly they just appeared once a year in guest appearances on sitcoms or starring in productions of the ubiquitous *Love Letters* on the condo circuit in Florida. Their income was barely enough to keep up their SAG/AFTRA health-insurance premiums. But the older they all got, the more demanding they became, insisting on such contractual impera-tives as a box around their names in print ads and in *Playbills* or last-place billing preceded by AND ALSO STARRING... It wasn't hard to see that the less important one's name was in Hollywood, the more crucial it was to amplify the appearance of status.

Suddenly paranoid about his own career and future, Michael was certain the entire town either didn't know his name or knew who he was but laughed behind his back about his shabby client list. If it weren't for his assistant, Troy, Michael wouldn't even be able to get a table at the Ivy. As a matter of fact, he could only get a table at the Ivy *because* of Troy, who was movie-star handsome and had dated most of the servers at the Robertson Boulevard restaurant. Michael justified the situation matter-of-factly. "With a name like Troy, you just automatically get laid, like a Tito or Trampus or Tristan. Not much he can do about it." Michael hated his too-bright son-of-a-bitch assistant because everything came easily to Troy. That's what good looks and half a brain will get you in Hollywood—everything.

Troy Everett was an up-and-coming player himself. In fact, unbeknownst to Michael, Troy's ambitions were coming to fruition faster than his well-planned long-game timeline. He was a mere several paces away from overtaking Michael's career.

All of Michael's clients adored Troy. More often than not, they preferred to deal with him because he was always better able to answer their pathetic insecure questions about pilot season or a show that they'd heard was going into production and how right they thought they'd be for this or that role. Troy could appease them, usually by getting them invited to premieres or at least preview screenings of soon-to-be-released films. Without exception, each of them encouraged him to seek an agent's position of his own, if not with Actors and Others, then elsewhere. And they all promised to follow him if he ever decided to jump Michael Stone's sinking ship. However, Troy had his eyes only on new and exciting talent. Once he left Michael and Actors and Others, he planned to leave the old farts behind for the coroner's office to eventually collect in zippered body bags.

Tossing *Daily Variety* aside, Michael picked up the morning edition of the *LA Times*. A blind cryptic item in the Calendar section of the paper jumped out of a column: "As the gophers continue to burrow under the 'green grass' of this star, we have it on good authority that his top-secret tell-all will dig deeper, grave-size holes in the careers of Hollywood's hottest!"

Michael's blood was already boiling, but now he was at serious risk for a massive stroke. He gnashed his teeth, guessing right away that the news item referred to Peter Jacks. *I haven't agented any goddamned book deal! What the hell is Peter trying to pull on me?* Michael seethed. *Fifteen percent of a big book advance was what?* Michael couldn't do the math, but he knew it was a serious chunk of change. After five seasons on a top-rated show, the small-fry comic from Nowhere, Oklahoma, was almost as big a star as Jerry Seinfeld had been in his heyday, and Jerry got ridiculous multimillion-zillion dollar advances for his books. Five million dollars wasn't an impossible sum to consider for Peter, especially now, what with the gossip-hungry world craving every bit of dish about his personal life.

Michael barked at Troy to get his now-professionally-destroyed client on the phone. "Oh, how Hollywood loves to see the mighty tumble," he groused as he crumpled the newspaper and once again yelled at Troy to get Peter on the phone, even as Peter's cell phone was ringing.

Michael's voice oozed comfort and caring as he put on his wireless headset and greeted Peter. "My poor cookie," the agent purred. "What a pity about that damned video getting out. And the show. And all that money! And the lawsuit filed by the mother of that sixteen-year-old from Pacoima. Oops, you hadn't heard? Check out today's *Times*, second-to-last paragraph. Happy to send a PDF. What'ya say I pick up something from House of Siam to nosh and bring it over. It'll cheer you up. We've got to make some career plans, cookie, baby. 'Bout an hour? Terrif!"

Before hanging up the phone (without so much as a good-bye), Michael snarled at Troy, "Get Panda Express to deliver a bunch of stuff here, pronto. When it arrives, put the food into something decent. No leaky cardboard containers in my Bimmer! Then bring the car up from the garage. Oh, and throw in a handful of scripts that I've rejected, too."

Peter Jacks wasn't thrilled to receive Michael's call. They hadn't spoken since Peter threatened to leave the agency a few weeks previously for another agent—anyone who might truly care about jump-starting his feature-film career. Michael had calmed Peter down, then promised him a special sex worker as a re-signing bonus, and that he'd work extra hard at getting Spielberg or the Coen brothers, A-list directors, and producers for sure, for his "favorite cookie."

This had appeased Peter for about a week. Now, he thought, perhaps Michael was coming to the house to officially drop him from the agency. And perhaps Michael had deciphered the coded item in the *LA Times* about the clandestine book deal. "How do these things get out?" Peter groused to himself, trying to remember whom he might have mentioned the book project to while he was drunk. Then Peter decided to try to view this from a different angle. Perhaps Michael actually had some career-enhancing guidance to impart—a film deal maybe. He sang, then whistled, an impersonation of Eric Idle being crucified in *The Life of Brian* but still always looking on the bright side of life. But he knew that there was an agenda to this unusual meeting, because Michael never paid house calls—except to catered parties.

Peter was anxious about all the possibilities of Michael's calling on him. He decided he'd better shower, shave, and put on his cleanest pair of Calvins. The younger and more appealing he looked, the better he felt. He looked around his vast mansion and sighed. Soon he would have to downsize, now that the big paycheck from *The Grass Is Always Greener* would no longer be rolling in. Nor would the large sums from his Ford truck endorsements. Even the lucrative Japanese commercials might be history. Everything seemed in limbo—a state Peter loathed because he had no control over it.

Off Mulholland Drive, between Laurel Canyon and Wrightwood—not the most prestigious location in town but better than most—Peter Jacks's six-bedroom estate was nestled atop a long, steep, cobblestone driveway, hidden behind an electric gate and surrounded by tall pines and palms. The pool, which was only steps away from the back door, was clean but needed resurfacing. Because of the profusion of pine trees, very little sunlight ever got through, so the pool was seldom used and gave lie to the urban myth, perpetuated by porn videos, that all pool boys in Los Angeles are blond calendar models—tanned, muscular, and impatient to strip and service their clients. Peter thought he must have been living in a parallel universe, as was evidenced by his own pool boy. Or pool *grandfather*, as in this case.

The old man came once a week and did meticulous work. However, Peter had only to answer an ad on *Eros*, a website he regularly visited, and his Slovenian "full service" pool boy (or pool girl depending on his mood) would be in the cabaña and out of a swimsuit in a flash. Different pool boys (and girls) showed up, but none of them so much as dipped their skimmer into the water. It was doubtful they even understood the correct pH level for the water. At five times the expense of the pool grandfather, the *Eros* escorts would probably have to be downsized, too.

By the time Michael Stone arrived at Peter's mansion, the master of the house had showered, dressed, and was stirring his third martini of the day. Michael would later recall that the man who answered the door when the bell chimed the theme song of *The Grass Is Always Greener,* didn't seem to be a man who was a pariah in Hollywood and the hot topic on *The View*. Peter had a bemused smirk on his face when he greeted his agent, and consciously reached into his tight jeans to adjust himself.

"Laughing on the outside, crying on the inside, are we, cookie, baby?" Michael chirped.

"We?" Peter hated the nickname "cookie."

"We're a team. We've both gotta be strong. But first a little sweet and sour pork," he said, waltzing into the vast kitchen carrying a plastic bag containing takeaway tubs of chow mein, fried rice, beef with broccoli, and egg rolls. Peter could see he'd been lied to about where the food would be procured. The entrees were obviously not from the trendy House of Siam, but he kept silent. He really wasn't in the mood for eating, anyway. It was too late for lunch and too early for dinner. However, another martini would be filling enough, so he prepared himself one. He didn't offer a drink to Michael.

As Michael put food on a plate, he asked rhetorically, "What happened to Hugh Grant when he was arrested for participating in lewd conduct with a prostitute? How 'bout Eddie Murphy mixing it up with a transexual prostitute?"

"Where are you going with this?" Peter asked.

Michael, balancing a plate and chopsticks in one hand and a stack of scripts in the other, continued babbling as he moved out of the kitchen and toward the library/den. "And what happened to Rob Lowe when he was videotaped screwing a possible minor? And Michael Jackson when he was caught having sleep-overs at Neverland Ranch with little white boys?" Michael stopped short. "Scratch that one. It's not a good example. Anyway, what I'm getting at," he continued, "is Hugh's still in films. Rob got *The West Wing*, and he's still around. With the right strategy, you'll be back on the tube—or even the big screen —in no time."

Peter whined, "I want to work in movies. I want Hugh Jackman's career." His speech was beginning to slur. "I want a fucking Oscar. Just one. Is that too much to ask from this fucking town? If someone like Nic Cage can get one... Haven't I paid my dues? I came from nowhere, and look where I am now."

"Nowhere again, cookie," Michael said with a wink.

"Do I have to prove that I'm a *fucking* survivor before I get the *fucking* recognition I deserve? Is that the *fucking* lesson I'm to learn from all this crap?"

Michael looked around the vast library, his eyes drawn to Peter's two Emmy Awards perched on either side of the fireplace mantel under pink spotlights. "My friend, 'fucking' is what got you into this mess in the first place. Unless you clean up your act —and your language, for Christ's sake—and do things my way, not only will there never be an Oscar, but you'll also be hawking those Emmys on eBay!"

Peter began to cry.

Oblivious to Peter's pain, and envious of Peter living in this gorgeous mansion, Michael took a seat in a wing-back chair opposite the fireplace. "Here's what I want you to do. First of all, read these scripts. They're all tentative projects that require packaging. But don't read 'em with the idea of playing the lead. I'm going to have to reintroduce you first in supporting roles."

"Supporting…"

"Don't argue with me about this, Peter," Michael insisted. "All the best shows have supporting characters who make the stars look better than they are. Just look at Ruth and Wyatt on *Ozark*. Or Susie Myerson on *Mrs. Maisel*. I think you'll be especially good in this one. It's a feature film."

Michael tossed him a copy of a script called *Blind as a Bat*. "My assistant likens it to Mr. Magoo, only the star character is a near-sighted former Wall Street executive who is now reduced to being the super of a building on a run-down street in New York. The role Troy says would be good for you is the new gay tenant who is trying to gentrify the neighborhood."

"Gay?" Peter was aghast.

"Let me finish. Everybody knows that *real* men, *straight* actors that is, play gay better than gays. But the public doesn't know that there really aren't any *straight*"—he used his fingers to indicate quotation marks—"actors in Hollywood. Scratch the surface of any actor and you'll find an actress," he repeated the line that had come to him earlier in the day. "Audiences think that *straight*"—again with the air quotation marks—"actors are comfortable enough with their own sexuality that they haven't got a problem playing gay. No offense. It's all Scientology... or sociology. I get those two confused."

Peter sobbed again. "Scientology, my ass! If I joined up with that church, I'd be better taken care of than I am with you. Just look at what they've done for Tom and John and Juliette, and who knows how many others."

As Michael finished his plate of orange chicken, he offered some traditional agent-client wisdom: "Trust me." Then he added, "So what's your fortune?"

"You know I spend everything." Peter sighed. "And now Lydia wants to sue me for palimony."

"No. Your fortune cookie. But here's a twist. Whatever it says, you have to add 'in bed' to the end."

Peter, in a gin stupor, didn't quite follow as he held a Panda Express fortune cookie in his hand.

"Here," Michael said as he crumbled his cookie and demonstrated what he wanted Peter to do. "Oh, mine's a goody. 'Luck will visit you on the next full moon... *in bed*.' Ha! Now you try it."

Peter cracked open his cookie and munched on part of it. He took out the small slip of paper with red printing. Through double vision he read: "'Don't judge by appearances and good luck will come to meet you...'"

"*In bed*." Michael completed the sentence.

Peter looked askance at Michael. Even halfway to being drunk, Peter could see he had a bonehead for an agent.

Then, as a coda, Michael said, "By the way, how's the tell-all book coming along?"

Peter turned ashen.

After scurrying back to his office following the disastrous meeting with Stephanie, Bart told his assistant, Brian Kovack, that he was on deadline and would be behind closed doors until he'd completed yet another rewrite of the press release.

Brian was a schizophrenic actor with equal parts talent and deep-rooted issues of resentment and hostility toward his boss in particular and mostly everyone in general. Many years ago, he had won the Golden Mask Award from some storefront acting academy in Akron, Ohio. He subsequently got a job in a Honda SUV television commercial and was on his way—as it turned out, to oblivion. Lately he'd been reduced to playing the Monty Woolley role in a church basement production of *The Man Who Came to Dinner* with the Los Angeles Rainbow Theatre Experience.

Brian divided his time between crying over his bitterness that he had to work at a movie studio as an assistant rather than as a star and attending a half dozen different twelve-step programs, including Alcoholics Anonymous, Overeaters Anonymous, Sexaholics Anonymous, Overspenders Anonymous, and

Alien Abductees Anonymous. Bart wished there were a program called Oversleepers Anonymous, because Brian couldn't be on time if a curtain call depended on it. And overhearing a Monday-morning chat between Bart and Mitch, standing at the coffeemaker in the break room, talking about how great Bette Midler's concert was at the Hollywood Bowl on Saturday night, could ignite a tirade from Brian about how much more famous he could have been than Bette. "Bette just got all the breaks," Brian groused.

"Honey," shouted Mitch Wood, "to paraphrase Mama Rose, 'If you coulda been... you woulda been.'"

To Bart, Brian's most annoying habit involved his personal telephone calls. Trained to enunciate and project in the theater, he unwittingly subjected Bart to every syllable uttered from his cubicle just outside Bart's office. All the whining and crying and personal conversations with his ex-lover, the artistic director of the Los Angeles Rainbow Theatre Experience, grated on Bart.

Brian's saving grace was that he was fairly good at his job, and he saved Bart much time by fielding unsolicited telephone calls. Bart couldn't risk losing him. Moreover, any other assistant might have ratted to accounting that Bart's expense reports didn't always truthfully reflect whom he dined with at expensive restaurants in Beverly Hills. Brian was at least loyal. Plus, he knew more about Bart's intimate life and the personal writing projects he sometimes worked on—during company time.

Now, with his office door closed, Bart sat down at his desk and stared at his computer screen. Tears of frustration began to blur his vision. The first draft of the press release was as good as any he'd ever written. The second draft was merely a variation on the same theme. The third draft was simply Bart retyping the same material, barely using different words.

He decided that Stephanie was toying with him, testing how far she could push before Bart said or did something that would give Stephanie a reason to fire him. To challenge this theory, he went back to the first draft and retitled it "Fourth Draft." He would print it out, waiting until it was nearly past filing deadline at *Daily Variety* before taking it back to his miserable boss. With the trade publication about to go to bed, Stephanie would have to approve the release as it was or rewrite it herself.

In the interim, Bart decided he needed a diversion. He picked up his phone and opened Plunder, his hardly-ever-used dating app. Sure, he didn't actually have time for dates and was usually too exhausted to think about going out with anyone, but he liked a lot of the photos of sexy young men.

But this time when he opened the app, Bart ignored all the nude pictures because there was actually a message waiting for him. He hadn't been on this site for weeks, but he now tapped on Caliente4U. Bart had just finished reading the succinct message, "Nice profile," when he heard a trill, and a message appeared: "You're hot."

Bart tapped Caliente4U's profile:

Name: Don't ask.

Location: In your dreams.

Birthdate: All candles still fit on one cake.

Marital status: No ring.

Hobbies: Yes, I have a BIG one.

Occupation: My brain is in my pants.

Bart responded: "So are you." He waited what seemed a full minute, and then Caliente4U added, "I'm unlocking my pix. If you like what you see, we can negotiate."

With trembling hands, and the fear that Stephanie could be knocking on his office door at any moment, he tapped on the photo album, then emitted an involuntary gasp at the image on his screen. If he were a cartoon, his eyes would have popped out on springs. Caliente4U was physically unlike the guys Bart had dated in the past, the accountants and doctors, the type of man

Bart imagined he'd eventually marry. No, this was definitely a sex-fantasy man: a swarthy Latino with a dangerous-looking scowl on his face.

Caliente4U's pictures were all variations on the same theme: a body that God created specifically to drive men and women insane with lust. He was lean and dark and well-toned. His stomach boasted a hint of six-pack abs. His shoulders were strong and wide, and he had tattoos around his neck that looked like gang insignia. His chest and pecs glistened from oil or perspiration. He had a gap between his two front teeth. But it was his eyes that mesmerized Bart most. They were deep, dark, and intense. They stared out from the pictures and seemed to bore right into Bart's soul. His stare was angry and menacing. The addition of beard stubble made him the sexiest man Bart had ever seen—and the most threatening, too. The combination was exhilarating.

Bart dashed off a quick message. "Excellent. Maybe meet up sometime?"

When there was no immediate response to his message, Bart panicked. Didn't his own picture measure up? He only had one photo, but it was of him in the woods in a hiking outfit: boots, short shorts, a white tank top slung over his shoulder, exposing his lithe torso.

Bart waited anxiously, his eyes glued to his phone's screen. At this very moment Stephanie was likely flying down the hall on her broomstick. But Bart was frozen in his chair. He couldn't move from his desk for fear he'd miss the hoped-for response from Caliente4U.

Bart waited. Nothing.

Anxiously, he typed: "Still there?"

Nothing.

Finally, the announcement trill came. "I want to touch you. BTW, I charge. Is two hundred okay?"

Bart made a face. Forget it! No way was he going to pay for sex, for crying out loud. That was absurd. "Can't afford it," he replied.

Just then, Bart's door burst open, and he clumsily fumbled the phone. It leaped out of his hand and landed screen down on the desk. Stephanie, hands on hips, stood in the portal. She was barefoot, with painted red toenails. "Bart, I've had it with you! I swear I've never had more problems with a fucking staff writer! Where's that fucking rewrite?"

"Hot off the printer, Stephanie," Bart managed. He was red-faced and afraid that Stephanie would catch him playing around and see the naked man on his phone screen. He diverted Stephanie's attention by getting up from his desk and handing her three double-spaced pages of text. Stephanie grabbed the press release, turned around, and stormed out without closing the door. "I hate the quote you gave me!" Stephanie bellowed over her shoulder as she padded back toward her office. "I don't talk like that!"

Desperately hoping that he was still connected to whatever the Latino equivalent of Adonis was, Bart returned to his desk and picked up his phone. There was another message. "Price negotiable."

He quickly typed: "Address?" The reply came quickly: "27 Heather View Circle. Go around to the back of the house. Wait at the sliding-glass door."

"I'm an hour away."

Logging off from his computer, Bart shouted to Brian, "It's six o'clock. I'm outta here!" He smiled to himself and said under his breath, "And I might even get laid."

4

Paco Castillo, aka Caliente4U, wasn't what he appeared to be. If you happened to look over your shoulder and register this buzz-cut, beard-stubbled dude in a dingy tank top that revealed tattoos and muscles walking down the street behind you—day or night—you'd quickly look for sanctuary. Paco appeared as though he should be mugging old ladies for their Social Security checks, or Jehovah's Witnesses—just because. Jessica Rabbit said it best, "I'm not bad... I'm just drawn that way," and Paco had sketched his barrio-clone persona to attract a certain kind of man (and woman) and to repel every other type.

In the privacy of his own space, however, he was a quiet twenty-five-year-old who worked up to eighteen hours a day doing whatever was required to support his three passions: the gym, sex, and writing screenplays. At his young age, he already had five feature-film scripts completed—romantic comedies in the tradition of his hero Nancy Meyers. They were neatly stacked on the desk beside his computer in the small room he rented in a house owned by a former movie bit player who needed a boarder like Paco to make ends meet.

But making men and women sexually excited was in his genes. Before he was kicked out of his house at age sixteen, he'd learned all he needed to know about self-awareness and street smarts from the people who raised him. He learned that he had to seize opportunities and rely on his instincts, as well as his sex, to get what he wanted from life—and from the people who wanted him.

Paco was steadily employed three nights a week as a bartender at the Trap, a popular bar on Santa Monica Boulevard in West Hollywood, where he worked shirtless, in jeans that were a size too large at the waist—which guaranteed they'd ease down his hips enough for drooling customers to see where his pubic hair began (and prove he wasn't wearing underwear). He served beers and shots of tequila, handpicking the covetous patrons who packed the place on Friday and Saturday nights hoping to have sex with him against cases of Budweiser in the stockroom. For two hundred bucks he could be easily seduced. "One does what one has to do to survive in this world" was Paco's mantra, handed down by his gangbanger dad, who was still a kid himself when Paco was born. Two other nights a week he bused tables at the Cobalt Cantina on Robertson from 4 p.m. until closing. On his free nights and during the days, he worked on his screenplays.

Paco might not have liked his present circumstances, but he considered it honest, if not altogether legal, work. More important, it kept his days free to work out at the gym and write. To Paco, the gym=sex, and sex=cash. But his primary focus was on his writing.

Every morning, he woke up believing success was just around the corner. He knew that in Hollywood lives changed with the blink of an eye. He remained confident that he would eventually meet an industry-connected person who could get one of his scripts made into a feature film or offer him a job as a staff writer in episodic television. True, it wasn't likely that he'd run into Shonda Rhimes or Steven Spielberg at the Trap, but perhaps the keys to the door to success would appear in the guise of a less-well-known player who would come for a drink and leave eager to read his work, recognize his talent, and offer to mentor him.

The house in which Paco rented a room by the month was a one-story shingle-and-stucco structure, circa World War II, dirty white in color, and had a peculiar, if valuable, feature: The sliding glass door in the back that led to his room was laminated with a reflective Mylar tinting. It enabled Paco to see outside, but nobody could see inside. This gave Paco an opportunity to size up any customer he'd trolled for on Plunder or Tinder and decide if they were worth the time and two hundred bucks, or whether he should jack up the price to three hundred dollars just to get rid of someone creepy.

He also liked to watch clients preening at their own reflection in preparation for meeting him. Most of the customers were too stupid to realize it was a two-way mirror. Men would tuft the chest hair out of the top of their T-shirts or flip open the top button of their 501s, reach inside, and give themselves a quick pump in order to show off how much they were packing. Women would check out their hair, their teeth, and adjust their clothes. This amused Paco, who was completely confident about what he himself had to sell. Anyone who had experienced his sexual apparatus would agree that the service was worth the price.

As it was Monday night, one of the two nights a week Paco had off, he was free to peddle his physical wares. Although he'd rather spend the time writing, it was the sex work that allowed him to keep his days free—and also provided unlimited character studies. Old Mrs. Carter, who owned the house and was once married to a minor movie star who, after fifteen years of marriage, traded her in for a younger actress, seldom came all the way to the back of her home, where Paco's room was located. She usually stopped midway down the hall at their shared bathroom.

But although she was generally unobtrusive in Paco's life, Mrs. Carter wasn't an idiot. She knew what was going on under her roof. It was clear since her tenant's customers usually had to use the one bathroom, which was directly in view from where she sat in the living room, reclining in her La-Z-Boy with her cat, Mr. Boots. It was a blessing to Paco that Mrs. Carter was practically deaf. She kept to herself, watching television day and night, with the volume cranked up so loud it could be heard clear down to Paco's room. Thankfully, the sound of the TV also covered the often-animalistic noises emanating from his bedroom.

The drive from Burbank to West Hollywood took an inordinately longer time than usual for Bart. An accident had taken out the traffic lights at the intersection of Barham and Cahuenga, so the usual ten-minute drive from Sterling Studios to the Cahuenga Pass took a grueling forty minutes.

Once he finally passed over the 101 Freeway, Bart turned left and drove down past the Hollywood Bowl and the American Legion Post, which looked like an Egyptian temple, to Franklin Avenue. There he turned right, passing the big Methodist Church, with its huge red AIDS ribbon illuminated by a bright spotlight, the way the gargoyles on Notre Dame Cathedral in Paris were blasted by halogens at night.

Bart passed the Magic Castle and then the Highland Gardens motel, where singer Janis Joplin had overdosed on drugs and died so many years ago. At La Brea Avenue, he turned left. Just a few blocks farther down were the former Charlie Chaplin Film Studios, which was later A&M Records Studios, where the now also-dead Karen Carpenter had recorded her biggest hits. Once when he passed this way, Bart found himself listening to a CD by the seventies pop duo, feeling almost overwhelmed by sadness because he loved the velvet-voiced Karen, whom Bart's grandparents had often played on their stereo when Bart was growing up. But like Janis Joplin just a few blocks back, Karen was obviously self-destructive in her own way.

At Hollywood Boulevard, Bart turned right. The other direction would have taken him to all the famous landmarks: the Chinese Theatre, the restored El Capitan movie palace, and the Egyptian Theatre, and of course, the Walk of Fame, where more than twenty-five-hundred household names and long forgotten has-beens were embedded in the sidewalks. Nearly every star from the Golden Era of Hollywood was represented and spat upon by inconsiderate tourists or urinated on by shopping-cart transients. Neil Armstrong and his Apollo XI crew had their star at the corner of Hollywood and Vine, and they weren't spared fewer indignities than Lassie a few blocks back. The newer celebrities who received recognition on the Walk of Fame were now mostly inaugurated for publicity purposes—the pomp and circumstance paid for by studios to promote a new film. Therefore, a few mistakes were made in the hallowed pavement, such as adding Donald Trump to the mix. Cough up enough money and the Hollywood Chamber of Commerce could vote you a spot in front of the Hollywood Palace Theatre, Amir's Discount Souvenirs and T-shirts shop, or the Allied Parking lot. So far, the chamber had managed to evade a Kardashian's name.

Cruising down to Fairfax Avenue, Bart pretty much knew where he was going. At least he was familiar with the neighborhood. It was close to the Sports Connection (also known as the Sports Erection), the popular gym on Santa Monica Boulevard where he took yoga class on weekends.

Heather View Circle turned out to be a side street just a couple of blocks behind the health club. Finding a parking spot in this part of town was always murder. The city of West Holly-wood had strict parking policies, and even if you were lucky enough to find an empty space, you had to read the confusing and often conflicting street signs two or three times to under-stand if and how the parking was restricted.

It was after seven when Bart finally found the house where Caliente4U said he'd be waiting. Popping a handful of Tic Tacs into his mouth, he rolled along looking for an open spot into which he could slide his '99 Mustang convertible. Soon, he was standing, as instructed, outside the back of the house under a bright porch light, opposite the mirrored sliding-glass door: checking his hair, teeth, clothes, and opening another button on his white shirt, he was perspiring from the anticipation of what was to come.

Bart timidly rapped his knuckles on the glass door. No answer. He saw his own look of panic reflected back at him under the overhead house light. Tense about what he might be getting himself into with a stranger, Bart found himself looking up at the grimy light fixture with its accumulation of dust and dirt sifted out of the LA air, as well as shadows from dead and decaying insects inside the light globe. "Dead," Bart said to himself as if the collection of insects might be an omen. "Am I so desperate to take my mind away from my job that I'm willing to risk God-knows-what to have sex with a guy I met online? Yes!" he whispered aloud, although he couldn't believe he was actu-ally on the brink of following through with this fantasy.

Then, as if there were a devil/angel advocate colliding in his head, Bart thought: *This isn't my modus operandi at all. I play the virginal ingénue. I'm turning into Mitch!* Bart winced at that thought. However, his apprehension was quickly overruled by the excitement he'd felt in his stomach ever since Caliente4U's picture flashed on his phone screen. He decided that for once in his life he wouldn't be Victorian about the propriety of sex. His stupid, puritanical sense of morals was to blame for him being chaste for so long in the first place. Now was the time to take a chance. This could be a once-in-a-lifetime opportunity.

Even if the guy was only half as hot as his picture, Bart decided it was worth the possible danger just to feel a man's skin against his own again. Quite frankly, he admitted, he was turned on by the potential for a bit of peril. It had been way too long since Bart had been intimate with anyone, and he was practically going insane with lust. "I'm no angel," Bart whispered to himself, now ready for the previously unthinkable act of actually paying for whatever was about to take place behind the mirrored-glass door. *D'ya think he takes American Express corporate cards?*

Returning to his reflection, he tapped on the glass again. He could hear the muted sound of a television coming from the front of the house, and wondered if perhaps Caliente4U was there and couldn't hear him knocking. But just as he stepped back and was about to try the front entrance, the outside light went off. A long moment later the glass door slid open.

Backlit by the illumination of a lamp on the floor of an otherwise dark space, the male figure standing before Bart was impossible to see clearly. He didn't bother to introduce himself, and simply said, "Hey," then stepped aside, indicating for Bart to enter.

Although Bart had never paid for sex before, he had heard somewhere that such transactions were usually made up front, though money was never actually handed to the hustler. Apparently, the etiquette was to place the cash on a dresser or table. He stammered, "Before we... I mean... we didn't discuss... I mean... I don't know if I brought enough..." he mumbled.

"Whatever, man." The voice held a distinct Latino accent.

"I thought your photo was awesome... man." Bart felt himself slipping into an unfamiliar character and began using what was to him a foreign vocabulary. He didn't often speak in sentences that required him to use "man" when addressing someone or saying things like "awesome" unless he was describing the Grand Canyon or an actor's performance. It was as though his entire personality had shifted to match the environment, the way it did when he was at the opposite end of the social spectrum, wearing a tuxedo, holding a flute of champagne, and being overly courtly toward some of the world's most recognizable celebrities at an awards banquet or film screening.

Bart's eyesight adjusted to the duskiness of the room. A bedroom. The furnishings were utilitarian. A queen-size mattress lay on the floor. A fitted sheet covered the mattress. Two corners of a top sheet were tucked in between the bottom of the mattress and the carpeted floor. A desk, which was just an old door laid across two sawhorses, supported a laptop computer, a small flatscreen television, papers, pens, pads of yellow Post-its, and several books.

Bart decided that either there had not been time to make the place presentable for guests, or perhaps this was all part of the mystique of anonymous sex. In any case, the mess actually added to Bart's excitement. Images of other bodies having been on the very same sheets flashed through his mind, which at once turned him off and turned him on, too. Mostly on.

Then he got a full view of Caliente4U: He was probably just under six feet tall. Scruffy. He had a space between his two upper front teeth. His nostrils were flared, and he had well-defined cheekbones. Over his bare torso he wore a yellow reflective vest—the type that construction workers wear. A baseball cap on his head was worn backwards. But again, what Bart noticed most were the man's eyes. They were dark and deep-set and intense, like photos he'd seen of serial killers. They absolutely hypnotized him. Caliente4U was not handsome in the traditional sense. And yet, he was the sexiest man Bart had ever seen. He was holding a bottle of tequila.

"Want some?" Caliente4U said, holding out the half-filled bottle.

Bart nodded and coughed as the fluid burned the lining of his throat. The guy poured a good amount of the liquid into his own mouth, then pushed his lips against Bart's, forcing the tequila to surge into his. Bart felt a rush of heat and lust unlike anything he'd ever experienced before.

"Time's money," Caliente4U said, taking off his baseball cap to reveal a head of short hair that looked more like fur. "Do you want me to force you to strip?"

The mild-mannered and innocent persona that served as Bart's public identity quickly fell away. What emerged from deep within was a thirsty and demanding vampire. Within moments, Bart and Caliente4U were on the sheets, both aggressively exploring each other. "Look into my eyes and tell me what you want me to do," the man insisted. "I'm here to make you excited and to give you what you want. I won't do anything that you don't like," he said, his eyes fixed on Bart's.

Then, overcome by the guy's musky scent, Bart melted into his partner. "I'm so ready!" Bart nearly begged.

After they had exhausted themselves, they lay beside each other, breathing erratically, while their heartbeats slowly returned to normal. Although Bart had had a few sexual partners in the past, he had never been with a man who was so completely out of his erotic fantasies. Until this night, sex had never been a major motivating force in Bart's life. He knew that if he wanted to, he could probably sleep with any one of a dozen guys at the studio. But who had time? With his demanding career schedule of fourteen-hour workdays and the intense stress he was under from the demonic Stephanie, sex was relegated to the back burner. Sure, he checked out attractive men as he dashed from one movie screening or celebrity interview to another, but he seldom had time to exchange even a flash of eye contact.

On the rare occasions when he actually had a date, Bart was too timid to make the first move toward sex. He'd been emotionally incinerated by his first lover, who, toward the end of their yearlong affair, called him a "grab-ass" and shoved him away one night when Bart tried to initiate sex.

Now, after a few moments of silence except for the sound of breathing, Caliente4U finally said, "I'm Paco."

Bart panted, "I'm Bart, and you're the most amazing..."

"'Fuck.' Say it." He chuckled playfully. "I'm the most amazing fuck. You do know the word, you little Ivy League fuck?"

"You're... amazing."

After they had both rested for a few more minutes, Bart got up. "Bathroom?" he asked.

"Down the hall."

Still naked, he stepped barefoot out onto the hardwood floor of the corridor. Mrs. Carter was coming out of the bathroom with her cat. She disinterestedly sized up the young man and walked back toward the living room and the televised cacophony of *Wheel of Fortune*.

Returning to Paco's room, Bart made small talk as he dressed as slowly as possible. For some reason that he couldn't fathom, he was stalling to remain in Paco's presence for as long as possible.

"What do you do? Other than... I mean..." Bart asked.

"Bartend. Work out. But mostly I write."

"Work out. That's obvious," Bart said. "I write, too. What do you write?"

"Screenplays."

"Really? I work at Sterling."

Even if Paco had been strapped to a lie-detector machine, there wouldn't have been the slightest response on the polygraph to indicate his sudden piqued interest. He was a master of inscrutability. "What do you write?" he asked nonchalantly.

"For Sterling? Publicity stuff for movies. For myself? I'm working on a novel. But then, who isn't, right?" He chuckled self-consciously. "Do you have an agent? Have you sold anything?"

"Can't seem to get in the door."

Bart knew that almost every sentient being in Hollywood had a screenplay they were writing or "shopping around." From gardeners to cater/waiters to the guys who detail celebrities' cars, everyone seemed sure that they had a brilliant idea for a script, and if they could just pitch their idea to a creative executive, they'd be rich and famous. Screenwriters were more ubiquitous than Starbucks coffee shops. Before Bart realized what he was possibly getting himself into, he took a big leap. "Maybe I know someone who could look at your stuff," he said as he slipped into his shoes.

Paco snorted. "A lot of people have said that to me before," he said truthfully. "Nobody in this town keeps a promise. Half the time the dicks I meet online don't even show up."

"I can at least get a friend in the story department at the studio to do coverage on one of your scripts," Bart said. "If you want. He sorta owes me a favor."

"Cool," Paco said, still reserved and distant. "It'd at least give us a chance to see each other again, too. When you get the coverage back, I mean."

"Hey," Bart said, still not having completely decompressed from the sex, "can I take you out for a drink? Like now? To talk about your script... and stuff?"

"Nah. I can't. Got someone coming at eleven."

Registering Bart's obvious disappointment and knowing that

the opportunity of getting one of his scripts read by a legitimate story analyst at the most prestigious studio in Hollywood could hinge on keeping Bart around, Paco added, "So far, I don't have anyone booked for tomorrow night. Why don't I block it out, and we see each other again? Gratis this time."

Gratis, Bart repeated to himself, thinking it was not the kind of word a simple street hustler would use. "Great. I'm off at six. I can be back here by seven-ish."

Paco picked up a script from the top pile on his desk and handed it to Bart.

"*Blind as a Bat.*" Bart read the title aloud.

"Yeah. Gave it to an agent from Actors and Others. The guy is a freak-o who comes into the Trap every Friday night. You know the place, down the street on Santa Monica? It's where I tend bar. He's never mentioned the script again. Probably never read it. Like I said, nobody in this town keeps a promise. But I have a feeling you will. Won't you?"

"Absolutely."

Paco smiled. "Hey. By the way, if you thought I was great, so were you. You really kept up with me. Some people can't last that long. They say they want it, even beg for it, but after twenty minutes or so..."

Bart felt himself getting excited again.

Paco was a hustler and a first-class manipulator. It was surprising he hadn't gotten further in his writing career by now by sheer will and aggressiveness. Even a marginally talented hack can be a success in Hollywood. And Paco was better and brighter than most. "So. Tomorrow. Seven... *ish.*" He smiled again. Then he came forward and planted his mouth onto Bart's and slipped his tongue between his lips and teeth.

They inhaled deeply, nearly giving mouth-to-mouth resuscitation. Not only was Bart eager for another tryst with the sexiest

man he'd ever met, Paco was possibly getting the career opportunity for which he had been waiting years.

At last, they pulled away from each other. Paco unlocked the
door and slid it back on its track.

"Tomorrow, man," Paco said.

"Tomorrow, man," Bart parroted.

5

"Tell me how you feel about that," said Bart's therapist, Dr. Ecle, responding in his best neurotic Sigmund Freud impersonation to Bart's latest career crisis. Bart was sitting on Ecle's black leather couch, detailing the latest scenario of Stephanie publicly castigating him during a staff meeting. Bart's supposed transgression this time was that he had insulted one of the studio's biggest stars, Zarita Holcombe, by altering her previously approved bio in the publicity materials for the musical-comedy movie *Nuns Are Sisters Too*. The film costarred Jonathan Burk as a monk constantly failing to remain celibate, and old-time star Gretchen Stein in a cameo as the imperious Mother Abbess.

"How do you think I feel?"

"I won't know until you tell me."

Bart rolled his eyes. This Jungian or Freudian or Gestalt passiveness wasn't why he was paying a hundred fifty bucks an hour. "I was humiliated, of course. The entire New York office was on video conference, too. Stephanie embellished the whole situation. She claimed she received an outraged call from Zarita. It's too bad the world outside of Hollywood doesn't know what a dreadful person Zarita really is. She would have made Faye Dunaway look like a smudgy orphan in *Annie*. And I'm sure that Stephanie was lying. Zarita would never have made any such call herself. She'd have her lackey manager complain on her behalf. That woman is constantly afraid she'll lose her cash cow. Trust me, I know. I've worked with Zarita and her type too many times. It's amazing how many people can't see through her phoniness."

"And you feel Stephanie was out of line and exaggerated the details of the call?" Dr. Ecle asked.

"Hugely!"

"What seemed to be the root of the problem?"

"Root? Stephanie publicly scolded me, claiming Zarita had threatened to pull out from doing all publicity to support *Nuns*. Specifically, because I, Bart Caine, made *appropriate* changes in her self-aggrandizing bio."

"So you see yourself as a victim and a scapegoat?"

"Exactly. Everybody in town knows how Zarita likes to hold studios hostage. Early on in negotiations for her to star in a film, she agrees to do all the print, radio, and television media publicity we flacks drum up. Then, at the eleventh hour, after the press junket has been set and the hotels reserved, the premiere party planned and the press invited, she backs out. She says she's too exhausted or the film sucks. Which in this case it does. But then she comes around saying she could possibly be persuaded to work on behalf of the movie if the studio buys her that multimillion-dollar Monet, Chagall, or Mapplethorpe she's had an eye on."

Bart whined, "Now I'm supposed to buy a magnum of Cristal champagne, no expensing it, and personally go down to LAX tonight and find Zarita before she takes off for New York on the studio's corporate jet. I have to present her with this token gift and, on bended knee, apologize for editing her bio. It's my *job* to write and edit talent bios, for crying out loud."

"What was wrong with the bio in the first place that made you change it?" Dr. Ecle asked.

"The hyperbole was excruciating. It gave me bleeding hemorrhoids. Honest to God, this is how she wants it to read. I've memorized it verbatim because it's so lame: '*What a moviegoer gets from their two hours in the dark of a cinema house depends entirely on the dazzling, effulgent star Zarita Holcombe. The Academy Award-nominated, Tony Award-nominated, Emmy, Grammy, People's Choice, and NAACP Image Award-nominee Zarita Holcombe is the most successful Haitian-American actress in the history of all time.*'

"'In the history of all time'? What kind of cockamamie redundancy is that!" Bart cried. It goes on to say, '*She loves telling you, her loyal, devoted fans, a real story and fully developing her characters.*'

"Well, I would hope she'd fully develop her frigging characters! She is, after all, an actress. Excuse me, *star*. There's a difference." Bart sniggered.

"'*So, we all leave the theater enriched and overwhelmed by her unforgettable roles and excitedly await the next great story she will share with us on-screen.*'"

"And you feel that's all wrong?" asked Dr. Ecle.

"It might be acceptable in a *Saturday Night Live* parody sketch. One in which Zarita accepts a Golden Loom Award from the International Ladies Garment Workers Union, for one of her publicity-perfect humanitarian efforts. But it's not fine in a motion-picture publicity press kit. At least not in materials that have my name on them as the writer."

Dr. Ecle pressed his hands together. "I sense you're filled with anxiety, Bart. Even with the Xanax I've prescribed."

"Anxiety?" Bart said sarcastically. "No kidding. It's my maniacal boss who got me on this drug in the first place. There's way too much pressure. And now that I should be with the only man I've ever met who's off the Richter scale of earthshaking sex, I'm forced to work overtime on arbitrarily created assignments. It's as though Stephanie knows all about Paco and she won't let me have a personal life. Anxiety? It takes on a whole new meaning!"

"Follow that thought about sex," Dr. Ecle suggested, his prurient mind making the segue to a more lascivious issue. It was the first time since Bart's session began that the shrink became seriously attentive. "What's going on there?"

Bart finally smiled. He closed his eyes and flashed on Paco's dark-skinned body hovering above him in all its naked anatomic glory, hard as steel in all the right places. "You'll think I'm nuts."

"That's what I'm here for."

Bart sighed. "Well, for most of my adult life, I've equated sex with love. This is the first time I'm experiencing sex as *play*, as extracurricular activity. I've always had to at least think there might be a future with a guy before wrinkling the sheets with him. With Paco, it's just so damned much *fun.* He's the perfect stud! The fact that I can't be with him all the time is driving me out of my mind. I want to stay in his bed all day, even if he's not there, and wrap myself in his dingy sheets and hibernate."

"Bart," said Dr. Ecle, "you're beginning to display rather overt signs of becoming obsessive. You realize that, don't you?"

"Obsessive? Over Paco? You bet your prescription pad, Doc. I even stole a pair of his underpants. When I put them on... well, let's just say that I get a really great feeling. It's like they have some magical aphrodisiac property! Next, I want one of his perspiration-soaked tank-top gym shirts."

Bart paused, then: "I told you he's a wannabe screenwriter? Coverage came back on one of his scripts that I sent to a friend in the story department. The guy gave it an *Excellent.* It means Paco has real talent. I'm obsessed with a guy who's a stud *and* talented at the same time. That's a first for me. A breakthrough, wouldn't you say?"

Dr. Ecle shrugged. "That diagnosis is yet to be determined. But tell me more about the sex."

Bart let out a sigh of pleasure. "I've only been with him a dozen times, but he's awesome. When I arrive at his house—or, rather, the room he rents—he merely slides open the glass door... I walk in, and he immediately pins me against the wall. It's as if I'm the only one he's seeing. I know I'm not. He rents himself out, so to speak. He always has a bottle of tequila on hand. We start by taking a couple of swigs. I've gotten used to the taste. Then I start by slowly disengaging my lips from his and dragging my tongue from his Adam's apple down his chest, over to an armpit. I become like I'm a cat licking its coat. I go for his brown nipples and gnaw on them. Then I make my way down his chest, which has a green-and-blue tattoo of some sort of symbol on the right side. Gang-related, I suppose. Then on to his taut stomach. I usually linger at his navel. He's got an 'inny.' Then it's on to the main course, which is feathered in a bed of black alfalfa sprouts and anchored with the pits from two ripe avocados."

"How vivid," Dr. Ecle said, his mouth agape. He looked like an asphyxiated fish.

"We eventually make our way to his bed and... and... you know."

Dr. Ecle swallowed and snapped out of his reverie, disconcerted by the abrupt end to the scenario.

"I think he intuitively knows he's brought me out of my shell, and I'm an animal. I'm no longer the mild-mannered little angel that people think I am. Years ago, I had a guy say to me he wanted to 'screw me until my head caved in.' Nothing out of the ordinary happened with that jerk. We had sex, but my head was still intact—just brain-dead from boredom. Paco makes me feel my head actually will explode. He's perfect. Except..."

"Except?"

"Every time after... you know... after the first climax..."

"First?"

Bart smiled mischievously. "After the first round, he gives me the third degree about his script. He does it indirectly. Like he's merely making after-sex, lovey-dovey small talk. First, he laughs and says, 'Man, you're wild.' Or 'Did you have as bitchin' a time as I did?' Then he always whispers in my ear, 'Hey, any news about our project?' I confess, I've been sort of evasive."

"Haven't you told him? About the coverage?"

Bart shook his head. "Not yet. I keep telling him to be patient, that I'm sure my friend will come through soon."

"So, basically, you've been stringing him along."

"Not *stringing*... per se."

"Why do you think you're withholding this information?"

"I don't know."

"Yes, you do."

"No, I don't," Bart parried.

"I think you do."

"Then *you* tell *me*."

"I can't give you the answers, Bart," Dr. Ecle said.

"But that's why I'm here, isn't it?"

"Are you afraid of something?"

"Like what? That I'm being used? That when he gets the coverage, it'll be *adios, amigo*?" Bart paused and thought for a long moment. "Maybe," he admitted for the first time aloud.

"Who's using whom?"

"Hey, he's lucky to have me. I'm his entree to the biz."

"But isn't *he* your entree into the world of sex for play? You've bitched about not finding anyone special ever since we started these consultations."

"There's more to it than that," Bart insisted. "I can't explain it in words." He paused. "Do you think maybe I'm falling in love?"

"You tell me. The answer, Bart, is deep in your subconscious."

"Why must it always be the *subconscious?* It's my *consciousness* that I'm aware of."

"We're going to have to do a lot of excavating to find the answers to your questions. Very arduous." Dr. Ecle sounded like a Gestapo agent preparing a prisoner for torture.

"I don't usually do this," Dr. Ecle continued, "but let me tell you about another patient of mine."

"Isn't that a tad unethical?" Bart said, looking at Dr. Ecle, who was staring into space.

Dr. Ecle wasn't what most young people would admit to finding sexy. But until Paco came along, Bart's idea of sex appeal in a man wasn't necessarily linked to physical appearance. Bart gave more weight to how intellectual, talented, or witty a guy was. Dr. Ecle was most definitely not a six-foot-five, broad-shoul-dered, blue-jeans-wearing cowboy, but to Bart he seemed smart. He was more a latter-day Professor from *Gilligan's Island,* including the white dress shirt opened at the collar and down a couple of buttons.

Bart used to get excited just thinking of the strands of chest hair revealed through the nearly diaphanous fibers of his shrink's shirts. Although he wasn't anywhere near runway-model handsome, he was what Bart had considered "marriage material." He seemed stable. Had a thriving Beverly Hills prac-tice. Drove a sleek fern-green Jaguar. He looked like a guy with whom Bart could comfortably trade sections of the Sunday edition of the *New York Times* in bed in their jammies each weekend.

Bart's impression of Dr. Ecle changed when Paco came into the picture. Now Dr. Ecle seemed more like a bifocaled pug dog.

"I'm not naming names," Dr. Ecle continued. "I just want to suggest that as part of your therapy, you continue to keep a diary as this one patient did as a means of catharsis. It may give you a better perspective on how you respond to the people who *appear* to have authority over you."

"Like Stephanie? And Paco?"

"Or that last major crush you had. Layne, was it?"

"Thane."

"Yes. The one with the wife and three kids."

"Ex-wife. And three cats."

"Right. Well, the individual to whom I refer is the grandson or granddaughter of a great big movie star from the old, old days. Doesn't matter who the star was, but his or her towels could be monogrammed BD or JC. Confidentiality prevents me from telling you the real name—of the star, I mean."

"MGM old?" Bart asked, ready to play twenty questions.

"It isn't important."

"Warner Brothers old?"

"Anyway, I suggested he or she—the nameless grandson or granddaughter—write down every sordid detail about the way he or she was mistreated by one of Hollywood's legends, who happened to be his or her grandmother or grandfather."

"BD? JC?" Bart pondered aloud the monogram initials clue. "Bo Derek? Jane Curtain?"

"Star. Not just celebrity," Dr. Ecle said. "And that's enough hinting. The journal he or she—my patient—kept is about to be published as a book and has already been optioned for a movie. This person now has beaucoup bucks or—as you've said in the past—'fuck-you money.'"

Bart immediately bolted upright, as if he'd suddenly had a presentiment about who murdered JonBenet Ramsey. "Bette Davis or Joan Crawford! You treated one of their granddaughters or grandsons?"

Dr. Ecle's face turned beet red, as though Judge Judy had caught him in a big fat lie. "Jane. John. Son. Daughter. Who knows? Who cares?" Dr. Ecle exclaimed.

"You know I'm a slave to Joan Crawford! A guy I knew had her dog's ashes in a coffee can!"

"Hour's up," Dr. Ecle said defensively. "Anyway, I never said it was anybody you've heard of," Dr. Ecle cried nervously. "It could have been Julie Andrews, for all you know."

"Wrong initials."

Dr. Ecle looked around his office as if half-expecting a parade of members from the California State Board of Psychology to burst through the door and confiscate his Perma-Plaque degrees, like Rose Hovick pilfering Papa's solid-gold retirement award in *Gypsy*.

Bart stood up from the couch and left the office. To him, Dr. Ecle had looked as frazzled as Dr. Frasier Crane after a mix-up with his tickets for orchestra seats on the aisle at a Seattle Repertory Theatre production of *The Lisbon Traviata*. It was amazing how much life really was like TV.

6

The gates at all the Hollywood studios officially open at nine every day—except Disney, where a former studio head once said, "If you don't come to work on Sunday, don't bother coming in on Saturday!" Or was it the other way around? The admonishment was so stupid, no one ever quite figured out what he meant. The saying was as cryptic as the lame "Love means never having to say you're sorry" on the poster copy for the old movie *Love Story*.

For Bart, "business as usual" at Sterling meant that he arrived each weekday morning at six. Today was no different—despite the fact that he had been up until 2:00 a.m. with Paco. Over the years that Bart had worked at Sterling, he was always the first one in the office. The studio was notorious within the industry for its understaffing, thereby wringing every drop of blood and sweat from its employees and creating nervous breakdowns, and even a few suicides. Still, Bart enjoyed getting out of bed before dawn because it meant quietly jump-starting the day in peace, even though his sadistically overwhelming workload actually required the long hours.

There was an unspoken, companywide assumption that

since Sterling was one of the most prestigious entertainment empires in the world, hundreds, if not thousands, of would-be Eve Harringtons were waiting in the wings to replace any lackey who deigned to show a lack of gratitude for the privilege of his or her employment. In the blink of an eye, anyone who wasn't a team player could be history. But though unequivocal loyalty was expected from each worker, Sterling had no reciprocal allegiance to the cogs that ran the big wheel. Anybody courteous enough to resign with two weeks' notice was swiftly escorted off the lot that same day by studio security.

Bart was good at mimicking what was expected of a team player. "Yes, sir." "No, ma'am." "I'll volunteer for that unpaid assignment, even though it's in opposition to the collective-bargaining agreement between Sterling Studios and my union and even though my mother's funeral is at the same time..."

But as much as possible, he tried to leave the brown-nosing to the overly enthusiastic interns who didn't complain about the slave-like treatment and less than minimum wage, and the just-out-of-college assistants who mistakenly thought if they proved themselves tireless workers, they'd enjoy a meteoric rise in Hollywood and make the leap from being under a thumb to being the *Thumb*. Invariably, they were all in for a surprise— especially at Sterling.

Bart's mornings were ritualistic: coffee in an environmentally responsible cardboard cup. Read the emails that had collected overnight. Listen to whining voicemail messages from minor actors or their agents complaining because they had not been asked to do publicity for the film in which their single thirty-second scene was their big break. Then there were memos to write. Post-its to plaster on Brian's computer screen with instructions to call personal publicists to get approval of their clients' bios or photos for use at some upcoming film festival.

Lately, however, Bart had a new objective for arriving early: his diary.

With his notebooks in which to capture fleeting thoughts and feelings, Bart unleashed a torrent of frustrations and run-on sentences of venom and resentment toward his colleagues, family, and friends. He was stunned by his own vitriol and use of what he'd been raised to think of as vulgar language.

He devised codes for his various colleagues in case his notes fell into the wrong hands. For instance, "JtH" was "Jabba the Hut," in reference to behemoth Harry Pence, the most frighteningly obese person he'd ever met. Harry Pence was a Harley-Davidson motorcycle enthusiast who led the Hogs-on-Hogs contingent at the annual Fourth of July Parade and fired assistants as soon as they proved to be smarter than him and quite capable of doing his job. JtH was threatened by demonstrations of intelligence among his support staff, especially since he had the IQ of an ice cube—and he knew it.

His journal entries were almost like automatic writing—the words not coming *from* Bart but rather *through* him. The sometimes-unintelligible sentences reminded him of one-sided conversations of a schizophrenic homeless person whose words poured forth with no continuity of thought.

Nine o'clock came too quickly, usually when Bart was on a writing roll. He resented having to put away his scrawled notes and begin his workday, preparing questions for interviews for a new press kit or feature article. By 9:05 the trade papers and Bart's mail were delivered. He finished the dregs of his coffee and scanned *Daily Variety*.

Several interesting stories peppered the paper today. Something about Robert Downey Jr.'s old jailhouse uniform being auctioned on eBay. Some wunderkind studio marketing chief in his early twenties losing it at the shoulders when his latest movie starring old-time star Michael Douglas flopped at the box office.

Bart shook his head. "Poor guy. Washed up at twenty-three!" He really wasn't worried about the studio marketing guy. There was an unwritten law in Hollywood: You can only fall upward. If you get fired from one studio, you always go on to a bigger and better job at another one, regardless of what offense caused your termination. Lying. Cheating. Embezzling. No sin in Hollywood goes unrewarded.

Take producer David Begelman, for example. Still the poster boy for dirty tricks in a town with more scandal than Washington, DC, Begelman had embezzled a fortune from Judy Garland and Cliff Robertson and God only knew who else. But like countless executives before and after him, Begelman was commensurately rewarded with better-paying jobs. The Devil finally caught up with him, though, taking his soul in a suite at the Century Plaza Hotel and making it appear to be a suicide. "Ah. Karma," Bart said triumphantly when he'd read of the incident in some celebrity biography.

Each day, the mail boy also brought a stack of résumés from eager freelance writers hoping for a chance to do some work for Bart and thus add Sterling to their list of credits. There were also the screenings and invitations to film premieres from his counterparts at rival studios and announcements about awards banquets. Stacks of crank letters from disgruntled filmgoers completed his daily haul from the US Postal Service.

One of Bart's myriad duties was to personally respond to people who had nothing better to do with their lives than complain about the tarnished image of Sterling Studios. Nine out of ten letters quoted the Bible and ended with some unimaginative, cliché prophecy that the studio's famous grandfather-like founder was "spinning in his grave." *He's frozen, you dunderhead!* Bart often screamed silently at the semiliterate letters. *Ever hear of cryogenics? He ain't spinning unless he's on a spit roasting in hell!* Which was a definite possibility, considering the several biographies that brought up evidence of his Nazi affiliations.

Bart's written responses to the sometimes-hostile letters were unfailingly polite. He protected his professional integrity while maintaining the appropriate image and preserving the rich culture and history of the studio, which had been built primarily on the success of the country's biggest-ever hit song from one of Sterling's early short films from World War II. The ballad "Meet Me at the Zoo (When the War is Through)," from the film *Service from the Heart,* was still raking in royalties more than seventy-five years later.

Bart's letters sometimes sounded as if they were written by an automaton with the same affected congeniality as a recorded voice at Disneyland admonishing parents to keep a tight leash on their dysfunctional brats. He had long ago run out of original ideas for his responses to these letters. Now they were all pretty much uniform:

Thank you for taking the time to write. We appreciate your patronage and promise to continue to strive to live up to your highest expectations for the finest in family film entertainment... you cock-sucking shithead.

That tag never made it into any of Bart's correspondence, but he often fantasized about insulting the cretins who took up his valuable time with their lame protests and threats to never again buy tickets to Sterling's movies or spend their yearly vacations at any of the company-owned water parks and spa resorts. Instead, he strove to sound as sincere and sickly-sweet as possible when he imagined the ignoramuses who bitterly complained about profanity in the studio's films or asked why the young hero or heroine in so many stories were always fatherless or motherless or orphaned. Nine out of ten times that loathsome phrase "family values" appeared in their idiotic missives.

It was a testament to Bart's tact and professionalism that he was able to respond with diplomacy, especially the time when a barrage of thousands of letters with nearly identical sentences were delivered by the sackful from the Coalition for Traditional Nuclear Family Unity, a faction of the so-called Religious Right. They were having a field day with Hollywood in general and with Sterling Studios in particular.

"Yeah, yeah, and you don't hate the sinner, only the sin," Bart jeered, parroting evangelical Pat Robertson-like rhetoric.

Bart bet that if the writers of these letters knew about the bulletin board outside his office door, where he posted the week's most asinine complaints for all to laugh at, there'd be fewer letters for him to answer.

But EVP Stephanie insisted on reading every one of Bart's responses, especially since the *WACs in the White House* debacle. "Too arch!" she scrawled with her Sharpie across one of Bart's typical replies. "Your condescension is obvious!" she wrote in the margin of another. "Don't patronize!" she declared on still another.

Bart picked through the rest of his morning's mail. To his surprise, there was an invitation-size envelope with his name and address handwritten in elegant calligraphy.

"I hate weddings," was Bart's muttered first response as he sliced the top edge of the envelope with a serrated opener. However, when he withdrew the ecru-colored engraved card, he was surprised to discover it was an invitation to a black-tie soiree.

Your presence is requested at the home of Peter Jacks,
February 9th 7:00 p.m.

To commemorate and screen the final episode of The Grass Is Always Greener.
Regrets Only.

A handwritten message was scrawled at the bottom of the Benneton Graveur stationery card. It read, "Mitch says you've got the cutest dimples. Please attend." It was signed with the initials PJ.

Bart looked again at the date on the card and then checked his calendar. As a rule, he hated Hollywood parties. But on a Saturday night Paco would be working at the Trap and, rather than sit at home alone wearing his underpants and fantasizing about his Latino lover, Bart decided he should probably accept the invitation and at least make an appearance. But he really didn't want to show up alone. He didn't want to give the apparently lecherous Peter Jacks the impression that he was *available*. Bart wondered if he could persuade Paco to switch shifts with another bartender. "It would certainly be a novelty having an actual *date* with Paco," Bart thought aloud.

Thus far, Bart had been content to keep the relationship on a purely sexual basis. The "old-fashioned boy" shackles that Bart had cast aside since meeting Paco made the idea of dinner and a movie not an option if, instead, they could spend their time on the sheets, igniting each other into a sexual conflagration.

Dates are for people who are testing the waters or are tired of making love to each other, Bart thought. This was his time to quench his nearly insatiable thirst and appetite for Paco's naked body, and he didn't want to share Paco with anybody.

Reevaluating the party situation, Bart thought, *In a town that pays absolutely no attention to me, if I make a grand entrance with Paco on my arm at Peter Jacks's, even Hollywood's most jaded movers and shakers would probably do a double take. We'd be king and queen of the prom.*

Bart confessed to himself that, just once, he'd like to know how Eliza Doolittle felt when she appeared coiffed and in couture at the top of the palace staircase as royalty and servants alike whispered to each other, trying to deduce her real identity. The same thing might actually happen at Peter Jacks's party. "Who's the lucky guy—and the stud he's with?" Bart could practically hear the covetous crowd murmuring.

By 9:30 the office was alive with the sound of the copy machine spewing out film reviews emailed from the New York office, and phones ringing everywhere. Assistants usually preceded the arrival of their bosses in order to make coffee and flag meetings and luncheon appointments on daily calendars and clip stories from the major daily newspapers and trades about the studio's films and stars. The exception to this rule was his assistant, Brian. He sauntered in whenever he damn well pleased, and more often than not, it was Bart who got Brian *his* coffee. If he was going to the commissary for a cup, he figured he might as well be gracious enough to bring him back a decaf. Brian always thought he was getting the real thing, but he was generally so wired, Bart didn't want to contribute to a meltdown from more caffeine.

After returning with Brian's java, Bart called Mitch to acknowledge he'd been invited to Peter Jacks's party.

"That's my handwriting on the envelope, silly," Mitch said, pleased with his penmanship and social clout.

"You also told Peter I have dimples? There's just the one."

"How do I know you don't have one hidden on another cheek... one in your jeans?"

"Save your lines for the water-delivery guy." Bart laughed. "You'd better be there to protect me."

"Trust me, Peter'll be too drunk on martinis to be a bother. He'll just embarrass himself, as usual." Mitch sighed. "But you'll meet some stars. Totally A-list. It's a who's who of Hollywood leeches. They'll be bloodsucking Peter for the last time. Fortunately, I've spiced the list with an assortment of the cutest bag boys from Gelson's."

Bart couldn't care less about the stars or the bag boys, although on second thought, the human resources director at Gelson's market was known for having a sweet tooth when it came to hiring soap-opera-beautiful young men. The grocery store was a good place for sexually frustrated older women to get *themselves* bagged. But Bart loathed Hollywood and its pretentious parties. He often vowed that once he found a way out of Sterling, and Hollywood in general, he'd never accept an invitation for anything but intimate dinners for no more than eight. And he'd never read another edition of *Daily Variety* or the *Hollywood Reporter*.

When did my attitude change? Bart occasionally wondered about his intense dislike of Hollywood. *When did my wondering childlike enthusiasm disappear?*

From his earliest memory, Bart had wanted to work in show business. He didn't want to be an actor, but he wanted to be surrounded by creative people. The stifling mediocrity of living in a small town and growing up with family and friends who were dull and passionless gave him no other choice than to pursue a totally different life. He identified more with the kids on the television show *Glee* than with anyone in his own school. And there was never a question in his mind that he'd somehow make a success of himself.

Bart had left home and gone off to UCLA to study English lit. In his sophomore year, when a chance came up to do temp secretarial work at Paramount Pictures, he accepted the assignment and left school. He thought he'd never look back, and for a few years he felt right on track with his life. He'd even burst out of his virginal closet and fell in love. Then he was hired at Sterling Studios, and the intense daily pressure blew the fairy dust right out of his eyes.

It was still fun to have Meryl Streep or Glenn Close call him personally to discuss their publicity responsibilities for whatever film they'd just made for the studio. And to be in the marketing department's restroom and find Chris Hemsworth at the urinal beside him gave Bart a small reminder of the excitement he once felt about making his dreams come true in Hollywood. Bart's real issue with the biz was the gargantuan egos of talentless senior executives and the flash-in-the-pan actors and their maniacal representatives—as well as having to write trivial bile about them day in and day out.

"Maybe it isn't so much that I hate Hollywood," Bart mused aloud. "Maybe I'm simply burned out."

His reason for attending Peter Jacks's party was almost like peeing next to Mr. Hemsworth, only it had a more historic significance. Peter had been America's #1 comedy star and was still the country's most talked about celebrity in a week that also boasted such headlines as the *Globe*'s "Megan and Harry Screw the Palace."

"If nothing more, we'll have fun dishing the crowd," Mitch assured Bart. "I'm planning to get Tom Holland and Armie Hammer together, then separate them from the crowd to see what happens. An experiment. Sociology 101."

"I think they're both straight-*ish*," Bart said. Bart knew that in Mitch's mind every man was considered gay until proven otherwise. He lived by his motto: "I never met a man who didn't like to get his dick sucked, sweetums."

The rest of the week seemed endless. Between meetings and writing press releases and press kits and cast and filmmaker bios and photo captions and film synopses and answering complaint letters and talking to agents and personal publicists, Bart had little time to think about Paco or Peter

Jacks's party. Besides, the only time he could telephone and leave a message on Paco's machine was when Brian was away from his desk. His ears were as acutely tuned as a Doberman's. Bart couldn't risk him overhearing any plans he made with Paco.

It hardly mattered. Paco never answered the phone before three in the afternoon. That was when his writing time ended. When he knocked off, he played his messages. If Bart had called, Paco would return the call right away. Brian had begun to suspect something was going on, because whenever Paco phoned and he asked in his rapid-fire cross-examination, "Bart-Caine's-office-who's-calling-please-and-thank-you?" Paco would say, "It's personal."

By now, Brian recognized Paco's voice. "*Personal's* on line two," he announced with a deadpan smugness. Bart picked up the line and whispered his conversations.

Every time *Personal* phoned, it was obvious that Brian was eavesdropping, because things became utterly quiet outside Bart's office. Bart could sometimes see the silhouette of Brian's shadow as he leaned closer to the frosted-glass door and took mental notes about the one-sided conversation he was hearing. Bart had to keep everything he said to Paco cryptic and ambiguous. A code evolved. Bart spoke in brief, monosyllabic sentences. Paco understood. Brian thought he did, too. He was always projecting what he *thought* people were thinking... especially about him.

That night, another traffic snarl turned into a harried drive to Paco's room. The moment Bart arrived, he could tell his lover was not in the best of moods. The sex was perfunctory. Paco was physically present, but his sexy, scruffy, and buzz-cut head was off spinning somewhere in another universe.

Finally, Paco heaved a heavy sigh of dissatisfaction.

"What?" Bart asked.

Another sigh. "How long before your friend reads my script?" Paco whined.

Oh, shit, Bart thought, *no more fooling around.* "As a matter of fact, you sexy, talented stud, I wanted to surprise you."

Paco rolled onto his side and propped his head up into the palm of his left hand. "Yeah?"

"Good news. I talked to him today." Bart smiled, drawing on his best PR bullshitting skills. "He apologized for taking so long. Lots of other scripts to read. But he loved *Blind as a Bat.* In fact, he said in his report he gave it an *Excellent.*"

"Cool." Paco was obviously thrilled but didn't want to sound overly enthusiastic. "So what's next? Will the studio buy it?"

"You can't even officially submit it without an agent," Bart said, quickly bringing down Paco's euphoria.

"But if the guy likes it, can't he recommend it to one of the studio's creative execs?"

"He could get fired for reading unsolicited material."

"Then what's the use?"

Bart made a snap decision. "I've got a plan. There's a party on Saturday... at Peter Jacks's house."

Paco whistled. "Peter Jacks. Wow. I saw his video. That's one sick dumbass."

"So he has a couple of sexual kinks. You're not exactly Mary's innocent little lamb when it comes to a few perversions. Anyway, there'll be plenty of stars and agents and managers there. If you switch your night at the Trap, you can join me. To meet people. To network. Parties are where it all happens."

"I'll definitely get the night off," Paco quickly agreed. "So what exactly did he say about the script?"

"He's going to send me his written report," Bart lied again, having received the coverage over a week ago. "But he did say it was one of the best scripts he'd read in a long time."

"I'm totally jazzed, man. And this guy's legit? He's good at his job?"

"He's been at it for a long time. The studio takes his coverage seriously. As soon as I get the written report, I'll bring it over. We'll celebrate."

"Come here, you little shit. I'm celebrating now!"

With those words, Paco rolled over onto Bart's still-sticky-with-sweat body, and the two began to deep-kiss again. The feeling of hard muscles and velvet flesh made any further thoughts about anything other than physical pleasure disappear. Paco was back to his old self again, giving his undivided attention to sex.

Before dressing to leave, Bart met Mrs. Carter and her cat in the hallway. Apparently, she was getting used to seeing Bart—because for the first time, she stopped and smiled. Her eyes scanned Bart from top to bottom. When Bart returned to Paco's room, he dressed and said, "By the way, you need a tuxedo for this party. I'll pay for it if you like."

Paco took the offer in stride, as if he expected the invitation would come with all additional expenses paid for. Bart added, "Just go down to Garry's Tux Rental in Burbank tomorrow. The studio has an account there. And don't forget the shirt and shoes, too."

"I'll be Prince Charming at the ball," said Paco.

"Ever been to a glittery Hollywood party?" Bart asked, knowing the truth. "You're in for a shock... or treat... depending on how you look at it."

"What's the big deal? A lot of phony baloneys all dressed up for Peter's funeral."

"Do you have business cards?" Bart asked.

"I don't even have a website. Too expensive."

"You should, to hand out to everybody you meet. I'll have our graphics department make up a box for you."

"De rigueur?"

Paco surprised Bart with his choice of words. What one minute seemed like a limited monosyllabic vocabulary with a heavy Latino accent, the next minute became a mouthful enunciated with a genuine French inflection. That was the writer in him, Bart surmised. Or the actor.

"If I could just meet an agent and get him to represent the project, I'd be set," Paco said.

Bart cautioned, "These things take time in this town, so don't be too disappointed if, after all the alcohol and drug-induced bonhomie, you don't hear from anyone right away. We may have to go to a lot of these things before people start to get used to you. Just stick with me, Mr. Sexy."

Although Bart wasn't in any hurry to leave, he knew it was time to call it a night. Plus, Paco said that another online customer was due to arrive soon, which made Bart furious, although he tried not to show it. Bart was, if not *in love* with Paco, at least *conquered* by him. He was envious of the other people Paco was having sex with—for profit. He wanted to be his only partner, just as Paco was his only partner.

"Can I ever expect to be the only man you're interested in?" Bart asked, surprising himself with his blunt question.

"Hey," Paco said, enfolding Bart in his arms, "I'm really grateful for you."

"Because I came through with my friend at the studio?"

"Yeah," Paco said. "But also because you still excite me. You definitely came along at the right time in my life."

"All I can do is open the door. It's up to you to walk through it." Bart tried to sound like a benevolent mentor. "You came along at the right time for me, too," he added before a long, passionate kiss goodbye.

7

The next morning arrived too quickly. Before Bart even had his coffee, Stephanie was on the warpath. She'd left a voicemail message on Bart's cell phone the night before, insisting he call the moment he received it. Bart hadn't responded. By the time he'd gotten home after seeing Paco, it was way too late, although he thought that calling Stephanie at 2:00 a.m. and waking her up would have been a fun prank.

An identical message was on Bart's office answering machine: "Rumor has it that you're not finished with the press kit for *Gratuitous Explosion*," he heard Stephanie's husky voice shout through the phone's speaker.

"Fuck you, Stephanie," Bart said aloud. It was still early, and the office was fairly empty, so no one heard him.

"If I come in there tomorrow and find that's true... well, you can only imagine how I'm going to strangle you, you little shit. Think about it."

Is this harassment? Bart wondered as he reached for his bottle of Xanax and dumped twice the prescribed dosage into the palm of his hand. He chased the pills with a swallow of coffee.

Bart stared at the framed poster from the sci-fi movie *The*

Day the Earth Stood Still that was hanging on the wall opposite his desk. "*Klaatu barada nikto!*" he said aloud. They were words from the film, an alien pronouncement to summon the robot policemen of the universe to zap criminal Earthlings with a deadly ray. Bart wished that he could rid planet Earth of Stephanie with a ray gun. He would have loved to see a giant robot cornering Stephanie, making her scream and faint with terror, like Patricia Neal did in the movie. Or better yet, the blaster beam could totally disintegrate Stephanie altogether. Imagining Stephanie reduced to a pile of ash amused Bart.

The press materials were indeed late, but as usual, it wasn't due to Bart's lack of diligence. Stephanie herself had held up production for a full two weeks by failing to read and approve the written copy. Call after call to Stephanie had resulted in little action. Stephanie seemed determined to undermine Bart's reputation and make him look incompetent. But because Stephanie had the ear and support of the chairman of the studio, there was no one Bart could go to for help.

With Stephanie, there was always an excuse. "I left your press-kit notes on the airplane." Or "It must have dropped out of the cab in New York." Or "The sentence structure was so poor I couldn't go on. If they were done properly in the first place, I wouldn't have had to make any comments."

It was a no-win situation for Bart. Nothing he did would ever please Stephanie. But at least the Xanax was kicking in, so he decided he might as well just be himself and stop worrying about his personal Cruella de Vil.

In Bart's imagination he envisioned a time when Sterling Studios would be making a film adaptation of one of his novels. As executive vice president of publicity and marketing, Stephanie would have to be involved with the project. In Bart's fantasy, he walked into the executive conference room with the director, the producers, and Stephanie, who would be all smiles,

taking credit for having been a mentor to Bart during his forma-
tive years in the industry.

As the meeting begins, Bart, with a glass of sparkling Pelle-
grino in his hand, suddenly stops the proceedings.

"This is the film with the highest budget for any movie
you've ever made," he announces triumphantly. "I'm so
delighted that you outbid Warner Brothers, Disney, Amazon,
and Netflix. It's great that we've got Meryl Streep, Leonardo
DiCaprio, and Angela Bassett. I love them all. Wow! I smell
Oscars for almost everyone in this room. I always thought this
would happen. I just never imagined that my alma mater, Sterling, would be the studio to make the picture.

"With that said, please indulge my one artistic idiosyncrasy,"
Bart continues. At this point he stands up. Stephanie is shocked
to see that Bart has grown from five seven to a wide-shouldered
six five just since their arrival in the conference room. His
piercing blue eyes look first upon the director, and he smiles.
Then to the duo of inconsequential producers. Finally, his face
freezes. His eyes bore into Stephanie. Pointing a well-manicured
index finger, he roars, "If this fucker is on the project—in any
capacity—I walk away from final negotiations this very minute.
Paramount, Universal, Hulu, and everybody else in town are just
as eager to make this film as you are. *No Stephanie Hough!* Do I
make myself perfectly clear?"

By now Stephanie has withered away in her chair, a child
swallowed up in a grown-up's clothes. Security arrives to escort
her off the lot and out of Hollywood altogether. *Vanity Fair*
magazine runs a cover story about the incident, and the whole
town applauds.

Bart's reverie was interrupted by the ringing telephone. His
heart raced when he saw whose number appeared on the caller
ID: Ext. 666. Stephanie.

Giving his most effusive, bullshit-publicist greeting, he

answered, "Morning, Stephanie! I was just about to return your call from last night. Got in too late to disturb you at home. What? Who's spreading that silly rumor? The press materials will definitely post online this week. Of course. Right on schedule. Don't pay any attention to what Brian says. He's in rehearsals for an all-male version of *The Women,* so he's a bit distracted. Yes, of course, they'll be up by Friday. Great. See you at the staff meeting at ten."

Bart replaced the telephone receiver on the cradle. "Bitch!" he whispered.

When Brian finally wandered to his desk at 9:45, Bart could hardly control his impatience. "*Afternoon*, Brian," he mocked, his tone dripping with sarcasm.

"Sorry I'm late," Brian panted as he turned on his computer. "Had to wait for the plumber. I accidentally flushed my emotional support hamster down the toilet, and it clogged the pipe. Major flooding." It was one of his more creative excuses for being tardy.

"Last week your parrot was decapitated by the ceiling fan. Before that, your dog went into cardiac arrest when he ate a plate of marijuana edibles. Whether fact or fiction, I wouldn't tell those stories on myself if I were you," Bart suggested. "They really make you sound like you're a few planks short of a full stage. Anyway, I need you to call Graphics right away and find out when the title treatment for *Gratuitous Explosion* will be ready to post. You apparently told Stephanie the press materials weren't available, but I told her they'd be up pronto. Please don't make me out to be more of a liar than I already am."

The day was not starting out well. Not only were the press materials for *Gratuitous Explosion* not ready; other projects, such as the synopses for the studio's entire slate of films for the remainder of the year, weren't ready. The other publicists in the department needed this material to pitch stories to the so-called muffin magazines and mommy bloggers. It was time for Bart to stop thinking about Paco and start concentrating on the fearsome deadlines he was facing.

But as soon as Paco called to confirm he'd been able to switch with another bartender and could go to Peter Jacks's party after all, Bart fell back into his lackadaisical "God, I don't want to be here working today" mode. Hearing Paco's voice just made him crazy with lust. If it weren't for Paco's unbreakable writing schedule, Bart would surely run over for a nooner. But Paco was extremely disciplined. He had his unwavering routine: Writing. Gym. Hustling. Bart. In that order. Bart felt doomed to be a puppet to Stephanie—and to Paco. *Please, dear God, let things change after the Peter Jacks party*, he silently begged the universe.

Perhaps once he and Paco were seen together in a social environment, people would automatically jump to conclusions and think of them as a couple. Bart hoped that Paco, too, would start to see them as partners and begin to think of their relationship as more than a business arrangement. Bart wasn't ready to rock the boat by making domestic demands of Paco, but the prospect of being Paco's only man was definitely high on his wish list. If they were a success at the party, perhaps Paco would keep him around.

Saturday afternoon finally arrived. Bart—dressed in a tuxedo—drove to Paco's place. Parking was easier now that Paco had arranged a city street-parking pass for him. After the glass door to his room slid open and revealed Paco in all his black-tie splendor, Bart gushed, "Ricky Martin has no competition in the sex-appeal department." Paco always looked sensational—wearing anything—or nothing at all—but seemed especially attractive in a tuxedo.

"Fancy, eh?" Paco said, not fishing for a compliment so much as giving himself a thumbs-up. "The guy who did the alterations paid me a hundred and fifty for sex after hemming my pants." Paco laughed, pleased with himself.

It was typical narcissistic Paco behavior, and Bart was never in the mood to hear about his sexual exploits with others. Whenever Paco flaunted how much sex he had, it cut to the core of Bart's insecurity and fear of rejection. He knew he could never expect Paco to be monogamous. Hell, he made a good part of his living by people paying to get physical with him. But it was way too late for Bart not to feel possessive. "Amusing," he said sarcastically.

"It was. What a kick watching from three different mirrored angles. Isn't it wild what people will do for sexy people?"

"Yes, wild. I suppose I should be grateful that I no longer have to pay you for the honor."

"You've paid me enough with all your help getting the script read and taking me to this party," Paco said, his tone registering genuine appreciation.

"Speaking of which," Bart said, holding out a manila envelope, "here's the official coverage on *Blind as a Bat.*"

"No way! How cool is this, man!"

Paco grabbed the four typewritten, single-spaced pages. The detail into which the script reader had gone was extremely analytic. Under the heading "Synopsis," Paco's entire story and characters were boiled down for quick reading. Paco skipped two pages of synopsis and flipped to the one that was headed "Comments."

It read:

BLIND AS A BAT appears to be a tightly woven screwball rom-com from start to finish. It's filled with memorable characters, enhanced by witty dialogue. There is a payoff at the end that heightens the emotional farewell between main characters Jesus Parez and Joanna Wren. The writer brilliantly puts a perfect spin on the contemporary issues of love and romance in the 21st century. In terms of overall appeal, there seem to be many fresh and intriguing elements to this project. Again, the writer (and story) offers much in the way of fresh imagination and inventiveness. The principal characters are nicely drawn, and the dialogue throughout has energy and humor. The writer is obviously good at devising poignant "moments" and character reactions.

At the bottom of the page, under the heading "Script," was the single word *Excellent*. The next line down, beside the heading "Writer," was another single word: *Brilliant*. Under "Comments," the analyst had typed: "Don't let this one get away."

"'The characters are *nicely* drawn'?" Paco said with incredulous disdain. "How could he say they were *'nicely drawn.'* They're *perfectly* drawn, for Christ's sake."

Bart was shocked. "Paco, that's the best script coverage I've ever read! 'Nicely drawn' is a good thing. How can you take those two words out of an entire document that practically hails you as the Second Coming? You sound like an actor who gets rave reviews from all the respected critics, then a little wuss in some freebie throwaway says his performance was rigid or something equally stupid, and the actor's ego is destroyed. What you've got here is gold! You're validated as a screenwriter! You can probably take it to any agent in town and get representation!"

Paco realized he was overreacting and admitted he had never expected anything so glowing. He knew it was one of his better scripts, even if that cocksucker from Actors and Others hadn't

recognized its merit. But he truly hadn't expected quite the effusive reaction from a professional reader.

"So now we get in the car, drive to the party, and start
making contacts," Bart said. Then from his pocket, he took out
another surprise: a small rectangular white box tied with a red
bow. "Open it," he said, handing the package to Paco.

Paco looked quizzically at Bart, then untied the bow and
lifted the cover off the box. Inside, he found two hundred white
business cards. Each engraved:

Paco Castillo
      Screenwriter
      (310) 555-2847

Bart said, "After all our time together, I still don't know if I
have the correct spelling of your last name. Is it right? I can have
it changed."

"Yeah, man." That was all Paco could say. He was seriously
touched by Bart's generous gesture. "I've never had business
cards before."

"I guarantee they'll go fast," Bart said. "Everybody at this
party is going to want to know who you are. Once the right agent
gets a copy of the script and the coverage, everybody will know
who Paco Castillo is. Believe me."

8

"**A**nd all the stars, there never were, are parking cars and pumping ga-a-a-ass! I've got lots of friends in San Jose..."

The car radio was blaring an oldies station, and Paco was singing along to that old Bacharach/David song—the Carpenters' arrangement—as they pulled up to the valet sign at the bottom of the private road that led to Peter Jacks's mansion. Paco pointed to the two young valets. "Think these guys are 'all the stars that never were'? They're parkin' cars. And probably pumpin' ass." He laughed at his own sexist joke. "But who'd be caught dead living in a place like San Jose, for Christ's sake." He was still on an emotional high from reading and rereading the coverage and anticipating his first big Hollywood party. The two good-looking blonds in red vests rushed to either side of Bart's Mustang and opened the doors. "Jacks party?" one asked as Bart stepped out of the vehicle and was handed a pink-colored claim ticket. The valet did not expect a reply to the obvious. He nodded toward a waiting Rolls-Royce at the entrance to the driveway. "The car will drive you up the hill."

"How do I look?" Paco nervously asked Bart. "Is my tie straight? Is my breath okay? Should I have worn underpants?"

"You look great. I guarantee all the women and gay agents and managers in the place will be choking on their crudities the minute you walk in the house. As for the underwear—wouldn't want your panty lines to show."

The two of them got into the backseat of the Rolls for the short but elegant ride up the hill to Peter Jacks's estate. At the top, dominating the center of the circular drive, was a three-tiered water fountain bathed in lights of red, green, and amber. As two more red-vested valets opened the car doors, Bart and Paco stepped out from opposite sides of the vehicle. The sound of water cascading and gurgling in the fountain, combined with a miasma of voices and music emanating from within the mansion, gave the evening a fairy-tale aura.

A card table was set up at the bottom of the steps leading to the front door. A burly black man dressed in a dark suit, white shirt, and black necktie was seated on a folding chair, checking off names on a guest list. On the table beside the list was his walkie-talkie, which emitted mostly static, but every now and then, incoherent voices.

"They have a list?" Paco said nervously as he and Bart stood in a short line and approached the table.

Bart smiled at Paco's naiveté. "All the news about Peter's sex play probably makes him a sitting duck for religious fanatics. Plus, more than half of Hollywood is here tonight. It's free food and booze. But blow this place up and the whole town goes with it."

"Then my script would *never* get made," Paco said, always thinking of himself first. "What if we're not on the list?"

"We're on. I've got the invitation. Plus, one of my studio colleagues is Peter's friend. He set the whole thing up."

When the couple ahead of them had been cleared, Bart

announced, "Caine... and guest."

The guy at the table took a while to go down the alphabetical list to find *Caine, Bart.* "Doesn't say you're bringing anyone," he said, speaking in an imperious tone with a West Indies accent.

"You always bring a guest," Bart said testily. Was the guy an idiot? "Nobody expects you to come alone."

"Apparently Mr. Jacks did." The black man's jaundiced, bloodshot-but-knowing eyes looked up at Bart, judging him to be just another privileged Hollywood elitist.

Other guests were waiting behind Bart and Paco. "What's the holdup?" someone asked, as if a restaurant maître d' had the impudence to make Mr. Big wait for his usual high-profile table. These were industry people unaccustomed to cooling their heels for a fraction of a moment for so much as a Starbucks coffee.

"This is ridiculous," Bart said. "Call Mitch Wood on your walkie-talkie thing," he said dictatorially.

The security man sighed insolently and picked up his walkie-talkie. He spoke to someone inside the house.

In a short moment, the front door flew open, and Mitch practically danced down the steps to the table. He gave Bart a peck on the cheek, hugged Paco, and went behind the table. He grabbed the pen out of the security guy's hand and, next to *Caine, Bart,* wrote: *Plus One.* "There! Everything copacetic? Come, kids," he said, and led Bart and Paco into the house.

The mansion's entryway was *Architectural Digest* perfection. In the center of the polished marble foyer was a nearly priceless, round, Lalique pedestal table. Its cut-crystal foundation of Erté-like vestal virgins, standing side by side in a circle, formed the plinth on which the beveled glass top held a tall vase containing a colossal, colorful spray of ranunculus, roses, peonies, and lilies.

"Welcome to 'Peter's Patch'! Definitely not to be confused with Valentino's 'Falcon's Lair,' up on the other hill," Mitch explained. "My, you two look so-o-o-o yummy together," he gushed, taking in the seductive Paco. "It's definitely the man who makes the clothes, not the other way around," he said, giving Paco a long, lascivious look; then he actually growled.

The house was a jaw-dropping stunner in every respect. As they followed Mitch to the top step of the sunken living room, both Bart and Paco were taken aback by the most breathtaking view of the city either of them had ever seen. Los Angeles was revealed through floor-to-ceiling glass windows, a 180-degree expanse like the view one might see from an airplane on approach to LAX. A Santa Ana wind was blowing, so the lights of the city below were a shimmering sequined cape laid out like one of Bob Mackie's bugle-beaded costumes for Cher but magnified by a zillion.

Two steps below, the room was packed with recognizable faces from television and movies. Most of the women were wearing New York black, but a few—assistants from agents' offices, no doubt—had slipped in wearing red or teal. They were there to be noticed by any straight man attending—of which there was a definite dearth.

Silver trays with flutes of champagne were passed among the wall-to-wall guests by an array of handsome, smiling, blond caterer/waiters. Mitch made an almost imperceptible signal to one of them, and Bart and Paco were offered their first drinks of the evening.

"Cristal, of course," Mitch preened, boasting about the quality of the champagne.

"And where's our infamous host?" Bart asked *sotto voce*.

Mitch raised an eyebrow. "This way, sweetums," he said, cocking his head.

Mitch, acting as cattle catcher, took Bart by the hand, and he took Paco's. Together, the trio wended their way through the crowd toward the terraced garden outside. Soon they were poolside. It was a perfect, balmy Southern California night. Adding to the magical atmosphere, a full moon was hanging over the city. Even Bart was impressed. Paco was bowled over and could hardly maintain his well-trained facade of indifference, especially when he inadvertently pushed up against Julia Roberts as she nibbled on a stuffed mushroom. She was about to complain, but when she looked at Paco, it was as if she'd just been baptized and seen the light. She absorbed the full spectacle of Paco and smiled. "No worries."

Opposite the trio, across the pool, lounging on a chaise, was the man himself—Peter Jacks. Holding the stem of a martini glass, the base of which was resting on the arm of the recliner, Peter was surrounded by a group of attractive and successful-looking men and women all dressed in formal wear but looking as comfortable as if they were in jogging togs. Bart could tell that Paco envied their composure. For the first time, Paco understood what was meant by "to the manner born."

Mitch led his charges forward, but he stopped the train a few paces before reaching the depot. He paused to point out the particular people who were fawning over Peter. "The tall one is Brent from over at Fox. Who's he kidding with his so-called fiancée on his arm?" Mitch clucked. "I had him at last year's White Party in Palm Springs. And that one's Pucky." Mitch pointed to another young and attractive man. "Cute, and he knows it—if you get my drift. Untouchable now. He belongs to his boss, or vice versa. I'm surprised he's not wearing his collar and leash; master-slave, that sort of scene. He's with Writers and Actors Agency."

Bart gave Paco the elbow and a nod, indicating he should keep Pucky in mind for a pitch of his screenplay.

"Standing next to Pucky is what's-her-name, the new exec in

charge of prime-time programming at NBC. There's no way she didn't have something to do with dropping Peter's show. Surprised she's showing both of her faces here."

Then, practically jumping up and down, Mitch said, "Goody! Speaking of man hungry, but doesn't want Mommy and Daddy and the industry to know, is that scummy Michael Stone from Actors and Others. Ick." Mitch improvised a shudder.

"Shit," Paco whispered to Bart. "That's the guy who comes into the Trap each week. The one I told you about—the one who promised to read my script and then never mentioned it again."

"Michael thinks he's a hotshot just because his uncle, who's the chief counsel for Actors and Others, got him a job at the agency," Mitch declared. "The other agents all hate him. Even his clients hate him. Unfortunately, Peter's too stupid to drop him. Oh, I can't wait to see Michael's reaction when he sees you here, Paco. Let's go make a splash, shall we?"

Mitch led the way, and in a short while they had circumnavigated the pool to the place where Peter was holding court. "It's the man of the hour!" Mitch sang out as the trio neared the master of the manse. "And here's the man I wanted you to meet. Bart Caine, meet Peter Jacks."

"Bart?" a voice cried with indignation. "What the hell are you doing here?"

"Stephanie!" Bart stammered, startled to see his boss away from the studio and out of context. He turned to Mitch and whispered harshly, "Why didn't you tell me she'd be here!"

"You'd never have come." Mitch rolled his eyes, then spat, "Oh, Stephanie! For fuck's sake. Back off! It's a party."

"What the hell are you doing here?" Stephanie demanded of Bart again, her nostrils flaring and her eyes moving up and down Bart disdainfully, as though Bart were covered in slime.

For the moment, Bart ignored her as he redirected his attention to the evening's host and extended his hand to Peter. "I'm an ardent admirer," he lied. "Do you know Paco Castillo, the screenwriter?" he said, introducing Paco.

Paco burst into a wide smile when he heard Bart's generous introduction.

"Screenwriter?" Peter's rheumy eyes met Paco's. "Do you have anything I could look at?" His words were a double entendre and not lost on Paco or the small coterie pretending to pay homage to Peter.

"Thanks for inviting us," Paco said, holding out his hand.

"You're welcome. Anytime, I'm sure." Peter showed a wry smile. He was obviously drunk. He slurred his words and couldn't make an effort to stand and greet his guests. He kept staring at Paco and thinking maybe they had met before. He'd entertained so many prostitutes and hustlers at the house.

Mitch piped in, "Peter, Bart's the one I mentioned. The publicist at Sterling Studios? Dimples?"

"Right," Peter pretended to recall. "Guess I could use a good publicist right about now, couldn't I, Hart? Heh. Heh. Heh."

"It's Bart. And I think you'll do just fine, Peter."

"Bart. Right. Oh, I'm terrible with names," Peter said. "But you're very cute, so I'm sure to remember next time."

Grasping for something to say to extricate himself from Peter, Bart caught Stephanie's eye. "And this," Bart said, looking at Peter and presenting Stephanie, "is the *Boss*. The lovely woman personally responsible for all the hits we have at Sterling Studios."

"Peter and I know each other quite well, Bart," Stephanie snarled. "We go way back, don't we, Peter?"

"If she's responsible for the hits, she must also be responsible for the bombs," Mitch said with a loud laugh.

"Stephanie, I just *love* your scarf," Bart said, trying to deflect her hostility and dissociate himself from Mitch and his bitchiness. There was something about being with his boss outside the studio environment that emboldened him.

"Hmmm," Stephanie said coldly. "You still haven't answered my question."

"Oh, I get out from behind my desk now and again. 'On festive occasions,' as Auntie Mame says."

"But his heart belongs to daddy," Mitch sang. "Meaning Stephanie and his job, of course. Bart gives Sterling his 100% undivided attention, don't you, Bart? Just like Auntie Stephanie asked, or shall I say, threatened."

Stephanie groaned. Looking over at Paco, she immediately summed him up and determined he would be scorching hot in bed, although, if he was with Bart, he was probably gay. Still, she thought she recognized him.

Noticing Stephanie's champagne flute was nearly empty, Bart asked in an overly courtly tone, "May I refill your glass?"

"I'll get my own, thank you," Stephanie said dismissively, and wandered off into the crowd.

Finding an opening in the awkward small talk, Mitch turned to Michael Stone and said, "You big important agent you. I had no idea that you and Paco here were old friends—almost kissing cousins. Or so the rumors say." Then, turning to Paco, he added, "Where again did you say you two studs got acquainted? Oh, yes, that B&D place on Santa Monica Boulevard. I always used to think that B&D stood for Black and Decker. Ya know, the power tools?" Mitch laughed at his own joke. "I know B&B is bed and breakfast. But what's S&M?" he asked for the crowd's benefit. "Oh, that's right, *sadomasochism*. I always wondered what went on in those dark rooms at the Trap. You must tell us all about it!"

Michael was demonstrably upset, and in a sociopathic talent agent, that can be lethal. The few guests who were still standing beside him—all people he knew from the industry—were looking from Paco to Michael and clearly wondering how well the two really did know each other.

Except for the tuxedo, Paco was the antithesis of everybody else at the party. Although he was more polished than anyone in his own family, there was no getting away from the fact that he was a newcomer to this circle of Hollywood players. And it showed. His discomfort among the other guests was obvious. Whereas Bart was effortless in his comportment and knew how to give and receive an air-kiss from anyone he hardly knew, Paco stayed behind Bart and tried to remain anonymous. If spoken to, he merely nodded his head to acknowledge the person.

Nobody other than Mitch or Bart made any effort to make Paco feel comfortable or accepted. The emotional high Paco had felt only a short time ago, after reading the coverage on his script and anticipating meeting the rich and famous in Hollywood, had vanished. In its place was the unsettling feeling that he was a party crasher. He wasn't a Hollywood player, and his discomfort and self-consciousness were compounded by the fact that he knew he was a diamond in the rough at best, with the emphasis on *rough*. After all, at some level, he would always be the personification of a dangerous Latino homeboy.

Not only had he little in the way of social graces, Paco knew he would never have been admitted into this rarefied circle on his own. He couldn't help feeling as though Bart were displaying him as a trophy. Paco grabbed the next flute of champagne that passed his way.

Somewhere between meeting Peter Jacks and downing his second glass of Cristal, he lost Bart and Mitch in the crowd. Now Paco stood by the edge of the estate and looked out upon the nighttime view below. He wanted desperately to get away from this superficial hellhole. He knew he didn't belong with these successful and talented people even though they were as synthetic as Styrofoam.

"Lovely view, isn't it?" A woman's voice behind Paco spoke in a little girl's whispery tone. Paco turned around. The woman was an attractive sixty-something Barbie doll dressed in a gold lame dress that stretched over her tight butt and revealed still lovely long legs. She made Paco think of the actress Connie Stevens, whom he'd seen on infomercials when he was a kid. She brushed a hand over Paco's ass. "Romantic, isn't it?" she purred, pouring half her glass of champagne into Paco's empty flute.

Ordinarily, Paco would have flirted with this aging beauty. He was a master sexual tease. However, this was not a good night for taking advantage of older but definitely still attractive ladies. He was too upset about the way the evening had disintegrated. All his previous *joie de vivre* had gone the way of an amyl nitrite high. The rush was over in a flash.

At that moment, one of the catering crew interrupted and announced that *The Grass Is Always Greener* was about to begin. The guests should all find a seat in the screening room.

Paco left the expensively coiffed and dressed woman without a word, not knowing she was a television celebrity dating back to the prehistoric 1990s. He went in search of Bart.

"Get me outta here," Paco demanded when the two finally met up in the living room.

"What's the matter?"

"Now, please! I wanna go—now!"

"Yeah, sure. I should just say goodbye to a few people."

"Now, goddamn it!" Paco cried defiantly.

Paco was so agitated that Bart had no choice but to lead him to the foyer and out the front door. They slipped into the waiting Rolls and rode down the hill. They waited in silence for the valet attendant to find Bart's Mustang. He tipped the guy five dollars and drove down to Mulholland without another word from Paco.

9

"They're just assholes. It's in their DNA." Bart finally broke the silence as they reached the intersection of Santa Monica Boulevard and La Cienega, nearing Paco's place in West Hollywood. Paco was still sullen and despondent from what he viewed as a fiasco of an evening.

"We didn't meet any big agents," Paco said. "Like an idiot, I passed out business cards to all the wrong people, including the lady washing dishes in the kitchen. She looked at me, then looked at the card, and looked at me again as if I were stupid. She shrugged her shoulders and put the card into her apron pocket. Then she said something under her breath in what sounded like Chinese and put her hands back in a sink full of dirty soapy water. It was an evening of free champagne and grazing food, and that's it. And I'm still hungry."

"That's not all of 'it,'" Bart retorted. "You should hear yourself. You've just been to a party that the whole town will be talking about for ages. You may even be in *People* magazine because you bumped into so many stars being photographed."

"Crashed into 'em is more like it."

"It was crowded. You can't be held responsible for colliding with people who take up more than their share of the planet. There were journalists from the *Hollywood Reporter* and *LA Times* and *Vanity Fair.*"

"I felt completely alone and out of place."

"You were far from alone. What makes you think most of those people weren't as self-conscious as you? The confident-looking ones have just found a way to not show their fear."

"What's your point?"

"My *point* is that you're unfairly comparing yourself with experts, people who have had plenty of practice in the limelight and making entrances and idle chatter at parties. The most outgoing personalities are often the most insecure."

Paco pouted. "I felt like everybody was staring at me. I didn't fit in. I'm nothing but a stud who hasn't got the social graces of a baboon."

"At least you give yourself credit for the stud part. Some pretty famous people were staring at you—in a good way. Even if you didn't notice."

"Of course I noticed."

"That old one who looked like she was once a Barbie doll? She happened to be a *famous* Barbie doll," Bart said. "And Julia Roberts choked on her stuffed mushroom when she got a look at you, silly. And don't tell me that Laura Langley with her arm around your waist wasn't a cool thing. And what about Chucky Chatterton? He paid more than enough attention to you. I was watching. You seemed stuck on each other."

"I thought he was just an old letch."

"He did some Broadway and TV sitcoms, and he used to be on game shows in the old days."

"Around the time that Lincoln was shot, I'd guess. I'm so stupid, I didn't know how to get him to take his freakin' hand off my ass without making a scene and having him accidentally on purpose fall in the pool. So, I just stood there, frozen."

"Welcome to hashtag MeToo," Bart said, patting Paco's thigh. "What I'm trying to say is, this was just an initiation. I'll bet, growing up, you never thought you'd find yourself at such a fancy affair."

"Sure I did. I always planned it. It just didn't turn out exactly as I always imagined."

"Things seldom do. 'Be careful what you wish for because you *will* get it,' I always say."

Bart empathized with Paco's situation. "When I first came to Hollywood and willed myself into the showbiz clique, I was as much of a hayseed as you seem to think you are. Talk about lack of social graces. I once nodded off to sleep in front of Kathryn Grayson while I was sitting in a chair in her living room during a dinner party with the Asshole—as she was singing some song from an old movie that made her famous."

Bart continued, "I know you probably don't know who Kathryn Grayson was. I didn't either, until the schmuck I was living with brought me to her house in Brentwood. But trust me, she was once a *huge* star. By the time I met her, she was just huge. I was forced to watch one of her old movie musicals. She was rail thin when she was famous. But I heard that she found Shirley Temple boning her husband one time, and it made her start bingeing on Ding Dongs."

Bart grinned. "Here's how I knew I didn't fit in. During dinner, I had to surreptitiously look out of the corner of my eyes to watch the other guests to see which knife and fork to use for each course of the meal. My family were bumpkins, and I was never taught how to properly tear a dinner roll and butter one piece at a time. I didn't even know the correct position to place my utensils on my plate to indicate I was finished eating. Who knew that was a thing? I also didn't know a wineglass from a water goblet. I was embarrassed as hell. What you went through tonight was nothing. Think of it as your coming-out party. You got your feet wet. From here on, every time we go someplace ritzy, it'll get easier. Trust me."

"You fell asleep while some famous singer was entertaining in her own home?" Paco backtracked.

"Yeah. She walked over and sang full blast into my ear to wake me up. Startled the hell out of me. The other guests laughed. I went home and cried."

"I probably missed a lot of big tips by not working tonight," Paco complained.

"Tips you can get every night for the rest of your life. How many people do you know had Kevin Spacey offering to get them another glass of champagne and asking where you work out and what supplements you'd recommend for a better-developed body? That doesn't happen to many people. Unless, I suppose, they look like you."

Paco smiled, finally warming to Bart's attempt to humor him.

Bart made a left turn off Santa Monica Boulevard down to Rugby Drive. By the time they found a spot and walked a block to the rear of the house, they were already smothering each other in deep kisses. Paco's tuxedo shirt studs dropped in the yard. "Never mind. I'll find 'em in the morning," he panted, anxious to shed his clothes and feel Bart's naked body against his own.

Bart was vibrating with anticipation. Every nerve ending in his body pulsated. He was desperate to feel Paco's chest and stomach with his hands and tongue. Paco was aching, too. The moment they entered the house, Bart wrestled Paco to the mattress and stripped him of his remaining clothes. Lying on his back, breathlessly looking up at the sight of what Michelangelo would have sculpted if he'd seen Paco before David, Bart was literally out of his mind inspecting every inch of Paco's muscular chest, thick arms, tight abs, tattoos, and prominent veins. "Oh, my God, you're amazing," he whispered.

Sometime during the night, Paco got up to pee. In the pitch-black darkness of the room, he automatically reached for his cell phone and saw that there were messages. As zealous as Paco was about his gym workouts, writing, and sex, he was equally devoted to his phone. He couldn't stand not to know who had called. It was like an unopened Christmas present. If he were not allowed to untie the bow and rip apart the paper, it would drive him nuts. But it was the middle of the night. He didn't want to disturb Bart with the sound of playing back what might be calls from customers begging to drop by.

Cautiously, and with as much surreptitious movement as possible, Paco made his way to the farthest corner of the room with his phone. He looked at the message log. There were two from the same number. He pushed Play and heard a man's voice. "Paco?" the voice inquired. "This is Peter. Peter Jacks. I'm glad you gave me your card. Very wise. I'd never have known how to reach you.

"Listen. I'm genuinely sorry. I'm extremely upset with myself for being inebriated when you and your friend arrived. I'm not a drinker, as a rule, but I was so sad about the reason for the party —you know, my last show and all. Things got out of hand very early. However, I wasn't so drunk that I didn't catch the fact that you're a screenwriter. When I asked if you had anything I could look at, I hope you didn't think I was being too forward. I say things sometimes that come out sounding differently than I planned. I mean, people sometimes think I'm mischievous or whatever. Anyway, I'm rambling here. Sorry for that, too. But I'm serious about looking for new material. Now that I don't have a TV series, I've got to line up other projects. I'd really like it if you would let me read something that you think I might be right for. So, here's my private number: three, one, zero, five, five, five, six, two, eight, zero.

"Again, I'm sorry if I came across as rude or anything this

evening. I noticed you left before the screening, and I wanted to apologize. Okay. There you have it. My apology. And my interest in your work. And my phone number. Guess that's it. Hope we have an opportunity to work together."

Beep.

"Paco. It's Peter again. This is so weird. You wouldn't happen to be the Paco Castillo who wrote *Blind as a Bat?* I have that script here. It says, 'Written by Paco Castillo.' I don't know of any other screenwriter named Paco, so I'm hoping this is you. My agent gave the script to me, so I guess we have the same agent. I hope it's written by you because it's great. I like it a lot. I'll have my people talk to your people. Oh, wait. Your people are my people. Small world. Weird. Anyway, great work. Glad we had a chance to meet."

Click. Buzz.

Paco walked back to the bed and settled onto the mattress. He lay on his back and stared into the darkness. "Fuck," he said in a low, incredulous whisper as conflicting thoughts crowded his head. *I've been cursing that Actors and Others suit for not doing anything with the script... I hated the party because nothing seemed to happen... Peter Jacks is interested in my work... I don't belong to the WGA... Is he serious about liking the material?... Why hasn't that lying Michael ever said a single word about it to me?*

Bart rolled onto his side and snuggled up to Paco, placing his right arm across Paco's hard chest. "Told you so," Bart said in a sleepy voice.

"What?"

"Peter Jacks wants you. I heard the messages."

"He wants to read my stuff. Then he discovered he already had."

"He wants you, babe. Probably on video. For his collection," Bart sleepily teased.

"Fuck you. He does not." Paco felt himself getting angry. "I thought you were the one who told me my stuff was good. Well, Peter's just saying the same thing."

"Don't get hostile, honey," Bart said, now fully awake.

"I'm not hostile. But you're accusing Peter Jacks of having an ulterior motive for calling me. Don't you think maybe he was telling the truth? That he needs a role and really wanted to see what I have to offer? It sounds plausible to me."

"I believe he wants to see what you have to offer, all right," Bart said, still teasing.

"And you know what? I'd gladly give it to him. If it means selling a screenplay," Paco said with a voice that spoke volumes to Bart about his lover's ambition and what he'd do to get ahead in Hollywood.

"I was just joking," Bart said in a tone that registered his hurt feelings. He turned and rolled over, his back to Paco. "Come to think of it, I've been a pretty good stepping-stone, haven't I?"

There was no answer from Paco, but Bart knew he wasn't asleep. In fact, Paco was wide-awake, eyes open and staring into his future.

As his mind raced with thoughts about his career and Peter and Bart, Paco had to acknowledge the truth to himself—that, yes, Bart was indeed a stepping-stone. But who wasn't? Everybody was upwardly mobile in their own way. Bart might have started out as a means to an end, but there was no doubt about Paco's physical attraction to him. And there was also no doubt that Bart could do, and had already done, a lot for Paco's career and ego.

Paco would have been content to keep sleeping with Bart as long as Bart served his purpose: someone who could help him get ahead. But as of this moment, it seemed Bart's time was almost over. They both had thought it would take a while before the right people noticed Paco's work. It was happening faster than either of them had expected.

Bart was practically reading Paco's mind. It made him feel weak and sick to his stomach. He realized he'd been falling in love with Paco; there was no mistake about that. But there was more. Although Bart had always previously been involved with serious, successful, intellectual, and accomplished men, they were practically interchangeable. The sex with each of them was, to varying degrees, almost always satisfying, but there had never been any man whose sexual energy radiated as intensely as Paco's.

From the first time they met, Bart got hard just thinking about being in bed with Paco. Everything from Paco's machismo attitude to his well-constructed body was in Bart's bedtime fantasies. He was now saddened to think that he might have to give him up.

"I love you, Paco," he said in a whisper. It was the first time he had ever uttered those words to him.

Although Paco heard the admission, he didn't know what to say. So he said nothing.

10

The light of Sunday morning began to spread through Paco's room. It was that early time just after dawn when, in the past, regardless of how many times Bart and Paco had enjoyed sex during the night, they both awoke with ravenous needs. This morning was miserably different.

Bart, who had been awake for hours, now sat up, rubbed his eyes, and looked over at Paco, who was lying on his back, still staring at the ceiling. He got out of bed and collected his clothes, which were scattered on the floor. The air was thick with unspoken thoughts and decisions, and he dressed in silence. His life had literally changed overnight. As he unlocked the door to leave, Paco said, "Later."

"Yeah. Later," Bart replied in a somber tone. They both knew that "later" didn't mean later that day. Or maybe even later this lifetime. The incredible joy that Bart had experienced over the past several months was sucked out of him. Part of his heart was missing. Empty. There was a huge gaping hole where he had allowed someone to occupy space. Now that someone had been ripped away from him.

Bart slid the door open and stepped outside. The cool

morning air revived him. Sliding the door closed, he stood for a moment, staring at his reflection in the mirrored glass.

He looked like hell to himself. His hair was tousled. He needed a shave. His eyes were puffy. He realized he was missing his wristwatch, but he didn't want to go back inside to retrieve it.

Most of all, he was feeling how much he would miss coming to this strange room. He'd even miss meeting Mrs. Carter in the hallway, and the sounds of television programs drifting down from the living room. Most of all, he'd miss being intimate with Paco.

Paco stared back at him anonymously.

Bart admitted to himself that it wasn't just the sex he enjoyed. There had been *real* intimacy. Or so he thought. But apparently, he had been duped into thinking that something deeper than orgasms were shared between them. He didn't want to think that Paco had used him, although it seemed pretty obvious now. He rationalized that he'd used Paco, too, used him for spectacular sex.

Bart turned and walked away.

As he moved down the walkway by the side of the house, he noticed a gold-plated cuff link on the ground, glinting in the weak sunlight. He picked it up, then gave a cursory look around for its mate. He didn't find it right away, so he gave up and walked off the property, holding the accessory as a keepsake. At the edge of the driveway, where the cracked sidewalk began, Bart stopped for a moment. He was trying to remember exactly where he'd parked his car.

To Paco, who had left his room and walked down the hall to the living room and was peering out the front picture window, it appeared that Bart was thinking about turning back.

The Mustang was a block away and covered with morning dew. Bart opened the driver's side door—which he discovered he'd neglected to lock the night before—and sat inside the car, warming up the engine as well as himself before driving to his apartment in the Silverlake area of Los Angeles.

Pulling out of his parking space, he drove along La Cienega Boulevard and up to Sunset, then turned right. The usual bumper-to-bumper street traffic was nonexistent at this time of morning on a Sunday, which made the stretch of city street an easy drive. He passed Fairfax, then Highland, heading to Western Avenue. After an inordinately long red traffic light at the intersection, he turned left, crossing Hollywood Boulevard, and headed up to Los Feliz. Bart passed Griffith Park, then drove by the early-twentieth-century mansions built for silent-film stars and studio moguls that lined the right side of the street. Somewhere along here Lily Tomlin and Jane Wagner had a place.

Bart had actually been in one of the old, gated estates on DeMille Drive, which was owned by a cast member of the old television show *The Waltons*. The actress was exactly like the shrew she played on the old series, which Bart had watched in reruns when he was a kid. If Paco had been to one of the parties there, he would have gotten the full impact of what it was like to be treated as if you didn't belong. It had happened to Bart when he accompanied a friend to an elegant dinner party at the home. As he remembered, the old woman's complexion was as pale as if a vampire had sucked out all her blood. Her hair was dyed Mars rust-red, and she wore brown lipstick and a dull red satin brocade ball gown that was appropriate for the refined ambience of her home but not for a modern-day intimate dinner party. She never once acknowledged Bart, even when they were introduced. Bart could have been invisible.

The actress was the most inhospitable hostess Bart had ever encountered. Well, almost. She'd rivaled another glacial personality: Audrey Christie. He remembered being taken by the same jerk who showed him off at Kathryn Grayson's house to a party at the tract home where Ms. Christie lived. The actress had played Mrs. Upson in Lucille Ball's film fiasco of the musical *Mame,* and she was also the crusty rich lady who snubbed nouveau riche Debbie Reynolds in *The Unsinkable Molly Brown* until Molly became a heroine when she gave her fur coat to a freezing survivor of the *Titanic.* Audrey Christie *defined* rude hostess. When Bart's jerk of a boyfriend mentioned to the hostess that the Coke that Bart had requested was flat, Ms. Christie made a big deal about this young man, whom she didn't even know, calling *her* Coke flat. It wasn't even Bart who'd made the initial observation. He would have been satisfied to drink whatever he was served. "What a bitch," he now said aloud. "Dead. Too bad. No love lost to the world!"

Once home in his Silverlake apartment, Bart shed his wrinkled clothes, leaving them on the floor beside his bed, and climbed in naked under the cold sheets. Being nude in bed had always made him sexually excited, as if at any moment some phantom lover would join him. But not this morning. To Bart, his fantasy had come and gone. He couldn't imagine ever having another to replace what had been physical perfection. He decided he'd stay in bed the whole day to recuperate—from last night and the past few months of not getting much rest. He had no other obligations. So that was just what he did. He slept.

Paco didn't waste any time getting in touch with Peter Jacks.

Shortly after Bart left, Paco brushed his teeth, made a cup of coffee, went to the gym, came home, shaved around his goatee, and showered. Then, at ten, he picked up his cell phone and called Peter. After three rings, Peter's outgoing message kicked in. "You know the routine," Peter's distinct voice advised.

Beep.

"Um, Mr. Jacks. Right. Ah, this is Paco Castillo. We met last night at your party. Then you called me. Sorry I'm just now getting back to you. Call me back if you feel like it."

Less than half a minute later, Paco's phone rang. It was Peter Jacks. "Sorry. I was still asleep and couldn't pick up before your call ended," he said.

"Oh. Sorry. I didn't mean to wake you up. I thought by ten it would be okay," Paco said.

"No, this is fine. I should have gotten up by now, anyway."

"So, you called me," Paco said. "You really liked the script? Oh, by the way, your party was great."

"Thanks," Peter said. "Sorry you had to leave early."

"I hope you didn't think we were rude."

"Not at all. And you can catch the show when it airs next week. That is, if you have any interest in my swan song. And yes, I really liked the script."

"I'm sure it's a great script. Final episodes of hit shows are usually a letdown, but I'm sure yours—"

"No. I mean *your* script."

"Oh. Cool."

"Is there anyone attached? To the script, I mean. Attached. You know, starring, producing, directing?"

"Of course. I mean, I knew you meant attached to the script. No one's attached that I know of," Paco said.

"I could easily see Kathy Bates in the role of the slumlord owner of the building," Peter said. "And how about Greg Edwards for the part of Gene, the new yuppie tenant?"

"Is he still doing movies?" Paco said. "He's kind of old. I sort of wrote it with Ben Wishaw in mind. But yeah, whatever. But it's not a sold script, if that's what you're asking. Michael, your agent, who gave it to you, isn't exactly my agent. He's just someone I kinda know. He never even told me you were reading it. You'd have to ask him what's going on with the project. Michael and I don't exactly talk anymore."

Peter was lying naked under the sheets in his king-size bed, holding his cell phone with one hand and unconsciously tugging on his chest hairs with the other. As he spoke to Paco, he was fantasizing about having sex with the Latino stud. Peter was only half listening as Paco was explaining the status of his screenplay and mentioning others he'd written that might be equally suitable for Peter's talent.

"My day's rather free," Paco said. "If you'd like me to drop by with some other stuff, I could do that."

At the very thought of Paco's coming by the house, Peter climaxed.

"Mr. Jacks? Are you there?" Paco sounded concerned.

Peter clenched his jaw in ecstasy, trying not to make any orgasmic noises. "Sorry," he finally said, breathing heavily.

"Is this a bad time?"

"No. I was just trying to find my glasses so I could check my calendar for today." He was lying. Peter had no plans. Sunday was usually the day a draft of the next week's script was messengered to the house. But now that *The Grass Is Always Greener* was history, he had the day completely free.

"Ah, would it be convenient for you to stop by around teatime?"

"Sure, that works for me," Paco said. "Around four."

"Great. See you then."

"Oh, and thanks again for the cool party."

Peter hung up, a satisfied smile on his face. Then he cleaned himself off with a couple of tissues from a box beside his bed.

_____

11

By three that afternoon, Paco still wasn't sure what to wear to his rendezvous with Peter Jacks. For the first time in his life, he wasn't certain what he was selling—his body or his "intellectual property," as Bart had called his work. He vacillated between his most provocative outfit—jeans and a tank top—or a more conservative look—jeans and a pullover crew neck T-shirt.

Thoughts of what Bart had said about Peter's motives kept resurfacing. What if Peter really was only interested in Paco for his body and not for his talent? Or maybe he was interested in both? Or maybe interest in his body could lead to interest in his work? People were willing to go out of their way to help sexy people. Bart himself had been proof of that.

In the end, Paco decided on jeans (sans belt and underwear), steel-toe work boots, and an unbuttoned, grease-stained, Shell gas station mechanic's shirt over a muscle-revealing tank top. The gas-station shirt was left over from a regular customer whose fantasy was to have sex with a grimy, sweaty, service station attendant.

After years of putting out for hundreds of different women

and nearly as many men, Paco thought he knew Peter's type pretty well. If Paco's intuition was correct, Peter would want to inhale the musky scent of perspiration. Therefore, before leaving the house, Paco did an easy two hundred push-ups and five hundred stomach crunches. It was a man's smell, one that turned on a lot of customers. Paco knew this. He was just playing it safe in case Bart had been right about an ulterior motive for Peter inviting Paco up to his house. However, Paco was confident that if this was the case, he could still wrap ol' Peter Jacks around his little finger and get him to do something about making a movie from his script.

At 3:30, behind the wheel of his clunky Ford Fiesta, Paco was trying to remember the exact location of Peter's secluded mansion. He knew the general vicinity, and he set out driving up Crescent Heights, which became Laurel Canyon. He followed the serpentine road all the way up to its Mulholland Drive crest, where he made a sharp right onto Woodrow Wilson. This was the tricky part. Most of the houses along here were gated and set far back from the street, hidden from the main road. Paco didn't recall the address, but he remembered that the tall gates to Peter's place were adorned with his monogram—PJ—set inside wrought-iron stars.

After driving along slowly and having to pull over several times on the narrow street to let other cars pass, there it was: the vaguely familiar, long, steep driveway. The gates were closed when he arrived. A buzzer and intercom box stood at car-window height. Paco pushed the white button on the box. He noticed brown-and-white plastic owls perched on the stone walls on which the gates were attached. He'd seen these things before. They were really disguised security cameras. The owls' eyes were telephoto lenses. He smiled for the camera.

"Come on up," a voice crackled through the intercom without asking who was there. The tall gates opened to allow his car to move up the hill. Paco was once again impressed with the water fountain on a patch of green grass in the middle of the circular drive, and he was happy to see that there was no security man waiting with a clipboard list of invited guests. He parked by the front entrance, picked up the four scripts he'd brought, checked himself in the rearview mirror, and climbed out of his practically worthless car.

Before Paco could reach the steps and ring the bell, Peter opened the double front entrance doors. "So nice to see you again," Peter said, extending his hand and shaking Paco's.

"You too, Mr. Jacks."

"Oh, please, call me Peter!" The handshake lasted a fraction of a moment longer than necessary as Peter's heart raced at the sight of Paco in clothes that advertised his physical endowments and planted the unmistakable suggestion of sex. Peter was wearing 501s and an expensive black silk shirt unbuttoned far enough to reveal a smattering of graying hair on his chest. "Please come in," he said with a hearty chortle.

As Paco entered the foyer of Peter Jacks's home, he noticed that the floral arrangement on the table in the center was just as abundant as the night before. The house had already been so thoroughly cleaned by the maids and catering staff that it was impossible to find any remnants from the lavish party that had been held on the premises just a few hours before. But there again was the staggering view of the city. This time it wasn't quite dusk, and the view was a pale pink rather than brilliant Christmas-like sparkling lights that had been so impressive the night before. Still, Paco nearly gasped again at the panorama of Los Angeles just beyond the precipice of the hillside.

"Let's go into the library," Peter suggested, leading the way.

They entered through twelve-foot-tall French doors molded with appliques of fleurs-de-lis in the center of each panel. The room was two stories high, with floor-to-ceiling bookshelves on two walls. A large fireplace dominated another wall, and hanging over the mantel was an oil painting of Peter dressed in a tweed jacket and seated in a wingback chair, one leg draped over the other. An Irish setter rested at his feet.

Peter noticed Paco's examination of the portrait. "The affectation of a wannabe baronial master," he said as if apologizing for the pretense. "Hell, I don't even own a dog."

The chair on the painted canvas was identical to the one in which Peter suggested Paco take a seat. Looking around at the grandeur of the room, Paco was awed by shelf after shelf of hardcover books, some bound in leather, others with their colorful paper dust jackets. There was also an array of awards. On opposite ends of the fireplace mantel, bookending numerous other shiny trophies, were two Emmy Award statuettes.

"What's the Grammy for?" Paco asked, impressed that he was seeing an actual Grammy Award in somebody's own home, not in a museum or clutched in Taylor Swift's hands on television.

"*Blow Me.*"

"Can't I get a drink first?" Paco chuckled.

"No. *Blow Me.* That was my first comedy CD. It won a Grammy."

Paco turned red. "That's embarrassing. My response, I mean."

"*Blow Me* went platinum. It's a line I made famous on the show. Like 'bite me' or 'sit on it' only more outrageous because the network was trying to keep up with the cutting edge of Netflix and Amazon series. I was supposed to record a sequel."

"*Blow Me Harder*?" Paco suggested sarcastically.

"You're joking, but that was to be the actual title." Peter smiled. "You're a clever young man. Now, with all that's happened in my personal and professional life, the record company has canceled the contract. We're suing, of course. We had a deal. I don't remember the Rolling Stones getting dumped by their label when they came out with *Sticky Fingers* way back in the seventies. You weren't even born then, but the album cover, designed by Andy Warhol, no less, was a pair of jeans—with a real zipper, for Christ's sake! Tell me that's not spelling everything out completely."

Peter uncorked a bottle of Pinot Noir and removed two Bordeaux glasses from a glass shelf behind the bar. "By the way, what do you make of all the fuss? Do you believe the tabloids? Do you think I'm a total perv?" He set the bottle down to breathe for a moment and opened a panel in the wall that revealed switches and dimmers. He pushed a button, and flames came to life in the gas fireplace. He pushed another button, and the recessed lighting in the ceiling illuminated the room. Pink spots directly hit the Emmy Awards and Peter's portrait. Another switch filled the room with soft classical music. Peter poured the wine and handed a glass to Paco. He sat down opposite him in an identical leather-upholstered wing-back chair.

Paco said, "First of all, not only do I *not* believe what I read—except in the *Intruder,* which is always right—I don't believe what people tell me. Everybody has an agenda. I only believe what I see with my own eyes. And I trust my intuition. Also, whatever you do in the privacy of your own home is your business. You may be a sick, kinky son-of-a-bitch pig—oh, not *you* personally, Peter; I didn't mean that—but I don't believe anyone has the right to judge anybody else who's a sick, kinky son-of-a-bitch pig."

Peter smiled again. "I don't think I'm kinky... well, maybe by radio psych Dr. Saundra's standards, but who wouldn't be. I'm no more a dog or a pig than any other sexual being—straight or gay or bi or transgender. We all have our needs. It's not fair that audiences think I'm just the character I play on the series.

People are so ignorant. There's so much more to who Peter Jacks is!"

"I know exactly what you're saying," Paco agreed. "People look at me and immediately think I'm hot and dangerous. Which I am. But that's not all there is to me. I'll bet everyone who meets me for the first time thinks my brain is in my pants. Most people would be shocked to discover that I'm a writer. As a matter of fact, the script you read was over at Sterling for coverage. The story guy gave it an *Excellent* and said, 'Don't let this one get away.'"

"My thoughts exactly," Peter said, trying hard to look directly into Paco's eyes and not give himself away by absorbing the fullness of his guest's sumptuous body and thinking, *Yeah, don't let this one get away.*

Peter took a long pull on his glass of wine. "I had no idea a studio had been approached. Michael didn't tell me that."

"Michael's an asshole." Paco snorted. "He didn't submit it to Sterling; another friend of mine did (*A friend. That's exactly what Bart was to me*, Paco thought for a fraction of an instant), although Michael will probably try to take credit. In fact, he didn't even tell me that he was giving you the script to read. I gave it to him six months ago, and he's *never* mentioned it since." Paco sipped his wine. "Now there's a sick one. I don't know why you, or any of his other clients, stay with him. You could do so much better."

"Michael discovered me. I believe in being loyal."

Paco finished his glass of wine and handed it back to Peter in a manner that said, *Top it up.* Peter nodded, taking the glass and thinking the afternoon (which was now evening) was going very well indeed. He had planned to come across as sympathetic, get Paco drunk, reveal just enough about his sexual fantasies, and then see what happened. So far, so good. He returned presently with a refill of the Pinot Noir. "Let's move over to the sofa. It's more comfortable than these damned chairs that my decorator insisted I buy." Peter indicated the twin sofas facing each other beside the fireplace. A glass-topped coffee table separated the furniture.

Paco moved as directed and placed the four scripts he'd been clutching on top of the table.

"Oh, good, more material for me to read," Peter said, looking at the stack of screenplays, each with a different-colored cover and three brass brads holding the pages together. "Tell me a bit about yourself, Paco. How long have you been writing? What have you sold? Do you have to wait tables like so many other actors and writers in this town? God, I'm glad I never had to do that! Not that there's anything wrong with being a server. Absolutely not. I just know I'd totally suck at it. I could never remember anybody's order!"

Paco gave Peter the most superficial details. "Always been a writer. No sales yet, but there's a lot of interest. As for steady work, I tend bar." He added, "Michael, your agent, is a frequent customer. You should ask him for the lowdown. I'm not very much at ease talking about myself."

"Oh, you writers. You're so introspective. You have the perfect career. You can be creative yet maintain your anonymity. Being a star like me is very, very difficult." Peter assumed a wistful, affected tone of world-weariness. "I can't leave the house without paparazzi stalking me. And forget traveling regularly scheduled commercial airlines. Oprah has the right idea—and money. Wish I could afford a jet like hers." Peter paused. "By the way, did anybody see you come to the gate?" He was suddenly panicked. "I should have warned you."

"No one that I was aware of."

"They're sneaky bastards, those photographers. They could be a mile away and, with a telephoto lens, get you down to the last detail of your tattoos. I imagine you *do* have a tattoo some-where, don't you?"

Paco smirked. Then he stood up and took off his grease-monkey shirt. Not only was his muscular body revealed through the diaphanous material of his athletic shirt, but also the gang insignia and inverted crucifix adorning his left bicep muscle.

"You're one hot stud, Mr. Castillo," Peter said. "You must have a happy girlfriend at home. Or a boyfriend?"

"Neither."

"Who was the man you brought to the party?"

"Just someone. We broke up last night." A twinge of regret flashed past Paco's mind as he referred to Bart as "just someone."

"Oh? I'm sorry to hear that." Peter didn't bother sounding sincere. "You both looked great together."

"He was jealous. I can't stand that."

"I don't blame him."

"Of you."

Peter snorted. "That's absurd. I'm flattered, but I'm hardly someone that anyone on the planet should be jealous of. I'm persona non grata now, not just in this town but in every American household. My Q-rating's a disaster. If I ever get a chance to make another TV series, it will be a miracle. I'll probably be relegated to a Saturday-morning sitcom like *Saved by the Bell* or some such network muck in sexually ambiguous roles that they used to call 'the funny uncle.' And that's if I'm really lucky."

Peter paused, then asked, intrigued, "Why was he jealous?"

Paco pondered the question for a moment, wondering how much he should reveal and how much he should embellish. He decided to go for a combination of the two. "Bart—that was the guy's name—didn't think my writing was any good, and he said you couldn't possibly want to discuss anything with me other than sex." For another split second Paco felt ashamed for lying about Bart, who had been nothing but completely supportive of his work.

Peter looked appalled at the very idea that he was thought to have had a hidden agenda for getting Paco up to his house. "You were right to dump him. You need someone who understands your creative nature. You're a brilliant writer. Someone has to appreciate your assets. Although, if you don't mind my saying so, I'll bet everybody *is* after your assets."

"Including you, Peter?"

Peter swallowed hard, and after a long awkward moment, and what sounded like a confession, said, "Listen, I need a job, and I thought you might have something that my agent could pitch to the studios. Then, when I found out you had written a terrific screenplay, one that I loved and thought was brilliant for me, I simply wanted to meet you and discuss possibilities. Sex was the furthest thing from my mind, I assure you. Until..."

Ah, Paco thought, *here it comes. The old man is making his play. What do I do? I don't want to jeopardize his enthusiasm for the project or have him blackball me to Michael or the studios if I rebuff him. Let's just see where he's going.*

Peter went on. "When you walked in here looking... well, you can't help it, but looking like someone out of Central Casting for a leading man in a hot daytime drama, only better... naturally I couldn't help but have only a quick fleeting fantasy. Just for a teensy instant. You know what you look like, so you have to agree it's not fair to those of us who are mere mortals. But I've regained my composure. I don't want anything to interfere with the possibility of our working together."

Paco, with a sleight of hand that would have made David Copperfield envious, had unbuttoned the fly on his jeans. "Would this be an interference?" he said.

Peter swallowed hard again. He was instantly mesmerized. After a long moment, he dragged his covetous eyes back to

Paco's tank top, tattoos, and goateed face. Then back to Paco's appendage.

"Seen one, you obviously *haven't* seen 'em all," Peter sputtered. "Would you mind if I—?"

"Think of me as a People's Choice Award. I am the choice of a lot of people."

Peter swallowed the rest of his glass of wine with one long pull. And by the time they entered Peter's lavishly decorated bedroom, they were both stripped naked.

Paco cringed when he saw Peter completely nude. His body was falling apart and morphing into Homer Simpson. He obviously didn't work out at all. *I've serviced worse, but this is going to be work,* Paco said to himself. *I'd better get something in return for messing around with this old fart.*

Paco had had to psych himself up countless times with some of the trolls who answered his Grinder or Plunder messages, but the stakes were much higher this time. It wasn't just rent money or saving toward a new computer printer for which he was now working. It was to obtain Peter's help with getting the script sold and made into a movie. Therefore, Paco knew he had to give the performance of his life and act as though Peter were the biggest turn-on in the world. The actor's ego demanded it. Paco's future rested on how much confidence he could instill in Peter, who, from the language he was now using, was exactly the sick, perverted pig he claimed he wasn't.

Having seen Peter's infamous sex tape, Paco pretty much knew what it was that this guy liked. He immediately took control, dominating the scene as the bangers on the video had done. Paco was tough but not too rough. He grabbed a necktie that was neatly folded on the back of a chair and lashed Peter's wrists to the iron slats of his headboard.

Paco gave him a slap across the face that was just a tad more than playful. Peter was in ecstasy. Paco was playacting as well as he ever had, something he never had to do with Bart. In fact, to get through this ritual, he started to fantasize about Bart and how much pleasure they had both given each other. Peter roared with pleasure. Finally, when Peter was totally spent, Paco asked if he was satisfied.

"Yeah," was all that Peter could say as he continued to breathe heavily. Paco untied him, and Peter drew himself into the fetal position.

Paco cast a magical spell over anyone he deigned to seduce. From the moment he invited anyone to touch and caress his hard body, they were under his control. There was no escaping his bewitchment.

Tough-as-nails Peter Jacks was no exception. In fact, as he now lay decompressing and sucking his thumb like a baby, his mind was racing ahead to the next time he could be with Paco, and the time after that, and what he would do to keep this Latino stud around for as long as possible. He had already decided he'd go to Michael and plead for him to get a studio to package *Blind as a Bat*. If Michael couldn't do it, then he'd call in a few favors. There was that Warner Bros. executive who had wanted to further his new young wife's acting career, and as a favor, Peter had given her a guest appearance on *The Grass Is Always Greener*. The Warner guy owed him big time.

There was also the closeted Sterling Studios creative executive who had propositioned Peter in the men's room at the Beverly Hilton Hotel during a break in a Salute to Angela Lansbury ceremony. Peter wasn't interested in a restroom hookup, and the guy pleaded with Peter not to tell anybody, especially his wife.

These were just a couple of the chits that Peter had planned to eventually collect when the time was right. If Michael couldn't come through, Peter decided he'd start making a few calls. Anything to keep Paco around.

When Peter had regained his strength, they put most of their clothes back on, and they returned to the library. The fire still roared, and the sound of Puccini filled the room. Their first bottle of wine was empty, so Paco took it upon himself to go to the bar and uncork another. Over just one afternoon he was starting to feel right at home.

Peter took a seat on the sofa and began staring into the flames in the fireplace.

"So, what do you think?" Paco said to Peter as he handed him a glass of wine, interrupting a reverie.

"About what?"

"The swallows at Capistrano being picked off with shotguns by eight-year-olds out on an NRA class field trip this afternoon. What do you think I'm asking you about? The sex, of course. You're a guy who probably gets laid a lot, and I just want to know if I lived up to your expectations," Paco said, playing coy.

Peter shuddered. "You were certainly born on the wild side," he said. Peter was masterful at acting out a character and getting what he wanted from people, too. Only his method was different from Paco's; he wasn't going to let on to this sexy, talented punk that he had practically died from rapture upstairs. "You're a very fine boy."

"A fine boy," Paco mocked, slightly irritated. "Thanks for the compliment. Would that be your recommendation to anyone who asked you if I was worth the trouble?"

"Trouble?" Peter sipped his wine. He looked at Paco, who had only dressed in his jeans and work boots. Starting to get excited once again, Peter reached out a hand and dragged his fingertips down Paco's chest and sternum. He grazed Paco's nipples and caressed the tattoo on his left arm. Peter's eyes spoke his thoughts loud and clear, that Paco was the most perfectly endowed man in a city that boasted the most gorgeous men on the planet.

Paco stared into Peter's eyes, and even though it was a total lie, he conveyed the thought that Peter was the sexiest man alive —which was the equivalent of telling Quasimodo that he belonged on the cover of *Men's Health* magazine. And clearly Peter bought into it. Paco's other gift was convincing the people who solicited him that they were equal in the looks department. That they did sex as well as he did. That they were the perfect partner for him—regardless of how incompetent or unsatisfying they might have been. Paco knew exactly how to make people trust him. And want him.

12

The next morning, Bart slept past his usual weekday waking hour of five o'clock. For the first time in memory, he arrived at the office after nine. Of course, Brian was nowhere to be found. The mail had been delivered and was still stacked by his office door. On his desk, the red light on his telephone indicated that messages were waiting. Settling in, he turned on his computer and found seventy-eight emails had accumulated since Friday.

"One thing at a time," he said aloud, thinking of the snail mail, the phone calls, the emails, and the conversation he was going to have to have with Brian *again* about what time he was expected in the office. Mostly, he was irritated with himself for being unable to ease into what was certain to be another frantic day.

Bart punched in the password number on his telephone to retrieve his messages. "You have four new messages," announced the pleasant, perfectly enunciated voice that lived inside the phone. "Start of messages," the voice said amiably. "Message one. From phone number 666."

Stephanie.

There was no message. "Bitch," Bart said to the answering-machine voice.

"Second message. From phone number 666." Again, no message. "Hag," he added.

"Third message. From phone number 666." Still no words from Stephanie. "Frankenstein." By now he was merely naming a bunch of evil villains.

"Message four. From an unknown number. 'I never said all the things you wrote.'"

The voice was movie star Mare Dickerson's, with an accusing tone, referring to the quotes attributed to her in the press notes for her new comedy, *Woodchuck Chuck?* also starring television's Courtney Traxton-Simonton and HBO comic John DeSalles.

"*Would Chuck, Chuck? Would Chuck-Chuck? Would Chuck, Chuck Chuck?*" Bart had played with the title for months, turning it into a title for a porn or snuff film.

"End of mailbox." The woman returned to her natural, nonregional voice.

"Oh, fuck both of you." Bart spoke to the machine, meaning Stephanie and Mare. He pushed the release button on the phone to disconnect the voicemail system.

"By the way, you so-called *actress*, I recorded our interview," Bart snarled. "Want me to play back the tape and prove my changes were for your own good?"

Of course, Bart couldn't say that to Dickerson. He'd simply telephone the aging star—and nobody but Margot from *Lost Horizon* had aged faster—and politely ask what the BAFTA-nominated bitch preferred to be quoted as saying about her experiences working on *Chuck,* as the film title was simplified and reduced for convenience at the office.

Bart had to be diplomatic, which was what he had tried to be when he changed one of Mare's quotes to read, "I'm an actor who enjoys her craft. I'm constantly striving for perfection. I accepted the role of Claudia because, although the character at first seems one-dimensional, I intuitively realized there was great depth to be found in her. Her story arc is such that audiences will relate to the struggles she must face in order to survive the devastating situations she ultimately finds herself trying to overcome as a prostitute in the gold-rush era of the Pacific Northwest. Thanks to our fine director and the support from the incredibly talented Ms. Howard-Giroux and Mr. DeSalles and the superb supporting cast, I'm very pleased with this film."

It wouldn't look good in the press kit if the star were quoted verbatim off her tape-recorded interview: "What kind of stupid idiot do you think I am, you little putz. I took the role for one reason, because they offered me a shitload of money. My motivation? It had only to do with the number of zeros they piled behind a number on my check. I don't give a rat's ass about the audience. I don't care whether they like this character or not!"

Yeah, Bart thought. *That would go over really well with Stephanie. The press would have a field day.* For him, there was no alternative to mollycoddling Mare Dickerson. It was a simple task of taking the high road and playing the obsequious toady. He was used to that. It was the life of most Hollywood publicists. They took orders and made jerks look like they were the Second Coming of Audrey Hepburn at a famine-relief center in Botswana. However, Bart had a feeling Audrey Hepburn had been a dream client and perfectly sincere in all her humanitarian efforts.

If Bart didn't already loathe Hollywood, this latest fracas with the star of *Woodchuck Chuck?* was just one more reason to think of gaining his freedom. There was the tempestuous

Stephanie, always accusing him of one contrived infraction or another. Then there were the stars who thought they were so far above the rest of the peons who served their every whim that they could be as rude as they wanted to be. Well, Bart decided he'd had enough of the Stephanies and the Mare Dickersons of the world. And he'd also had it with the fantasy of being with someone as unearthly sexy as Paco Castillo.

"I don't even have time for a nervous breakdown," Bart lamented. "This is a call for this little wuss to kick some Hollywood ass. But how?"

The easiest target would be Brian, who, by 9:45, still hadn't made an entrance. But not only was confrontation not in Bart's nature, he didn't want to emulate the jackasses he had to serve by being an ass to those who served him.

On the other hand, he thought, perhaps a lack of confrontation might be his problem. Look at what had happened at Paco's yesterday morning. There was no scene, no flying plates or words of anger that could be mollified by an apology and subsequent makeup sex. Perhaps if Bart had fought for what he wanted, he wouldn't feel as though his life were a case of the tail wagging the dog.

After scrolling through his emails for anything that seemed urgent, Bart came to a conclusion about the course on which he would reset his life. From this moment forward, he would buckle down and work extra hard to leave Sterling. Like Paco, he would concentrate on his personal writing—in particular the diary, which would become a roman à clef. Like a gossip columnist, he'd simply continue to dish whatever dirt he could dig up. And there was plenty of muck just lying around at publicity staff meetings, stinking up the place like Donald Trump's underwear after an all-night binge on his favorite Big Macs and KFC.

Bart used to have ethics, but they had been quashed by his working in Hollywood. Unlike the threshold that delineates when a kitten becomes a cat, there was no single moment that Bart could remember when he experienced the transformation from wondering child to amoral weasel. He had been an enthusiastic young man when he started in the business. No task at the studio was too small for him to accept with a smile. Simply walking between soundstages during his lunch hour or seeing a parking space stenciled with the name Michael Kane was almost compensation enough for the privilege of working in Hollywood. Even when he was a lowly assistant, he had felt he was contributing an important ingredient to what filmgoers would eventually view on-screen.

Now, sitting in his corner office, with his own sofa and mini-refrigerator as well as an assistant and an expense account and car allowance and weekly invitations to attend private movie screenings with the stars and directors of new films, Bart realized he was paying a colossal price for the so-called privilege of being privileged.

Bart had got into the movie business because he loved Meryl Streep, Angela Bassett, Jenifer Lewis, and Emma Thompson. Without exception, each of these stars was as professional and as pleasant as they were gifted. Unfortunately, the up-and-coming Streep/Bassett/Lewis/Thompson wannabes were poor imitations. It made Bart morose to recognize that his lifelong obsession for showbiz was merely the symptom of a disease.

He also decided to put himself on the dating market again. But this time he would go back to his original intent: to find a guy who was educated, emotionally mature, well adjusted, stable in whatever profession he'd chosen, and ready to settle down.

"All my men have had dysfunctional personalities," Bart realized. He rolled his eyes as if he couldn't believe his lack of being lucky in love—or his stupidity.

Prior to being involved with Paco, he'd only had one other

major love: "the Asshole," aka Thomas. He had moved into his house on Miller Drive, in the hills above Sunset Boulevard, in West Hollywood. The Asshole/Thomas was an aberration, albeit sexy—or at least Bart thought he was sexy, in a goofy kind of way. But as long as Bart lived, he'd have the horrible memory of the first time he found his so-called "lover" doing what he did best—destroying Bart's self-value.

It still gave Bart a jolt of sadness and anger to recall Thomas's numerous acts of infidelity. Bart always went semi-catatonic when he remembered the first time Thomas cheated on him. Or, more precisely, the first time he *caught* Thomas cheating:

It was an after-midnight hour, only a year into their relationship. The night had progressed like so many others. Bart had stayed up as long as possible, even though he had to be at work early the next morning, and finally retired to bed—alone. Thomas would never go to bed before 2:00 a.m. He said he feared never waking up. He stayed up to watch an old movie, which was his great passion. Soon, though, Bart was awakened by the dull report of their front door being closed and locked from the outside. Then the sound of the ignition turning over in Thomas's Volvo.

Bart recalled waking up a couple of hours later to find Thomas's side of the bed still cold and empty, the covers never turned down. Bart's first response was one of concern. But in the distance were unusual sounds, like hearing the ocean in a shell: muffled, unintelligible words heard through an air vent. Phantom noises came from beyond the closed bedroom door. Sounds that warranted investigation.

Calling out Thomas's name in a low tone, Bart moved from the bed, through the room, and out into the hallway. The door to a second bedroom was closed. However, the door had a peculiar attribute: A window had been installed to enable the previous owner to keep an eye on her baby without disturbing its naps. Thomas had never bothered to replace it with a proper solid door. Instead, he hung cheap, sheer drapes—the color and density of nylon stockings—over the glass.

Approaching the door with the trepidation of a survivor come to identify the remains of a loved one, Bart peered through the window past the diaphanous curtains. His eyes witnessed the first heart-stopping disillusionment of his entire life:

Thomas.

Naked.

Embracing someone young and blond.

Doing what he had taught Bart to do with him in the privacy of their bedroom.

Then the jaw-clenching, wounded-animal-like sound of an exhausting orgasm. The variety that is said to peel wallpaper in its steamy intensity.

To this day, the lingering impression in Bart's memory was that of arms and legs—flailing like breeding octopuses.

Bart's agony was too large to swallow. Hot misery restricted his breath. He wasn't even able to cry out in grief or express the volcanic rage that churned and melted his self-value. He was defenseless to confront Thomas or the interloper. Instead, Bart retreated to bed and buried his face in the pillow, sobbing for the loss of something intangible—fairy-tale dreams that could never ever come true. He wept for his own stupidity. And fear for his future, as he had very little money and nowhere else to live. He was trapped.

Morning arrived as slowly as payday. Horizontal bars of light, diffused through the slats of the bedroom's window shutters, revealed Thomas in his accustomed place, sleeping soundly on his back. The sheet pulled to his waist. The arrogant, conceited, son of a bitch was oblivious to the fact that he had destroyed someone's life. Bart's. Forever. Thomas, a failed singer but successful theater owner whom Bart had worshiped, was a stranger now. Unknown. Unknowable. An easy target for revenge—if Bart had had the guts. *Crimes of passion occur all the time,* he had convinced himself, thinking of the nutty movie actress who reportedly bonded her famous lover's penis to his leg with Krazy glue while he slept. The story, whether true or false, was memorable for its novelty.

Bart was still choking back tears later in the day when Thomas telephoned him at the office, their usual daily call. Thomas had thought he'd gotten away with the infidelity. From Bart came a cold, monosyllabic response to Thomas's cheerful greeting. When Bart finally explained his aloofness, Thomas was, at first, silent. Then he was remorseful and apologetic. Then angry at being made to feel guilty. By conversation's end, the circumstances of the night before were Bart's fault. "I can't be responsible for what happens when you're not around," Thomas said. "It wouldn't have happened if you had stayed up with me last night."

Ever since then, Bart had purposely avoided falling in love. His occasional dates were mainly for sex alone. Now, just as he had started to trust a man again, Paco had betrayed him.

"Time to grow up!" Bart announced aloud. "Forget Paco. Forget Thomas! Go out and find someone who deserves you!"

It wasn't meant to work out with Paco, anyway, Bart decided. In retrospect, he could see that they were on different life paths. Paco was determined to do whatever he had to do in order to become a successful screenwriter. He'd seduced so many clients while waiting for a patsy like Bart to come along, someone he could manipulate into helping him get ahead in the biz. The only thing Bart really wanted was to settle down with a life partner. The guy didn't have to be rich and famous. In fact, the man of Bart's dreams was successful but not in the motion-picture industry. Ideally, they'd both want a simple life on a farm in the country. Their evenings would be spent giving intimate dinner parties and making love three or four times a week. They'd hold hands in public.

13

"CGA!" Mitch exclaimed, running into the office supply room and coming to a screeching halt beside Bart, who was collecting a couple of red pens and a ream of paper for his printer. "CGA!" Mitch squealed again. *CGA* was his special code. It meant "cute guy alert."

"Did FedEx send a new deliveryman?" Bart asked with a knowing smirk and raised eyebrows.

"This one may not transcend your old beau in the looks department—not by a long shot," Mitch enthused. "But you're in no position to be fussy, my friend. Take what you can get."

"I've decided that I do need to be fussy," Bart said. "However, it seems I *am* in the market again. But a delivery guy? Hot or not, he's all yours."

"Aren't we the privileged class," Mitch mocked Bart's attitude. "Actually, he's not my cuppa. But I know you and your off-the-wall, bizarre sort of I'll take anything on the thirty-one flavors Baskin-Robbins ice-cream menu, please and thank you.' You couldn't care less if it was one of the guys on my Hot Hunks of the Fire Department calendar as long as they were 'nice.' Nice. What does that even mean?"

Bart's interest was piqued.

"If Dolly Levi could get on with her life and marry Horace Vandergelder, you can too," Mitch said, always ready with a movie or Broadway musical analogy. This time it was *Hello, Dolly!* "And here's your chance. Your very own Walter Matthau is in Stephanie's office, having a meeting right this very *moment-o.*"

"Not another actor!" Bart pleaded. "And I don't do wannabe screenwriters or producers, either. No more showbiz guys! When I start dating again, it'll be with someone from the top of my sensible list: a brilliant but boring seismologist from Caltech who will charm me with endless pillow talk about tectonic plates, the Richter scale, and volcanic eruptions."

"I could be a *size*-mologist." Mitch grinned. "And I know a lot about earthshaking volcanic eruptions, too."

"Or else he'll be an architect who designs interesting buildings, and his idea of domesticity is to build a Victorian dollhouse for us to live happily ever after in, and maybe make annual pilgrimages to Falling Waters and all the other Frank Lloyd Wright houses in America. We'll spend Friday nights playing Monopoly or entertaining other successful, monogamous, professional couples."

Mitch rolled his eyes. "Successful as in 'filthy rich' or as in the other doesn't know what their partners are doing on the side? 'Cause trust me, sweetums, show me a couple who claim to be monogamous, and I'll show you a pair who hide their porn and insist on getting the American Express bill sent to their office. Big yawn."

What was the point of being sexy, Mitch contended, if you didn't set your sights on *the* most beautiful partners available, not the average, everyday sort of Plain Joe that almost anyone could get. God, in His infinite wisdom, created gorgeous people for one purpose: for non-gorgeous people to walk into lampposts over, to stay awake at night crying about, and to do things together that one's mother would have a heart attack over if she caught them doing what she probably dreamed of doing herself. In other words, beautiful people having sex with equally desirable people. "You wouldn't think of sitting anywhere behind row twelve in the orchestra section for the ballet, would you? So why for an instant would you think of settling for a guy who wasn't at least the general population's idea of a sexual Adonis?"

"The general population seems to think Mick Jaggar was once hot," Bart said. "I don't get it."

"Nah. Me neither."

"That's my point!" Bart declared. "I never again want to date someone who'll be courted by every other beautiful person in town. I don't want the hassle or the eventual heartache." Bart paused. "But just out of curiosity, who is this CGA person with Stephanie, anyway?"

Mitch gave a casual *is anybody else around within listening range* turn of his head and twitched a come-closer finger for Bart to be taken into his confidence. "Stephanie's interviewing personal dog trainers."

"She's finally doing something about her barking and chasing after studio executives' cars?" Bart teased.

Mitch grinned. "Anyway, he certainly must be *someone's* type. I'm placing a bet he's yours. So go dig up a press release or a photo of Angelina Jolie that needs serious retouching, and bring it down to Stephanie for approval. Come on, now. This is one chance I won't let you screw up."

Mitch pushed Bart out of the supply room, and he reluctantly went back to his office, picked up a file folder with a draft of a press release announcing the new casting of the studio's soon-to-be-produced remake of *Mr. Peabody and the Mermaid,* then walked to Stephanie's office. "Just barge in," Mitch prodded.

Bart took a deep breath and sauntered with purpose into the

room. "Stephanie?" he said innocently, and then came to an abrupt halt in the middle of the room. "Oh, sorry. I didn't realize you were in a meeting."

Stephanie clicked her tongue in irritation. "What? Can't you see I'm busy?"

"Sorry. It's the press release you wanted. I'll just put it in your box. Would you please approve it as soon as possible?"

Mitch was right about the guy sitting opposite Stephanie. He was very definitely Bart's idea of attractive. There was a resemblance to Prince Charming from *Cinderella*, in a hazy, sort of out-of-focus way. Bart made a point of looking straight into the guy's green eyes as he was addressing Stephanie. The guy smiled and nodded his head, a nonverbal introduction.

"Just go away," Stephanie snarled. Then she reeled herself in, trying to control her tone of voice. To Bart it suggested she was doing her best not to fly off the handle in front of a guest.

"Again, sorry for bothering you," Bart said, still looking at the real-life facsimile of a superhero, sans cape. "So I'll just leave it here." Bart placed the folder on top of an overflowing stack of papers. He retreated toward the outer office, turned once, and saw the guy looking at Bart's departing reflection in the glass of a framed poster of *Marked Woman,* starring Humphrey Bogart and Bette Davis, behind Stephanie's desk. Bart had once looked that film up in *Leonard Maltin's Movie & Video Guide:* "Bristling gangster drama of DA Bogart convincing Bette and four girlfriends to testify against their boss, underworld king Ciannelli." Bart always thought that poster apropos hanging where it did.

Back in the ante-office, Bart said to Mitch, "Mmm. Yeah, an excellent choice. Stats?"

"Here," Mitch said, handing Bart a copy of the CGA's dog-training brochure. "It speaks volumes, especially if you read between the lines. Grrrr. Now go back to your office and study this in case you're quizzed when I send him down to you."

"Oh, don't. Please don't," Bart begged. "He smiled at me, but who knows? Maybe he's just trying to get a job. He could have been smiling out of sheer nervousness."

"He doesn't need a job. He's doing this as a favor to Anne Hathaway. Anyway, from what I can tell, *he's* interviewing Stephanie—not the other way around."

"Why do I feel like frumpy Agnes Gooch, and you're Auntie Mame sending me to the party with handsome Brian O'Bannion?" Bart said. "I'm going back to my office. But do not, I repeat, *do not* send him to me unless you've thoroughly cross-examined him. If he's found guilty of interest, then maybe. Promise?"

"On Stephanie's grave!"

"That's my real fantasy."

～

"I'm closing my door for a while," Bart said to Brian. "If a dog trainer comes looking for me, let him in."

"Since when did you get a doggie?" Brian asked in his usual have-to-know-it-all prying manner.

"I'm thinking about getting one."

"Poor little beast. You're never home. It'll be a latchkey puppy. It'll grow up to be as dysfunctional as—"

"As dysfunctional as you," Bart supposed was Brian's unheard assessment, as he closed the door and crossed to his desk chair. He sat down, turned on the music player on the credenza behind him, and filled the room with the soundtrack from one of his favorite old movies, *Somewhere in Time*. He looked at the brochure, which featured the CGA wearing jeans and a khaki safari shirt rolled up above his elbows. He was kneeling beside three dogs of various breeds and offering a blinding smile for the camera. The photo caption read *Dr. Ryan*

Stone... and family.

Bart began reading the text of the brochure:

RYAN STONE, PhD

Domestic Animal Behaviorist

A graduate of Exeter Agricultural Institute, with a master's in animal husbandry and a doctorate in veterinary medicine from UC Davis, Ryan Stone is one of the leading animal trainers—both wildlife and domestic pets—in the United States. His devotion to...

There was a knock on the door. "*Entrez vous,*" Bart called as he pushed the brochure aside and picked up a sheaf of papers and a red pen, pretending to be editing the text of a press release for Emily Keaton's new comedy.

The door opened, and the CGA poked his head in. "Bart?"

"Guilty." Bart smiled back, pretending not to recognize whom he was speaking to, let alone that they had just exchanged vibrations in Stephanie's office.

"I'm Ryan Stone. Mitch said you were having problems with your schnoodle?"

Brian howled from his cubicle. "Is that what they're calling it now?" He laughed a booming, hear-me-in-the-last-row-of-the-balcony voice.

Bart shook his head and made a "don't pay any attention to him" face.

"He just thought I might be able to be of service to you."

"Oh, you're the animal behaviorist from Stephanie's office." Bart feigned innocence but totally gave himself away by knowing Ryan Stone's professional title. "Sorry, I didn't recognize you. You were sitting down. I didn't know you were so tall. Come in. Close the door."

"Is this a good time? I don't want to interrupt your work."

"Yes. It's perfect. Almost time to wrap it up and get the heck out of Dodge, so to speak. Have a seat. So you train dogs? Stephanie's certainly an interesting breed, isn't she? She needs a muzzle—and some doggie downers."

Ryan rolled his eyes and smiled in nonverbal agreement. "Love your choice in music, by the way. That's actually my very favorite old movie score. Anything by John Barry is my favorite. And most of John Williams, too."

"The theme from *Schindler's List* is total genius," Bart agreed. "Dare I expose my ardent admiration for Karen Carpenter and risk a strikeout?"

"I've been in love with her since before I was born. Wish I'd been around back in the '70s so I could have seen her perform in person," Ryan said solemnly.

"My parents did. Several times."

Bart and Ryan stared at one another for a long moment, in that way people do when they visit the Louvre for the first time and suddenly turn around and unexpectedly find the *Venus de Milo*. The real, original *Venus de Milo*. There is awe and wonder that transcends words.

Finally coming up out of his reverie, Ryan began telling Bart how difficult it would be to train Stephanie's dog, since Stephanie herself could not be bothered with making the time to be present for any of the sessions. He explained how important it was for the owner to be there for each lesson and to work with the pet at home. "It's not like sending an inconvenient kid off to boarding school. A dog doesn't come home just for Thanksgiving and Christmas vacations."

As Ryan spoke, Bart surreptitiously broke eye contact for a nanosecond to glance at Ryan's ring finger. No wedding band. A signet ring adorned his right-hand ring finger. The furtive glance was not lost on Ryan, who took a moment of his own to look at Bart's hands. They both smiled at each other. If they'd been the stars of that old television series *My Favorite Martian,* this is where their alien antenna would have protruded from their respective skulls.

"So, about your schnoodle?" Ryan broke the spell but kept his effulgent smile.

Bart didn't want to play games or lie and then have to try to remember what he'd said that was half-true or completely false, so he leveled with him right away. "Listen. I'm really sorry. I don't have a schnoodle."

"That's too bad," Ryan said with a mischievous grin.

"Mitch sent you down here because—"

"You were eager to find a new schnoodle to replace your old schnoodle?" Ryan interrupted. "He said that you were in a quandary, that you don't want to make the same mistake and tackle a big schnoodle when perhaps a standard-size schnoodle would do."

"In a manner of speaking." Bart laughed as he blushed. "Oh, that Mitch. He always knows how to make a guy feel uncomfortable."

"I've known Mitch a long time," Ryan agreed. "He's definitely a bitch—in dog terms, I mean. But he also said some nice things about you. Since you're about to leave, what do you say we have dinner and talk about... schnoodles? Or just teaching old dogs new tricks?"

"Now that's the kind of training I could use," Bart said. "I need a little discipline—about leaving the office at a reasonable hour, anyway. Let's go."

Bart quickly cleared his desk, turned off his computer, put the telephone on Call Forward and opened the door, allowing Ryan to lead the way. "I'm outta here, Brian," Bart called to his assistant. "See you in the afternoon."

Exiting Sterling's publicity building, Bart and Ryan walked toward the parking structure and past soundstages 14, 15, and 16.

Along the way, Bart gave a brief history about the classic films that had been made on those stages and others on the lot.

"Anyplace in particular you'd like to eat?" Ryan asked when they'd reached the parking area.

"Anywhere we can talk... maybe with a bottle of wine."

"Italian all right? How about La Strega, over on Ventura? Great food and not too noisy."

"I love that place. Meet you there in about twenty. Depending on traffic."

"Don't try the freeway at this time of night," Ryan suggested. "Take Riverside to Coldwater, then up to Ventura. I'll call from the car and get a table on the patio. It's such a nice evening; we shouldn't be stuck indoors."

During the ride to the restaurant, Bart conjured up thoughts about Ryan: He wasn't just an average guy. He was obviously intelligent (if the academic credentials mentioned in his brochure were any indication), attractive, sensitive enough to work with animals, seemingly unattached romantically, and made the first move to suggest they have dinner. Bart had, just that morning, decided to consider the idea that he might begin to date again. But he didn't think he'd actually meet anyone so quickly. He had been busy and, frankly, just not terribly interested. Until now.

"Don't get ahead of yourself, Bart," he said as he drove along the route, losing Ryan's carnival-red Jaguar amidst the heavy traffic. "It's only dinner, for crying out loud. You might not even have anything to really talk about." But he suspected otherwise.

By the time Bart found a parking space along a side street and walked into the restaurant, it was five minutes after Ryan had been seated, under the branches of a tall tree and near an outdoor gas heater. Springtime evenings in Los Angeles were usually chilly. The desert cooled down at night except when the Santa Ana winds were blowing. The hostess escorted Bart to the table, and Ryan stood up as a gentleman would and leaned forward to offer a chaste kiss to his cheek.

Within moments of Bart's unfolding his white linen napkin and placing it on his lap, the waiter came over with a bottle of Cabernet Sauvignon. "I hope you don't mind," Ryan explained. "I took the liberty of ordering a bottle. You do like red, don't you? I can change it."

"Absolutely," Bart said as the waiter displayed the bottle for Ryan's approval. As soon as the cork was removed, Ryan advised the waiter that there was no need for the pretentious gesture of taste-testing the wine before being poured. "I trust you implicitly, Damien," he said, smiling, thus further ingratiating himself to Bart.

It was soon evident that Ryan was the type who charmed everybody he met. The lowliest bread boy and the restaurant's owner were equals in his eyes. They were all treated with the same respect and consideration. *Thank-yous* were distributed equally to the shy young man who poured olive oil from a cruet into a ceramic dish for dipping sponges of bread, to the waiter's recitation of the evening's menu specials, to the refilling of their wineglasses before they were empty, to the brushing of crumbs off the tablecloth, to the return of his American Express card after the check had been signed.

By the end of the evening, after exchanging respective, abbreviated life stories, including mention of recent disastrous relationships, Bart and Ryan couldn't believe where the time had gone. Both had enjoyed the same meal selection: chicken risotto, no dessert, and a cup of peppermint tea. To their mutual amazement, they found that although their careers were completely different, their appreciation of specific music and literature (classic and popular) and film and theater (they had both seen the same shows during their initial Broadway runs) was practically identical. There had not been a single instance during the evening when either pretended to agree with the other when it came to the merits of particular writers, artists, and political and religious figures, past and present.

"Well," suggested Bart, "we can't let this be the last of our conversations, can we? What's on your agenda for this Friday night?"

"You are," Ryan said, leaning forward across the table. "I'm clearing my calendar. This time, I'll cook."

"He cooks, too!" Bart exclaimed to no one in particular and yet to the entire restaurant. "What can I bring?"

"Sounds cliché, but just bring yourself. And your schnoodle." Ryan was wearing the roguish grin again. "Oh, that's right." He snapped his fingers in mock disappointment. "You don't have one. Darn. Guess we'll have to make do with my schnauzer."

Both were laughing as they exited the restaurant. Once outside, as Ryan was waiting for the valet attendant to bring his Jaguar around, he said, "One last confession before you go. When I left Stephanie's office, I was the one who asked Mitch who the guy was who had interrupted the meeting. You looked... adorable, although a bit intimidated by Stephanie."

Bart said, "You're the only good thing that's ever come out of Stephanie's office! Usually, it's just four-letter words that she hurls at me."

"You deserve more respect," Ryan said seriously. "We all do. After I observed her treatment of you and Mitch, I told her I couldn't train her dog. I don't work for the kind of people who give off Stephanie's low-level negative vibrations. There's too much odious energy emanating from her. I could feel it as strongly as I feel the opposite from you."

Bart was speechless, and aware that he was definitely smitten with Ryan. Especially with the man's positive outlook on life. Ever since beginning his job at Sterling, Bart had struggled with being surrounded by and bombarded with negative forces.

The attitudes of the upper-level managers to whom he reported as well as the egos of the stars and the downcast assistants combined to make the atmosphere of the publicity department redolent with cynicism and fear. These were among the reasons Bart hated working in Hollywood. It wasn't his job he disliked. The writing was, for the most part, fulfilling, although the deadlines were overwhelming. It was the difficult, unhappy personalities with whom he had to interact ten to fourteen hours a day that caused his anxiety. He was aware that these caustic attitudes and negative vibrations were attaching themselves to his own temperament, almost like brambles on clothing.

When Ryan's car arrived, he hugged Bart good night. Then he thanked the valet and handed him a five-dollar tip. Ryan raised his hand to acknowledge goodbye as he pulled into traffic on Ventura.

14

Paco closed the sliding-glass door to his room for the last
time as he sang "Movin' on Up," the theme song from
the old television comedy series *The Jeffersons*. He was
movin' on up, all right, to Peter Jacks's mansion in the Hollywood
Hills. Paco was leaving West Hollywood for good and never
looking back. After weeks of skillful maneuvering and
convincing Peter that their sex life was mutually extraordinary,
Paco got the invitation he'd been wrangling for—and charge
accounts at Aéropostale and American Eagle Outfitters.

Paco had quit his jobs at the Trap and Cobalt Cantina and
deleted his Caliente4U screen name from Grinder and Plunder.
He tried to maintain one important vestige of his past—his gym
membership—but Peter wouldn't hear of it and turned an
unused wardrobe closet (larger than Paco's old room) into a
weight-lifting and exercise area. Peter even promised to hire a
personal trainer. "For yourself, maybe," Paco said with indignation, then quickly realized he'd blundered. "I mean, you're never
too young to do cardio," he amended, feigning consideration for
Peter's health. He couldn't have Peter thinking that he had any

complaints about his troll-like body. That could spoil Paco's plans.

The work office that Peter had set up and decorated for Paco came complete with a brand-new laptop computer, a large oak desk, matching oak file cabinets, and a credit account at Staples for all the supplies he would need to continue his writing. Unfortunately, Paco's writing time was becoming less and less productive. Day after day he got to the computer later and later. Often, he'd no sooner be on a roll with a new scene for his rewrite of *Blind as a Bat* and Peter would show up with a martini and a seductive/suggestive grin.

As far as Peter was concerned, he was keeping Paco and was therefore entitled to sex whenever he damn well felt horny, which seemed like all the time. Paco, having no place else to go, as well as no job and no cash from the customers he used to court over the internet, was basically a prisoner, albeit on an extraordinary estate. "The Island of Dr. *Morose*," he called it. If he didn't submit to Peter's sexual demands, they had arguments, which ultimately led to Peter's feelings being hurt and Paco giving in anyway, just to appease Peter and maintain the status quo. It wasn't that Paco was afraid of being thrown out of Peter's hilltop manse. He'd find other digs soon enough. He was more concerned that *Blind as a Bat* wouldn't get produced if Peter lost interest in him. Nothing else but the screenplay mattered to Paco.

Peter's agent, Michael, was coming around often too, doing what he could to resurrect Peter's crashed-and-burned career, with what little clout he had. At Peter's request, Michael was supposedly representing Paco's work as well. As far as Paco was concerned, Michael dropped by way too often—especially when he'd arranged an audition for Peter and knew the time frame of when he'd be away from the house. Michael made it known to Paco that he, too, expected sex in exchange for prestigious

Actors and Others representation. "When the cat's away..." He grinned when he came to collect what he referred to as his "commission." And he came to collect often.

Over the past weeks, there had been a couple of close calls when Peter returned home sooner than expected. The first time, Michael and Paco were just finished with their business and were buttoning their shirts when they heard the bell indicating that the electric gates were opening. They had approximately two minutes to clear away evidence of their activities and act busy in the office, pretending to be discussing a scene from *Blind as a Bat.*

On another occasion, they hadn't noticed that the gate didn't automatically close after Michael arrived, and therefore, no warning bell sounded when Peter returned to the property. Fortunately, Paco had already dressed and was back at his computer. Michael, however, was still upstairs when Peter unexpectedly opened the front door and walked in. He stopped in Paco's office space and asked where Michael was, as his car was in the forecourt.

Paco, though startled, pretended to be typing away at a furious pace. He quickly offered the truth: "Upstairs. Bathroom." Paco faked being absorbed in his work and was typing nonsensical words into his computer. He added, "Maybe the flu. Heard him throwing up."

"He's not using *my* bathroom, I hope!"

"Who knows. He just raced upstairs."

"Why didn't he use the bathroom right here in the office?" Peter asked, scrutinizing Paco.

"For Christ's sake," Paco exploded, "you think I want to hear that freak hurling while I'm trying to work?"

"Sorry," Peter said, his hands raised in defense. "Don't fly off the handle. I was just curious."

And just then, unaware that Peter had come home, Michael

stumbled into the office, where he saw Peter standing by a book-shelf. Michael's shirt was untucked and only half buttoned, and his hair was disheveled.

Paco immediately took control of the situation. "Feeling better?" he asked in a tone that read: Play along with where I'm going. "I know you were burning up. Hope it's not a bug."

"Er, yeah, I'll be fine. I think my stomach didn't agree with something." Michael quickly buttoned his shirt and tucked the tails into his pants. He combed his hair back with his fingers.

"Probably that all-natural drink you were so enthusiastic about guzzling," Paco razzed.

"There's some Pepto in the medicine cabinet," Peter offered. "Maybe you should lie down for a while."

"No, I'll just go back to the office. I'll be fine once every-thing's out of my system." He glared at Paco.

Peter walked his agent to the front door. Before reaching the foyer, he asked, "Are you and Paco getting along? I know there was some friction in the beginning."

"He can be a self-absorbed little shit at times, but I'm keeping him busy—doing rewrites on the script, that is," Michael said. "It's none of my business why he's here, but it's probably for the best, at least for now—until the studio buys the screenplay and the film is a go. Until then, as long as he's happy, we're all okay."

"With all the changes we're making, I'd say we'll be in a decent position to eventually arbitrate with the WGA to get the screenplay credit." Peter grinned.

"Why else do you think I'm having him make so many changes?"

"I like Paco being around here just 'cause he's so fucking sexy." Peter chuckled. "The screenplay's a bonus. I may even keep him after we've sold the thing. By the way, the audition you sent me on sucked. Why do I still have to audition, anyway?

Doesn't anybody in this town know I'm a friggin' star who had a #1 hit TV show, for Christ's sake? It's so humiliating. I just know those casting assholes were mocking me as I left the reading today." Peter was almost in tears. "They were probably thinking of that video, which I'm sure they'd all seen. How come Frank DeSoto is working as a regular on three prime-time shows simultaneously; plus he has about five thousand national commercials all airing at the same time?"

"Because everybody likes Frank DeSoto. And he doesn't video his sexual fetishes. Well, at least none that have gone viral."

"Everybody used to like Peter Jacks!"

"Listen. Someday, when you get that Oscar, they'll be licking your boots. Even Frank DeSoto. Trust me."

Peter and Michael walked outside and down the steps toward Michael's Mercedes. "Anything else coming up—a part for me, I mean—that I might be right for? It's driving me nuts not to be working. I'm tired of staying in the house all day," Peter whined.

"Hell, at least you've got Paco," Michael said as he got in the car and buckled his seat belt. "A stud like that has got to provide hours of diversion. Better than just sitting in your screening room watching old movies and porn. We'll chat later about other projects." He put his car in gear and drove away.

When Peter returned to the house, he sang out, "Teatime," in a voice loud enough to reach the office where Paco sat staring at his computer monitor.

"Shit," Paco said softly. He cringed.

What Peter meant by "teatime" was that it was time for the first of his six or more martinis of the night. What it meant for Paco was that Peter would become disgustingly amorous. Paco would try to keep up with Peter's drinking just to anesthetize his loathing of the sex Peter would ultimately insist on.

It was during times like these that Paco missed the diverse people who had responded to his dating site profiles in the past. At least it wasn't the same old fart every time. Paco also conceded that there were many times when he actually missed Bart, who was both sexy and sweet. Bart never made demands. In fact, he was always the one trying to please Paco. Peter, on the other hand, was simply a mean, selfish drunk.

Killing Peter wouldn't have been difficult, and Paco had come up with several plot twists in the scenario of their life together. Considering the alcohol and drugs he consumed, a death could be easily accomplished. Peter could fall down the staircase and break his neck or drown in the pool. The sex games he liked could get slightly out of hand, and Paco could end up wringing the air out of him. Or he could be accidentally on purpose pushed over the steep hilltop precipice on which the mansion sat.

But Paco was a writer, not a killer. Although he knew that sometimes a person could be both; books by mass murderers had been bestsellers. But Paco could not see himself in prison, serving a life sentence like his own father. He wanted to be famous, not *infamous.* Therefore, whatever Peter wanted, Paco was resigned to giving him—at least for the time being.

Equally difficult as sex with Peter was going out to parties with him. On this issue Bart had been mistaken. Dinner parties especially did not get easier to attend. It was uncomfortable being the young stud living the high life off the spoils of an older man. Straight men could leech off their famous wives; women had been doing it to husbands for millennia. But two men—one young and devastatingly sexy, the other older, rich, and becoming fat—still raised eyebrows.

A few people he'd met actually tried to be nice to Paco, especially older gay men. Whether it was because of his extraordinary seductive looks or because they were being condescending in their own way, Paco could only guess. At any rate, he knew that people were talking about him.

Bart's personal scenario about scrutinizing other dinner party guests for common procedures of etiquette was nothing like what Paco had to endure. Paco's table manners had become impeccable. He knew a fish fork from a dessert fork and learned not to have too many glasses of wine with dinner, and to keep a respectful distance from the serving help. Inevitably, however, a rude guest would pose a question of the table regarding current political events or moral issues during coffee and dessert, then, in a patronizing tone, ask what Paco's thoughts were on the issue.

"Paco, dear," a face-lifted shoe store heiress had said, "you're from an ethnic culture that many of us have not had the privilege of experiencing except vicariously through our respective household staffs, bless their hearts. Perhaps you could tell us the views of your people on California's new strict crime codes for juvenile delinquents?"

Guests at the table would invariably become uncomfortably silent. Coffee cups would clink back onto their Dresden-china saucers. All eyes would turn to Paco, from whom they expected nothing more than, *"No hablo ingles."* Instead, after a theatrical pause for the curious to come to a prejudged conclusion, Paco would begin to speak. His enunciation was clear and considered.

"First of all, I am an American citizen, as are most of my—as you put it—'people.' *'Mi familia,'* as you might expect me to say. And of course, I will be more than delighted to offer my personal point of view on the subject you're obviously referring to: the new state legislation in which offenders—as young as fourteen—could be subjected to adult-like incarceration to fit certain crimes."

A simple declarative sentence, spoken with authority, as if from a professor of cultural anthropology, never failed to achieve Paco's desired impact: undivided attention and genuine interest.

"It's my opinion, and perhaps you might agree, that as a result of this law, youngsters—who are merely suspects and perhaps not guilty—will have their identities revealed in the media prior to actually being charged with a crime. They could be imprisoned in adult facilities. Perhaps we should consider alternative ways for rehabilitation rather than sending them to incarceration, a fate from which they may return as adult criminals."

By the time Paco completed his monologue, the other guests, predictably, were dumbfounded. The old bitch who'd tried to steer Paco into an embarrassing corner, hoping he would fumble and reveal himself to be a vapid intruder into their superior society, was the one who was revealed to be the fool. Paco's rapier responses to similar questions often posed to him wher-ever he and Peter went out together were the only aspect of these evenings satisfying to Paco. But he nevertheless knew he was on display as the stud Peter Jacks was keeping as a toy boy. He was a sideshow freak: a sexy stud with a brain and the verbal capacity to clearly express his thoughts.

"Now," he said, addressing his opponent, "perhaps you would care to share your views on the plight of Tibetans strug-gling against Chinese occupation of their homeland for the past seventy-five years?

"Not too keen on that one, eh? Then, surely you have a view on the new Taylor Swift doll from Mattel. She's costumed as Cleopatra. No...?"

That particular dinner ended early. During the drive home, Peter erupted, "Don't *ever* embarrass me like that in front of my friends again, you fucking little shit."

"Who's the fucking shit?" Paco hollered back. "The bitch who tried to make us both look like fools? Or you? These people aren't your friends. Tomorrow morning they'll all be on the phone with each other, gabbing about that sicko Peter Jacks and his new plaything... me. However, if just one of them says, 'You know, we misjudged Peter; he's found himself a kid with a brain,' living with you would be worth the goddamned effort."

"If I'm such an effort, you don't have to live with me!"

"Don't think I wouldn't leave you!"

"They're probably saying, 'That's the last time we ever invite those two freaks again,'" Peter yelled, drunk on martinis.

"Tell me, how many times have we been to the same home for dinner since we met? We only get one shot! They're all taking a turn to play host to one of the most famous ex-stars of our time!"

"Don't say that!" Peter cried. "Don't ever say I'm an *ex*-star!"

"Excuse me, *former* star!"

By now, Peter was blubbering. Paco maneuvered the Rolls along Mulholland Drive, finally arriving at the mansion on Woodrow Wilson. The gates parted, and they proceeded up the long drive. Peter had to be helped from the car and practically carried into the house, then laid out on the bed. On nights like these, Paco gave Peter one last drink to get him to quickly pass out, then stripped him naked and rolled him into bed.

By morning, Peter had usually forgotten the incident at whatever dinner they'd attended. "Did we enjoy ourselves last night?" he asked Paco, holding an ice pack to his throbbing temple. It wasn't the royal "we," it was an honest-to-God-I-don't-remember-a-thing question.

"Terrific," Paco said. "As usual, you were the life of the party. Don't forget to call Karen and thank her for the extraordinary filet mignon."

"Don't they know I don't eat red meat?" Peter protested. "Did I rave about how good it was? How many drinks did I have?"

"Just a couple. But you had a couple before we left, too."

"Who else was there?" Peter asked, making a mental note to let Karen Lopez know he really did have a wonderful evening.

"Let's see, Tish Channing, who lives down the street; Renee Patterson and Michael Wolfe came all the way in from Malibu; Sally Hartman, who I think also lives on the street; Tiffany Kazan, and Dominic Safari. Oh, and that bitch we keep running into, the department-store heiress, what's-her-name. The one who always tries to make me look like a fucking fool? But be nice when you call Karen. I like her. She treats me well."

"I suppose we have to reciprocate one of these days," Peter said. "We can't keep accepting invitations and not return the courtesy."

"Hell, you just had that big party when your show was canceled. That should keep us in good stead for a very long time! Any idea what that shindig cost you?"

"What do you care?"

"It must have been a bloody fortune. You don't know the value of a buck."

Peter rolled his eyes. Now that he didn't have a steady income from his television series, Paco kept reminding him that every big purchase was an issue. And if anybody knew the value of a dollar, it was Paco. For years he'd hustled for rent and gas money and enough change to buy a McDonald's cheeseburger. He thought of perhaps one day suing Peter for palimony, and he didn't want him spending everything ahead of time.

"Did we do it when we came home last night?" Peter asked with a grin.

"Oh, yeah, you were an animal," Paco lied, hoping it would keep Peter at arm's length for a few more hours. If Peter had thought he simply went straight to bed, he would have felt cheated. "I'm still worn out," Paco added.

Karen Lopez wasn't too thrilled to hear from Peter when he

called to express his thanks for a lovely evening. She was polite but distant.

"So glad someone enjoyed themselves," she said with a cold tone in her voice. She had already heard from nearly every other guest, all of whom complained about drunken old Peter Jacks and his insolent boyfriend. "How can you be friends with those two creeps?" the shoe store heiress had hissed. Karen had tried to smooth things over. "You know how it is; you put up with a lot when it's a star," she said.

"Yes," Karen said to Peter, "I'd love to have dinner with you and Paco one of these days. I'll call you when I get back from New York." She wasn't planning a trip to New York, but it sounded like a good excuse to buy time. She just hoped she didn't run into either of them at Gelson's supermarket.

As the weeks passed and the script began to take on a completely different storyline from Paco's original, he became angrier with Peter and Michael. The studio most interested, it seemed, was Sterling, whose story analyst had liked the script in the first place just the way Paco had written it. But still there was no firm deal.

"You read the original coverage, Michael. Why mess with what was considered brilliant in the first place?" Paco demanded.

"Hey, it's not me," Michael countered. "The creative exec wants to package this thing for Trent Bishop and Lizzy Osborne. They need specific changes before they can even approach them."

"Why not just send them the script the way I wrote it, for Christ's sake?"

"You don't know the business, you little bastard. This is how it's done, okay? It has to be properly packaged. You wouldn't put Kristen Bostik in a film with Julie Andrews, would you?"

"Wouldn't you? They might hit it off."

"Don't be an idiot," Michael scoffed. "Do you want to make a sale, or don't you? There are steps and procedures to follow. Got it?"

Paco was bursting with resentment. On the one hand, he had come this far and couldn't let something like "creative differences" interfere with success. On the other hand, all his years of hard work—especially on *Blind as a Bat*—seemed to have been wasted.

There was hardly anything left of the original story. Instead of a Mr. Magoo-like building superintendent in New York who causes all manner of trouble for the tenants and building owner, the main character was now a recovering-alcoholic plumber whose life is turned upside down when a distant relative dies and leaves the building to him in her will. However, an evil Donald Trump-like gazillionaire villain plans to raze it, and several blocks of brownstones too, to make room for the tallest skyscraper in the world and tries to pull a fast one on the plumber. To Paco, the new plot sucked.

Almost nightly, as Paco lay naked under the sheets beside a snoring Peter, he thought of two things: the screenplay and Bart. With every rasping snore coming from Peter's nose and throat, Paco was nauseated by the idea of having to deep-kiss the oinker in the morning, halitosis being such an unpleasant wakeup call. The only thing that saved his sanity was thinking about the imminent sale of his screenplay and maybe sleeping with Bart again.

Each night after Peter had passed out from booze, Paco thought about what a kick it would be if Sterling Studios actually bought the project. It would mean being his own man again and working with Bart, who'd surely be on the publicity team.

Bart would interview him for the press kit production notes, maybe even write a feature article. The title could be "Heart-throb Scribe at Bat." Paco smiled to himself as he considered his clever play on the title of his script, thinking about the publicity fanfare surrounding him when he finally became a famous screenwriter.

How would Bart handle the situation of our working together? he wondered, frowning. How could I make things up to him and let him know not to take it personally that I dumped him, that it was just a career move. "I didn't mean to hurt you, Bart," Paco whispered inaudibly. "Business is business."

The big guilt trip Paco suffered was knowing that Bart probably would not have done anything similar if given the chance, even for a big raise and promotion or a book deal with a major New York publisher. Bart wasn't the type to screw someone over for personal benefit. Paco knew this, but he tried to rationalize that anyone who didn't take advantage of an opportunity delivered on a silver platter was a loser. Bart included.

But that thought never stuck. Paco didn't think of Bart as a loser. He just wasn't a big winner the way Paco was determined to be.

15

I t was another late night in the office—nearly 8:00 p.m.—
when Bart's phone rang. He considered letting it go to
voicemail but decided to pick up on the second ring,
thinking any call at this hour might be important.

"I'm all alone in this big old house," the voice said without
salutation. "My agent's finally gone. Asshole's at a screening of
some new film that's about to come out. I'm a loser who thought
he'd get ahead faster if he slept with the right people. I feel like
Rita Hayworth in that movie you made me watch, *Cover Girl*, was
it? Remember how she thought she could get ahead as a dancer
by getting her picture on the cover of a magazine? I think that
story was a euphemism for sleeping her way to the top."

"Paco?" Bart hesitantly asked, interrupting the stream-of-
consciousness monologue.

"How many other losers do you know? Yeah, it's me. A voice
from your past."

Bart was in a drop-jaw state of surprise. Hearing Paco's sexy
voice for the first time in ages conjured up the most erotic
memories of his life. In spite of himself, his heart literally

skipped a few beats. "What's the problem?" was the only question he could come up with on such short notice.

"Nothing. Okay, everything." Paco sighed. "Actually, I guess life's great. I'm living it to the hilt. I just wanted to hear a friendly voice. I don't know why I'm calling. Guess I just had to take a break. Working on the screenplay night and day, you know. No time to make any friends of my own."

"I thought you and Peter had tons of famous friends. I just read the *People* magazine story about Barbara Levinson's big birthday bash in Malibu. Peter's name was mentioned, so I was pretty sure you must have been there too. Such fun!"

"Fun. Sure. We went. But I never met her. Too many other people. It was a freak show. A circus. I know she's super famous, but why would a hostess have a party, then not say hi to every one of her guests? Of course, you didn't read *my* name. I'm an A-list nobody."

"Every *somebody* was once a *nobody*," Bart said, trying to placate his ex-lover. "What about the screenplay? I read in *Variety* that Peter's close to making a deal for a film. I keep thinking it's *Blind as a Bat.*"

"It is. But it isn't. I mean, it's what *used* to be my screenplay. But they've made so many changes, you wouldn't recognize it."

Bart said, "Steven King probably complains about the same damn stuff, but he cashes his checks with no problem. That's the business. You'll have a bundle of money when this thing gets made." He paused. "Listen, I'm just about to leave. I have to meet someone."

"Bart? I don't know what to do," Paco said. "Everything should be so great. But it's the opposite."

"What can I do?"

"I was hoping you'd say that. You could come up here for a drink, for starters. Peter won't be home for hours. There's a party after the screening, and he's always the last to leave those things. Comes home stinking."

"I mean, there's nothing I *can* do about how you live your life. Paco, I'm running late," Bart said. "I'm seeing someone, and I have to be across town in half an hour."

"Seeing someone? As in dating?"

Silence.

Then: "He can't be as great as me," Paco said, sounding doubtful that Bart's romance was anything more than a rebound infatuation.

"There's no comparison," Bart said snidely. "Believe me."

Paco smugly thought that Bart meant no one could hold a candle to him. "Couldn't we at least have lunch or something? At the studio, maybe? I've got to work something out with this screenplay, and I need your help."

"Is that the reason you called? To get my help with your screenplay?"

"No. Yes. No, I really do want to see you again and make up for being such a shit. Also, I'm at a point where I need a talented writer to help me out."

"Paco, I'm sorry, but I'm all wrapped up in my own projects. There's Sterling and a new book I'm starting, and... everything."

"'Everything'? Meaning the new guy that you're seeing?"

"It would only hurt me to see you again."

"So you still have feelings for me, eh?" Paco chuckled. "I'm unforgettable."

"Unforgettable? Hell, you don't realize the pain you inflicted on me. No, you probably don't. That's so typical of you, Paco. Remember how you just let me walk away? How could you have done that if you even just *liked* me? I don't understand. I'll never understand."

"I don't understand either," Paco admitted.

Bart could hear Paco sniffling, as though he was crying. "Paco? Are you okay?"

"I hate Peter fucking Jacks! He's a total son of a bitch! I hate living up here! I used to call all the shots in my life, and now other people do. What do I have to show for it? *Nothing!* They promised they'd get my screenplay produced, and I believed them. So far, I just write and rewrite and rewrite the rewrites. Nobody's happy with what I produce. I know it's supposed to be a collaborative art form, but everybody wants to take credit for the good stuff and blame me for the bad."

"Who's 'everybody'?" Bart asked.

"Peter and that asshole agent Michael Stone. He's my agent now, too."

"The one who...?"

"Yeah. And just so you know, we still do it. But it's no fun anymore. I'm burned out. Listen," Paco continued, "let me at least give you my new phone number, all right? It's the only private form of communication I have. Depending on the circumstances, I might not be able to get back to you right away, but I promise I will ASAP if you'll just call."

Bart wrote the number down as he cradled the phone receiver on his shoulder and simultaneously slipped his arms into his coat, preparing to leave the office to meet Ryan for a glass of champagne at the Four Seasons.

Paco was pleading: "Promise me. Please, Bart. Promise me that you'll at least think about calling me. I need a friend. If it makes any sense, I'm really sorry for the way I put my freakin' career ahead of you."

"How early or how late can I call?" Bart asked.

"Doesn't matter. I keep it on vibrate so Peter doesn't know when I get a call. Not that I get any. Just leave a message. I check it all the time, but that woman in the phone just keeps saying,

'You have no new messages. You have no new messages.' Hell, I don't even have any *old* messages, either!"

"I'm really late," Bart said again. "You know me, punctual to a fault. If I'm five minutes late for anything, you may as well call 911 because something's happened. I can't keep Ryan—that's his name—waiting."

"Call me, man. Please?"

"I'll try."

"Don't try. Please don't *try*."

Still in a daze, Bart gave a cursory wave to the guard at the studio's main gate as he drove off the studio lot. Michael Bublé was playing through the stereo speakers, but Bart hardly registered the usually soothing sounds.

As he drove along Olive to Barham toward Beverly Hills, he didn't even notice the motion-picture union workers picketing outside the Warner Bros. gates or actor Brighton Fulsome in the Mercedes convertible next to him, even though the star kept looking over at Bart and smiling, probably because he was amused to see someone carrying on such an animated conversation with himself. Bart's thoughts were divided between Paco and Ryan and his conflicting feelings.

"Is it possible to be in love with two men simultaneously but for different reasons?" Bart thought aloud. "Sure. But this is stupid because one of them is a jerk. An incredibly sexy jerk. Ryan, on the other hand, is exactly the type of man I always knew I'd marry. Ryan and I don't just have sex; we make love! Paco was just fantasy sex. For crying out loud, you can have fantasy sex with any of hundreds of guys who advertise online. But, Christ, I'm so confused!"

"Get a grip!" Bart challenged. "There's *no* dilemma here! The only question is, are you going to let some sexy stud keep manipulating you, or embrace a good-looking ordinary mortal who treats you like you're the king of the cosmos? Which one can you quietly sit with in a room and read... and who makes you laugh... and who you can share interesting stories and friends with? There's no question, you idiot! How can you have the slightest hesitation?"

But Bart couldn't help thinking of the hottest sex he'd ever had—and the heartless way it all ended. He pounded the steering wheel again, this time accidentally pushing the horn and getting the finger from the driver of the car in front of him. "Sorry," Bart said to the pair of eyes he saw reflected in the rearview mirror of the vehicle he was following.

"Okay..." Bart continued his solitary debate. "You've known Paco for, what, six months? You've known Ryan only one month. You know exactly how Paco plays his games. You were just one of his suckers—literally and figuratively. Ryan doesn't have any ulterior motives. He's got the heart of a devoted puppy. While Paco is far better looking than the half-naked guy smiling in the Gillette shaving commercials, Ryan is just as beautiful—because he's Ryan. And his soul rivals Mother Teresa's, for crying out loud. He's perfect, in every conceivable way!

"There's only one logical choice," Bart finally declared. He made his way along Fountain Avenue and turned left onto La Cienega. Driving down to Melrose, he turned right and headed for the Four Seasons Hotel. He had made peace with himself. For the moment.

The champagne was Veuve Clicquot, of course. Dominic, the host at the Four Seasons' lounge, didn't even bother to ask for their drink orders anymore. As soon as Bart and Ryan arrived in the living-room-like bar area, two flutes of ice-cold, effervescing champagne were placed before them on the thick, beveled-glass coffee table in front of the sofa before either had a chance to take their seats.

Ryan, who had introduced Bart to the Four Seasons, enjoyed coming here for aperitifs because of the impeccable service as well as the elegant setting. There were few public places in Los Angeles or Beverly Hills where he felt more at home. That he was considered sort of a VIP among the members of the hotel's staff didn't hurt, but Ryan would have patronized this lounge even if he weren't treated like royalty. That he was unfailingly polite and respectful endeared him to the waitpersons. Also, he was generous with his allocation of tips.

"To another day of being together." Ryan smiled and raised his glass, touching it so lightly to the one Bart was holding out. "Such delicate, thin glass," Ryan observed. "And yet two equally fragile flutes are able to buffet one another and not result in the slightest crack."

"Like our sensitive souls," Bart added. "So far nothing's broken."

Ryan looked deep into Bart's eyes. There he saw a man who was as attractive on the inside as he was on the outside—a gifted, intelligent, intuitive, and tender human being. He had met too few of those during his life's thirty-year journey. Bart had made a strong, positive impression on Ryan from the moment they met in Stephanie Hough's office. That impression had never diminished; it had only expanded as they grew to know one another better.

Ryan and Bart. Two successful, confident, and attractive people living in Hollywood. Their obvious compatibility was becoming the envy of all the couples they met. Observing them in the lounge of the Four Seasons or dining together at Morton's, anyone could see that these two were clearly in love with each other.

However, if Mitch Wood could have been a fly on the wall, watching Bart and Ryan fuss over each other during dinner, he would have lost his grip and fallen to a welcome death. The two were like Chip and Dale. Or Alphonse and Gaston.

"Would you care for another roll, Bart?"

"Thank you, Ryan. May I refill your wineglass?"

"Thank you, dear. You have perfect timing."

"Doesn't the Chilean sea bass sound interesting this evening?"

"That's exactly what I was going to order."

"Shall we share a Caesar?"

"Good suggestion. Yes, let's do."

"And our waiter's an absolute doll. He's so attentive."

"That's because he has the privilege of serving you."

Mitch would have vomited, collapsed into a seizure or stroke, unable to withstand the torture of listening to one more cloying word of *snookey-ookkums* babytalk. But Bart and Ryan were having the best time of their lives.

Bart decided to tell Ryan about the call he'd received from Paco just before leaving his office. "You know about this guy," he prefaced the conversation. "He was the one I thought I maybe loved—until I met you. But he had other plans. He actually called me this evening, asking for some help. I'm not sure what to do."

"First of all, if it helps, I know he doesn't mean the same thing to you anymore," Ryan said. "The fact that you were once important to each other should still count for something."

"Even after he broke my heart?"

"It's no longer broken, is it?"

Bart smiled and shook his head.

"Sometimes what appears to be the worst thing that can

happen to a person turns out to be the best," Ryan said. "If Paco hadn't broken it off with you, we would probably never have met."

"I like to believe I still would have found my way to you somehow," Bart said.

Ryan patted his hand. "I think you want to help Paco, but you're afraid of how it might affect our relationship. Am I right?"

Bart thought for a moment. "I'd never do anything to jeopardize us. Believe me."

"I know. And I feel exactly the same way. Nothing short of murder could ever make me change my opinion of you."

Bart frowned. "I should at least call Paco back and find out how I might be able to help him. Is that what you're saying? He did sound awfully sad and desperate."

Ryan paused, becoming more thoughtful. "What Paco put you through was devastating. But it's in the past. It sounds like he's sorry. It's not healthy to keep feelings of anger. All that toxic poison festering inside. Release it. Throw it away. Call Paco and ask if he needs help... from either of us. It goes without saying, but if I can be of any service, just let me know."

Ryan was not in the least troubled by, or suspicious of, any amount of attention Bart might pay to Paco. Nor was he concerned about how he measured up sexually next to Paco, who, Bart had confessed, was the hottest lover he'd ever previously known. The only thing that mattered to Ryan was the feel and scent of Bart's smooth skin against his own hard body, the seal of their lips locked together, and the taste of Bart's delicious tongue. Ryan knew there was no competition for Bart's affection. They both recognized their mutual devotion with the same clarity.

The first time they made love, Bart was terrified he might accidentally call out Paco's name during a vulnerable moment of passion. He needn't have worried. From the moment he and

Ryan first kissed, Ryan proved to be such a virile distraction that Bart was completely absorbed in every moment of their time together. He frequently thought of that first night. Their lust was so intense, he could easily recall the precise details: arriving at Ryan's home, entering the house to the lilting sounds of Ella Fitzgerald wafting from the music speakers, dogs circling his legs, expecting to be petted, votive candles burning in a dozen different locations of the living room, the intense, loving look in Ryan's green eyes.

After formal introductions to the *family* and receiving a glass of Pinot Noir, of which Bart took only one small sip, they stood facing each other for a long moment, staring at each other and uncontrollably smiling. Their eyes spoke volumes about their lust. Bart took the for-him-unusual lead, unbuttoning Ryan's shirt. Placing his hands on Ryan's warm pelt of mossy chest hairs made him temporarily forget ever having been with Paco, or anybody else.

Now, a month later, the more Bart thought about Ryan, day in and day out, the more he realized he was in love with a for-real knight in shining armor. As jaded as Bart had become over the years, he was still sometimes afraid. He feared having to repeat the pain caused by his first lover, Thomas. He was afraid that so-called *love* might become a cycle of initial ecstasy followed by inevitable suffering. Bart didn't want to endure the nearly unendurable, soul-consuming grief that accompanied that devastating first breakup or the more recent one with Paco.

16

The security guard at the studio gate checked his computer list for drive-on passes and located "Castillo, Paco." He peeled off a temporary parking sticker, reached in through Paco's unrolled car window, and attached it to the inside of the windshield. "Know where you're going, Mr. Castillo?" the guard asked, looking straight into Paco's dark, deep-set eyes and illogically getting an erection.

Some of the most beautiful men and women on television and in feature films passed through this gate every day, so there was no justifiable reason for the guard to respond to Paco the way he did. Not only was he desensitized to the magnificence of Hollywood's hottest; he wasn't even interested in the cast of the sexy daytime drama *Shirts and Skins,* all of whom winked at him as they drove to work each day. They rarely failed to register more than a smile from the guard. So why was this guy who was going to see senior publicist Bart Caine so utterly distracting?

Paco, completely aware of his impact on the guard, feigned innocence and asked if the guard would mind personally showing him to the publicity building. "I can't leave my post," the guard said, quickly trying to figure out a plan to get away with Paco for a short time. "Tell you what, park your car, come back, and I'll see if I can get someone to take over for me."

"That'd be cool, man," Paco said with a smile that made the guard's stomach ache. A line of cars was impatiently waiting for Paco to move forward.

After exchanging a last lustful look into each other's eyes, Paco moved on. It took him a few minutes to find a vacant parking space in the jammed subterranean lot. By the time he walked back to the main gate, the guard, in his studio uniform of white shirt, gray slacks, black shoes and necktie with the classic *SS* logo, was waiting to escort Paco to the publicity building.

"What time's your appointment with Mr. Caine?" the guard asked, his heart racing a mile a minute. With a hand in his pocket, he tried to surreptitiously adjust himself. None of this was lost on Paco, who was a keen observer, especially when he was the center of attention.

"Lunch at one o'clock."

"It's only twelve thirty. How about a little sightseeing tour first? I've got the keys to all the soundstages. By the way, my name's Rich."

"Rich. Okay, cool." Paco pointed to sign on Stage 12 that read *Totally Kewl*. "That's the show with Jared Sumner, isn't it? Is he as hot in person?"

"Hotter," Rich said about the blond star of the hit show. "They're on hiatus now. Wanna take a look around there?"

"I'm all yours, Rich."

Rich was so turned on, he found himself leaking into his white briefs. The stage building was a huge beige-colored structure large enough to be an aircraft hangar. They entered through a side door with a large placard that stated in bold red letters: CLOSED SET!

Paco was overwhelmed by the enormity of the space. The Southern California afternoon temps were verging on ninety degrees, but it was actually cold inside the soundstage. And other than their footsteps, it was eerily quiet as they walked through the various sets of the living room and kitchen of the famous New York apartment that was immediately familiar to Paco from having watched the hit show a few times.

Rich led Paco into the bedroom set. "This is where, each week, Jared's character tries in vain to get his latest girlfriend to take off her clothes." He chuckled. It was an especially stupid running gag in the show because no one in their right mind— girl or boy, for that matter—would *not* go to bed with Jared Sumner, whose adolescent sexiness made him one of the hottest young men in prime-time television.

Paco looked around for any sign that they might not be alone. "It's a pretty big stage. Wanna see something else that's pretty big?"

Rich's breathing became harder. Paco reached out and took Rich's hand and pulled it to his crotch. "I'm ready for the rest of the tour," Paco said as he reached out for Rich's necktie and began to loosen it. Rich finished the job as Paco unbuttoned the security guy's white shirt. He then pulled his own black T-shirt over his head.

Rich literally almost drooled at the sight of Paco's brown skin and firm body. Knowing he didn't have any time to waste, he ripped open the buttons of Paco's 501s and fell to his knees.

When they were sated, and as Paco and Rich tucked in their clothes and left the soundstage, they returned to the glaring light of the early afternoon. Paco said he planned to be back on the studio lot frequently for meetings with Bart. "Now that we know each other so well, can you dispense with the formality of

Mr. Caine having to call in for a pass every time I come through the gate?"

"Totally against policy," Rich said. "However... as long as I'm on duty, which is every weekday from nine until six, you've got a free pass," Rich added. "Get here before your meetings. We can do repeat episodes on the set of *Totally Kewl*. Might even get Jared to join us when he's back for the season. He's into it. Trust me, he's nothing like his TV character. The things I could tell would have millions of teenage girls in America hanging themselves. He bags men by the six-pack, too. Even the studio's CEO, Rotenberg."

"So the stories are true." Paco smiled. "About Rotenberg, I mean. I kinda had him figured out. And I'm not too surprised about Jared, either. So, I'll be seeing you around." He left their next meeting indefinite. He really had no intention or interest in screwing around with the security guard again. This had just been another of Paco's ploys. Now he could get on the studio lot whenever he wanted. Without a visitor's pass. He'd heard that that was how Spielberg started at Universal Pictures.

Paco found his way to the publicity building and checked in with the receptionist on the first floor. Audrey, as her name badge announced, became cross-eyed when she saw Paco. He had that effect on everyone.

"Hi. I'm Paco Castillo. I have an appointment with Bart Caine." He smiled at Audrey as she went through the automatic motions of calling Bart's office to announce the visitor.

"I just get his voicemail, Mr. Castillo," Audrey finally said with a shrug to indicate she didn't know what else to do.

"Just Paco, please," he teased, a chess master in control of his pawn.

"Paco," she repeated lasciviously. "By the way, I love your accent. Is it French?"

Paco had to catch himself from rolling his eyes at her inane observation. "French?" He almost laughed aloud. *Is she an idiot? She lives in Southern California, which borders Mexico, for Christ's sake!* "*Es español, perra estúpida*," he said, pretty sure that she wouldn't understand that he'd just called her a stupid bitch. "Spanish." He smiled.

He could have said, "Your hair's on fire, or you've got green teeth," and she would have been too distracted by Paco's physique to have understood what he'd just said to her. Audrey's eyes never left Paco's eyes as she said, "Mr. Caine must be away for a moment. We're not supposed to do this, but since you have an appointment, why don't you just go on up and wait in his office. He's in room 1027. Get off the elevator, turn to your left, and go straight down the hall. There's a big poster of *Devil Girl from Mars* just outside his office. Can't miss it."

"You're so lovely, Audrey. Thanks for being so sweet and helpful." Paco moved away from the reception desk toward the elevator. When the car door opened, Paco stepped inside and turned to face the lobby. He waved to Audrey, who was smiling with as much lust as Rich the security guard had.

Audrey, too, was used to handsome actors and wannabe stars, but Paco was in a class by himself. Her heart was still pounding when Bart entered the building's lobby.

"Oh, Mr. Caine," Audrey called out as Bart passed by the reception station. "Paco, I mean Mr. Castillo, is waiting in your office."

Bart thanked her and pushed the call button for the elevator. He arrived on the tenth floor just in time to see Paco peering into his office. Brian had disappeared. He took every opportunity when Bart was in a meeting or away for any length of time to run off to God only knew where.

"Paco?" Bart said, coming up behind him. For just a moment Bart stood looking at the man he used to think of as the personification of the universe's greatest creation. "You look as good as ever," he finally said.

"Thanks, man. But I haven't worked out in two months. I'm getting soft."

"You were never soft," Bart said with a knowing grin. "You're still pretty damn sexy."

Paco smiled, the narcissist in him coming through. "I'm really glad you called, Bart. I was afraid you wouldn't. I've missed the hell out of you."

"I've missed you, too."

"But you moved on fast. This Ryan guy...?"

"How about you and Peter Jacks? That's quite a leap from when we first met. Let's go to the commissary and play catch-up over lunch."

As they left the office and walked out of the building toward the studio commissary, Bart couldn't help being aroused by a flood of memories of all the times they'd been flesh-to-flesh together in bed. Bart had thought he'd have his emotions under control. He was involved with the nicest guy on the planet, who was also a loving and sensitive sex partner. So why, he asked himself, was he still almost uncontrollably attracted to Paco? He decided he couldn't help his animal instincts. But he could definitely help how he responded to them. There was no way he was going to let Paco manipulate him, no matter what.

After ordering veggie burgers from the commissary grill and filing through the cashier's line, they decided to sit outside on the so-called Garden Veranda. The place was teaming with diners—assistants, middle-management executives, and a sprinkling of actors—and the noise level would allow them to talk openly without others eavesdropping.

As they made their way to a table by an ivy-covered brick wall, people who were used to keeping an eye on the door at restaurants, to watch the comings and goings of celebrities, couldn't help but look up as Paco passed by. All the women—and the gay men too—clearly thought Paco had to be an actor. Nobody as striking could get away from at least a momentary flash of stardom in Hollywood.

Those who knew Bart all wondered what the hell he was doing with someone who should be on *The Bachelor* or *Too Hot to Handle*. In Hollywood, perception *is* reality, and sexual magnetism counts for 99.9 percent of any individual's value.

Bart and Paco's preliminary small talk was casual: "Have you seen this or that movie or so-and-so's concert? Any vacation plans?" Finally, halfway through his meal, Bart asked the big question. "You mentioned problems with your screenplay. What's going on?"

Paco stopped in mid-bite and set his burger down. "It sucks," he said, his mouth full of whatever goes into a veggie burger. He swallowed. "Just like my life with Peter."

"Sucks. Literally and figuratively, I presume?" Bart refused to chide himself for being excruciatingly direct. He had often been told he would have made a fine therapist or prosecuting attorney because he was good at poking around and asking the sensitive questions, even if he wasn't always tactful. "Paco," he continued, "tons of wannabe screenwriters would kill to be in your shoes. People who can help you get ahead surround you. So what's the problem?"

Paco thought for a long moment before he finally spoke. "Things just aren't working out. What used to be *my* screenplay is now Peter's and Michael's."

"I don't understand."

"Neither do I. I don't think there's one original line of dialogue of mine left. Now, instead of being a romantic comedy that would have been right for a lot of famous talent, its turned into an edgy drama. Of course, there's a role for the great Peter

Jacks," he added snidely. "It's a big one. He and Michael have written that part themselves."

"All screenwriters have horror stories about the way their work is defiled," Bart reminded him. "How many books have been written on that subject by some of the biggest names in the business? William Goldman? John Gregory Dunne? You know what the game is. You're not the exception. Your so-called *problem* is run-of-the-mill."

"But none of those guys had to sleep with Peter Jacks's pimply butt on an on-call basis," Paco said, and continued eating his veggie burger.

The image of Peter Jacks that Paco created made Bart set his own lunch aside. "I really hate to say this, Paco, but it's called paying your dues."

"You mean paying off my karma. Talk about the wages of sin."

"The truth is, your ego is so large that you'll do anything, and I mean *anything,* to be successful. Why are you sitting here griping? This kind of behavior has been going on since time immemorial. Sex has been used the way you're using it by probably billions of people through the ages to reach their goals."

Paco stopped eating and placed the remainder of his burger on his plate. "God, I thought I could count on you for help. Why are you giving me so much grief?"

"I'm just telling you the truth. You know I'm right. You're essentially no more than a kept rent boy. Some stars keep their hustlers in red Ferraris. Others buy their boys Rolex watches and fly them all over the world. You see their names during the end crawl credits on movie screens. The credit that reads: so-and-so's 'assistant,' or thus-and-so's 'trainer.' What *you're* getting in the end—hopefully—is a produced screenplay."

"I've come to hate this town," Paco complained.

"It's also been pretty exciting for you, wouldn't you say?"

"I'm getting tired of putting out, thinking it's going to get me somewhere."

"It has already, hasn't it? Look where you're living? When we first met, you only dreamed about being part of this celebrity world. Now your fantasy has come true. Sort of."

Paco scowled. "I've hustled enough to know when I'm being hustled. I know I'm being used. I just thought it was a reciprocal deal. Day after day, I see how wrong I was. Those two bastards think they've got some idiot for a toy boy. The thing of it is, I am willing to put out—as long as there are long-term benefits. Right now, I don't see any."

"You've never been one to let anybody take advantage of you. Oh, you've taken advantage of plenty of people, me included, but I thought you were pretty good about not being a victim," Bart said.

"You weren't at any disadvantage," Paco sniped. "The date on the screenplay coverage was a couple of weeks earlier than when you gave it to me. You were stringing me along. Don't think I don't know."

Bart said nothing.

Paco became conciliatory. "I didn't mean to use you, Bart, honestly. And if I did, it was—it's just my nature."

Bart nodded. "I don't blame you entirely. And you're right, I got a lot out of our time together, too."

"At least with us it *was* reciprocal. And you always kept your word."

"Is it my imagination, or did we have the greatest time together? At least for me, the sex was amazing," Bart said, flashing back in his memory to a conflation of every night they'd spent locked together in each other's arms.

"Bitchin'."

"From start to finish."

Paco looked deep into Bart's eyes. "From start to—I don't

want us to be finished, Bart. I think we just got sidetracked, and I made an ass of myself. But I'm determined, for us, to get myself together."

Bart was flabbergasted. "Stop! Hold on! We've both moved on. We're seeing other people. You can't just call me up and say, 'Hey, how's it hangin'? I'm ready to let you back in my life.'"

"Why not? What if I say I love you, the way you did that last morning when we were lying in bed? I couldn't say anything then. I was afraid. The only people who ever said they loved me meant they loved sex with me. Am I stupid to think you'd make yourself available after I got my shit together with the screen-writing thing?"

"I think you're just tired of living with a creep, and life isn't going the way you expected," Bart countered.

"And I suppose *your* life is going exactly as you expected?" Paco lashed out. "You're still stuck at this goddamned studio in a job you hate. Do you still have that crazy, nympho, bitch-boss Stephanie? She still has it in for you? How much longer are you going to let her keep destroying you?"

Bart was silent for a moment. Then, with all the poise he could muster, he said, "As a matter of fact, I'll probably be fired within the month."

"What?" Paco was genuinely shocked. "Dude, that can't happen. You're a super writer." For the first time, Paco seemed to be sincerely interested in Bart's problems. The look on his face registered authentic concern for his happiness and future.

Bart explained, "It's all speculation, but it looks like there's a plot to get rid of the president of marketing, a really nice guy. I was actually propositioned."

"By the president of marketing?"

"No. And his name is Owen Lucas. He's a brilliant marketing genius and a good executive. It was Stephanie and her boss, Cy, who propositioned me. I look like a pushover to them. They wanted me involved in their scheme to oust Owen. And if I don't play along..." Bart trailed off, then continued, "They hate Owen because he's way smarter than they are. He's sexy and fun and has a great sense of humor and an extremely quick mind. There's one SOB—a supposedly straight guy named Josh, over in the Photo Stills department—who I hear is willing to make an accusation of sexual harassment just to get a promotion."

"Any chance you misunderstood Stephanie and Cy?" Paco asked.

"No. In fact, you can be the judge. I recorded the conversation."

"No way, man! That's too excellent! You could end up owning this whole friggin' studio!"

"Or dead." Bart laughed. "It's said that Cy Lupiano has East Coast crime family connections. I'll be lucky if I ever get to work at another studio after they blackball me."

"You don't get it, man," Paco said, looking as serious as he had the first night Bart showed up at his door, and he made him take shots of tequila from his own mouth. "We both have very valuable assets. You've got a recording that spells out a false sexual-harassment lawsuit... and I have..."

Bart looked quizzical as Paco scanned the Garden Veranda for eavesdroppers. "A copy of a manuscript—a book—that Peter's been writing. It's a wild exposé. It tells where all the bodies in Hollywood are buried. Or what closet they're hiding in."

Bart was intrigued.

"Yeah, it's a tell-all." Paco winked. "And I, unknown to him or anyone else, have a copy."

"You stole it?"

"I am not a thief."

"I'd call taking Peter's manuscript theft."

"Pilfering, maybe." Paco shrugged.

"Semantics."

"I walked into his office, looking for stamps for a letter, and happened to see *my* name on his computer screen. I had a right to know what he'd written about me, so I just printed out a copy to read. He has the original, for Christ's sake. It's not stealing."

Bart was intrigued, as Paco had been when he first came across the book. "What about this manuscript? What'd he say about you?"

"It's not so much what he said about *me*, it's more about all the people who run this town, including your very own nemesis, Stephanie Hough. The people he's met on the way up—and on the way down. It comes full circle in the life of a nobody turned somebody turned nobody again. It could be a primer for every wannabe in the industry."

"Is it a novel? A roman à clef?"

"He's used real names. Stephanie, Cy Lupiano, David Magnum, Harvey Weinstein, and Ron Howard."

"Ron Howard? Why would he lump Ron in with those creeps? He doesn't fit in among them."

"It's incongruous." (There was Paco again using one of his out-of-the-blue ten-dollar words.)

"He actually says only nice things about Ron Howard in the book. I met him once. He was actually really nice to me. But wait'll you read this thing—if you want to. I mean, I can't let it out of my hiding place, but if you meet me in private, I can bring parts of it with me. As for your recording, you'd better make a copy and stash it. You might be sitting on a gold mine."

"More like a ticking bomb," said Bart.

Lunchtime was nearly over, and the Garden Veranda was nearly empty. It was too dangerous to talk openly. If Bart had learned one unwritten rule of Hollywood, it was to never talk about anyone in a restaurant. There was some axiom of nature or universal law that made it a certainty that someone who knew the person you were talking about was within listening range. It had happened to Bart on occasion. Everybody knew someone who knew the best friend of the hairstylist who washed William Shatner's toupees.

Bart looked at his wristwatch. "I've got a screening in ten minutes. We'll have to pick this up later."

"I've got to go, too," Paco said. "Peter'll give me the third degree about where I've been." He rolled his eyes. "Every time I leave the house, he thinks I'm running off to see some dude." Paco paused for a moment. Then, as if taking Bart into his confidence, he whispered, "Frankly, I wish I could. I need to take the putrid taste of Peter out of my mouth. If you ever want to..." Paco's sentence trailed off.

"Wanting is one thing," Bart said. "I think my body will probably always *want* you, Paco. But there's a saying, 'If you want everybody, you'll end up with nobody.' Right now, I have someone really special. I wouldn't jeopardize my relationship with Ryan for anything." He checked his watch again. "Sorry, man, I've got to rush."

"Wasn't *I* special?" Paco asked as they simultaneously stood up from the table.

Bart looked at Paco for a long moment but said nothing.

"Never mind. Will you call me again?" Paco asked plaintively. "Please?"

Bart smiled. "Of course. You can call me, too. You can practically always reach me here at the studio. Sorry we can't talk longer, but I can't keep the director waiting."

As the two departed the dining area, they separated and slowly walked away in opposite directions—Paco toward the parking lot, Bart toward the Ella Raines Memorial Theatre. After so many paces, they turned around at the same time and waved to each other.

For Bart, the memory of holding Paco's hard body was a

painful distraction. *Damn it! But I've made the right decision! I know I have!* he insisted to himself, pushing away all thoughts that life with Paco could be even remotely better than with Ryan.

Paco, on the other hand, smiled, knowing that Bart was still physically attracted to him. In his mind there was always the possibility that they could get back together. Paco, too, was distracted by thoughts of his ex, and just as he reached the guard kiosk, he absently said, "Of *course* he wants me."

Rich, the security guard, overheard. "You flatter yourself," he said derisively. Paco hadn't heard Rich. He simply continued toward his car with a smirk on his face.

"Let's go over this again," Stephanie drawled in one of her slow-burn moods. She sat at her desk, facing Bart. "You're telling me that Owen Lucas came into your office one night and something happened? What?"

Bart hesitated for a moment, trying to visualize the scenario in his mind. "Okay. It was like this. So, I'm working late on the press kit for *The Last Chance,* with Russell Crowe. The office is empty. Even the cleaning people have left for the night. I'm extremely tired. Suddenly I'm startled when I see a shadow outside my office. At first, I think it's probably a security guard making his rounds. Or the ghost of our studio founder, Uncle Ralph, who's supposed to be frozen, but you never know about ghosts. Then I look up again, and there's Owen standing in the doorway."

"Doing what?"

"Just looking at me. Well, he's standing there with his shirt unbuttoned... down three or four buttons... and his jeans are unbuttoned at the top. The president of marketing wearing jeans to the office always surprised me. Not to mention his sexy hairy chest."

"Forget about your libido for a moment," Stephanie snarled. "Just tell me what happened next."

"For a moment he just leaned against the doorframe."

"He said...?" Stephanie prompted.

"Yeah. He said, 'Why don't you blow it off for the night, Bart.'"

"He said, 'Blow it off, Bart'?"

"Yeah. I didn't think he even knew my name."

Stephanie snapped, "I mean he said, 'blow it,' like it was a come-on, right?"

"I didn't think so at the time. I'm kinda naive about these things."

Stephanie rolled her eyes. "Then he came up and stood in front of you with his, his, his crotch in your face or something?"

"Yes, his mossy stomach. And he asked if I'd eaten anything."

"Dinner?"

"I suppose. At least that's what I thought at the time. I said I was too busy, that I'd probably grab something at Subway on the way home. Then he put his hands in his pockets and started moving them around, like maybe he was feeling for loose change or something. He asked me if I liked working at Sterling. I told him I'd been doing it for a couple of years, and it was great. I told him I liked my colleagues, and... and... I told him I especially liked that he had taken over as president of the department because he was a creative guy."

"Why would you tell him that?"

"Because I like him... I think he's sexy and—"

"*No! No! No!*" Stephanie convulsed. She stood up and paced the room like an angry prosecuting attorney, gesticulating with her hands to hammer home a point. "You're supposed to be a victim here, Bart, not some fucking cocksucker looking to score points with the boss, you stupid idiot!"

Bart blanched at being called an idiot. "Sorry. I'm confused. I've forgotten what I'm supposed to say at this point."

Stephanie plopped herself back down in her leather chair and exhaled with enough force for the breeze to scatter some papers on her desk, expressing enormous frustration because they had been at this rehearsal for more than an hour and still Bart wasn't getting the lines absolutely perfect.

"Once again! Final time!" she admonished Bart as if speaking to a stupid child. "This is where Owen tells you he's had his eyes on your performance, and he's really impressed with how much work you do and how well you accomplish your tasks without complaining and how you should have a promotion and that he'll personally see to it that human resources have a glowing recommendation from him in your files so you can find another department to work in."

"Oh. Right," Bart said, picking up the thread of the drill Stephanie and Cy had discussed with him earlier that afternoon. "Okay. So I asked him what he meant by a different department. And he said he was really sorry, but he always made it a policy at all the studios where he'd worked before to never have an employee that he found too attractive working for him because it was a distraction. And since I was very cute—"

"Oh, brother," Stephanie roared.

"—and I was all he could think about since coming aboard as president, he said it wasn't fair to either of us, because he felt like a lecherous old man—since I'm twenty-seven and he's forty —and was certain I'd be uncomfortable with him having these feelings, especially since he'd just made me fully aware of them. He said he didn't want to hurt me or create an unpleasant working environment. He had to think of not only himself and me but the entire department."

"Right. Good," Stephanie said. "And then you pleaded with him because you love your job, and you didn't know what else you'd be qualified to do. And that's when he asked how much you really do love your job and also what you think of him as a man. And what stuff you'd be willing to do to stay on as head writer."

"And I told him I just wanted to please him. And that if he wanted a blow job every now and again, I'd be happy to—"

"For Christ's sake, *no!* No! No! No!" Stephanie bellowed so hard that the poster of *Marked Woman* rattled on the wall behind her desk. "Jesus, Joseph, and Mary! The guy is forcing himself on you, you imbecile! Remember? You can't stand his guts. You think he's an ugly old troll."

It's your ugly old troll guts I hate, Bart thought. Instead, he said, "He's all of forty? I shouldn't say he's old, should I? Who'd believe that?"

"You've had nightmares ever since then, right?"

"Well, fantasy dreams, to be more accurate."

"That's more than I need to know, you little perv. Christ, you're as thick as a brick. Listen, are you with us on this project or what? I'll vouch for the fact that your job performance has slipped way down. You're worthless to the department because you're so traumatized and disgusted by Owen's affections."

"Isn't that taking it too far, Stephanie," Bart asked. "I mean, first of all, *you* scare me more than he does. Won't a jury find it unrealistic that I've rebuffed a powerful and sexy man? Will a jury believe this story? Secondly, the work I've done speaks for itself. There's no lack of quality in our publicity materials."

"No jury." Stephanie shook her head. "This will never go to any trial; I've told you that a dozen times; we're simply building a case against Owen because we know he wants to get rid of me and bring in his old team from Warner Brothers." Stephanie was trying to sob, but she lacked tear ducts. "I can't lose my job. I have a huge mortgage, and I'm supporting half my family. Owen doesn't like me. This is just for insurance. Besides, your publicity materials pretty much do suck."

"But you've been approving them, haven't you? What if the court makes me provide all your approval sheets?"

"No court! I've told you! All out of court!" She paused. "I'll write up some complaints for your personnel file."

"That's not necessary, is it?" Bart said in a wounded tone. As far as he knew, his employee file was impeccable. Never a day late. Seldom a day out sick. There were commendations from famous actors and directors offering praise for the work that Bart had accomplished promoting their films either through his writing or when he was on the steering committees for a fund-raising event with them.

Stephanie said, "Everything negative will come out of your file as soon as this is all over."

"So now you're going to lie about me, too? I'm not the one to focus on here, Stephanie. Perhaps I'm not the right one to go through with this after all."

"Too late, dipshit. And stop being such a sissy," Stephanie yelled. "This information will never go beyond my office. Trust me. We're just trying to turn up the heat and scare Owen to let him know we're not stupid. That's enough for tonight," she finally said, giving up. "We'll try again tomorrow. But get the fucking lines that we discussed straight!" She thought aloud for a moment. "Maybe we do need another gay guy to do this right... there are plenty in the office to choose from."

Bart felt depleted of energy. He walked back to his office and closed the door, then called Ryan. He didn't dare use the company lines because rumor had it they were tapped. The computers, too. It was suspected that all emails were down-loaded at night. When the names of the CEO or board members or even certain four-letter words in the text of a message showed up in an algorithm, the message was selected for review by corporate communications. Nothing was secret—or sacred—at Sterling Studios.

As usual, the extraordinary Ryan was completely supportive of Bart when he called to tell him about the ordeal. Although Ryan had already settled in for the night, he suggested they both meet for a late dinner and a bottle of wine. "Better still," Ryan said, "if you don't mind leftovers, my doggie bag from lunch at Langford Bistro is probably more than enough for you. I'll open a bottle right now. I'll let it breathe waiting for you."

Bart didn't hesitate to accept the invitation. Although they hadn't previously planned to be together that night, Bart wanted to be comforted and reassured by Ryan. Ryan, too, wanted to be near Bart and also to hear all about his horrific day. He was also eager to listen to the audio recording Bart had made from his latest tutorial with Stephanie.

It was a little after nine when Bart rang the bell at Ryan's home in the Fryman Canyon area of Studio City. The area might have been in the so-called *Valley*, which got its share of snubbing from those in Beverly Hills and the West Side of LA, but Studio City was home to many second-tier celebrities. "Sanctuary!" Bart exclaimed, imitating Quasimodo, and fell into Ryan's arms. "Yikes, what a day," he said, settling onto Ryan's sofa and looking lovingly at his man. "I still don't know if what I'm doing is the right thing, but I've recorded another session with Stephanie. She's giving me all these instructions about what to say in the deposition against Owen Lucas."

Ever since Paco first convinced him of the potential value of the recordings he was making of Stephanie's duplicitous activities, Bart decided to throw himself into the part of double agent. He'd act out his undivided loyalty to Stephanie and Cy and Sterling but simultaneously furnish Owen Lucas with the information. After consulting with Ryan and Owen, Bart had gone to Stephanie with his tail between his legs. He apologized to her for being a wuss. He had told Stephanie that to show how much he respected her and how honored he was to have such an important job at the studio, he would do whatever was best for everybody involved. Stephanie took the bait without a second thought.

"Let Stephanie and Cy think I'm going along with their conspiracy in exchange for a promotion," Bart had said to Ryan once his decision had been made. "I have this angelic face. I have a smile that makes people trust me. No one ever imagines I have the capacity for being disingenuous. See, these are the valuable life lessons one gets by working in Hollywood!" Bart laughed.

"She still has no idea that Owen is completely aware of all this clandestine business of hers and Cy's?" Ryan asked.

"She's definitely not the sharpest claw on the cat. She thinks I'm an idiot because I keep goofing up my lines. I just want her to keep reiterating her plans on the recording. I'm still sorta shocked that you and Owen are old friends. I think it's such a great 'six degrees of separation' thing."

"I never lose my real friends. We may not stay in touch as often as we'd like, but we always know we're there for each other. I'm in contact with most of the guys I knew in college. Owen's like a brother."

"But tell me again. How did Owen know that you and I..."

"I have a great relationship with my clients, too. They apparently talk about me. In this case, it was Warren and Annette. She told Gwyneth, whose dad was an old chum of Owen's father... yeah, small world... about me and my new relationship with you. When Gwyneth described you to Owen—cute young publicist-writer at his new studio, etc.—he put two and two together.

When he caught on to all the palace intrigue, he knew he could count on me for help. I'm just sorry for getting you so deeply involved."

"I'm thrilled to be doing something that will blow up in Stephanie's face. If we can just get enough recorded evidence, she and Cy will be history."

"We probably have enough now," Ryan said. "But don't forget, in Hollywood, the type of behavior that Stephanie and Cy are involved with is completely condoned. There's that old Hollywood maxim that when you get fired from one studio, you go on to a better job at another studio."

"That's usually after they get out of jail," Bart joked. "You know I don't care about my own career at Sterling. I have enough savings and stock options to quit anytime. But I won't be summarily kicked out for no good reason."

"And you know I'm not wild about interfering with the course of events in anybody's life," Ryan said. "But I also can't stand around and watch the people I love, Owen—and especially you—being abused."

Bart smiled gratefully. "I hate to admit it, but although I can take care of myself when it comes to weathering the storm of Stephanie Hough, I'm getting a lot of satisfaction from being part of the team to kick her ass."

Sidling closer to Ryan and nuzzling his lover's neck, Bart said, "When this is all over, I may accelerate my plan to kidnap you and run away to England. To that little farm in the Lake District that I fantasize about. The place where I can write, and you can take care of the village animals. We won't have to worry about Sterling Studios or Hollywood ever again."

Ryan had been hearing about Bart's desire to relocate to England or Scotland ever since their first date. Bart had had it all planned for himself before they met, and wondered what Ryan had thought of the idea. As with all things that were

Ryan/Bart or Bart/Ryan, there was harmony. They both agreed they would eventually settle abroad. England, Ireland, Scotland, perhaps a farm in the Hebrides. They weren't sure, but they planned to spend a couple of months traveling as soon as the situation at the studio was resolved.

Without further words, Ryan placed Bart's head in his hands and locked his lips onto his. Both were vibrating with electrical energy as they began their slow, passionate foreplay.

"The bed," Bart sighed.

The two of them rose from the couch, their lips still pressed hard against the other's, as they moved out of the living room and found their way to Ryan's king-size bed. Their kisses were gentle, then hard, then gentle again. This was the way they made love every time they were together—love mixed with lust, pouring from their souls.

The dogs wanted attention, too.

18

Peter and Michael were both high on martinis when Paco returned home from running errands.

"Paco," Peter cried. "Amazing news! *Perfect Love,* er, *Blind as a Bat* is sold! Sterling bought the script. We just heard from Cy Lupiano. Isn't this terrific? Have a drink to celebrate."

Paco was stunned. A tsunami of questions flooded the room. "Are you serious? What's the deal? Who's starring? The script's not even finished! When do they go into production? How much money? What's *Perfect Love*?" Paco hated martinis, but he accepted the one offered by Michael. "Shouldn't we have a toast or something," Paco said, hardly able to control his enthusiasm.

"Look at this kid here!" Peter said to Michael. "It's the greatest thing that's ever happened in his life, and we're responsible. Absolutely we should raise our glasses!"

"To *Perfect Love,*" Michael sang. "May it bring us all a shitload of money and Oscars all around!"

"*Blind as a Bat* or *Perfect Love* or whatever," Paco said incredulously. "I can't believe it sold!" Making a dramatic sweeping arc gesture high above his head, he announced: "*Perfect Love.* Original screenplay by Paco Castillo. From a story by Paco Castillo.

Executive producer Paco Castillo. Brought to you by the new Ford Explorer—and Paco Castillo!" He laughed himself silly. "Details! Details," Paco squealed after a sip of his gin. "And I didn't think the script was ready. I guess you pros really do know what you're doing after all. Tell me everything. How much money am I getting up front?"

Peter looked at Michael. Michael looked at Peter. They both looked at Paco. "There are still a million details to work out," Michael finally said. "This is just the first step."

"Don't count your chickens and all that sort of thing," Peter added. "It's bad luck in Hollywood. Like actors whistling backstage."

"But the script is sold," Paco said. "That means there's money. You *had* to talk money. How much am I getting? Just ball-park it."

Peter turned around and went back to the bar to pour himself another drink.

"Well, the thing of it is," Michael began, "since you're a first-time writer... you don't even belong to the WGA... for Christ's sake... things get complicated."

"Loan me the twenty-five hundred it costs to join the freakin' Writers Guild," Paco said, starting to feel uneasy. "Or better yet, just take it out of the check I get from Sterling. I only want to know how much. High six figures? Mid? What? It's worth every penny they're paying—and more."

"Well," Michael continued, "since the screenplay isn't really yours..."

Silence engulfed the room. "Isn't mine?" Paco said, feeling a knot tighten in his stomach.

Peter said, "Michael and I thought that..."

"Whoa," Paco said, holding up his hands, "*Perfect Love* isn't my title, but the script is *mine*. I've worked for months on all the rewrites of a perfectly good—no, excellent—original screenplay.

Of course it's mine. What are you talking about? I'm the author. You guys acted as consultants. I took creative direction from you, but I wrote the freakin' script."

"Let's talk about the specifics after we celebrate," Peter said. "This is a victory for all of us. You should be thrilled that something that began as a kernel of an idea—granted, you contributed to the start of this—is about to become a motion-picture reality, with a juicy role for me."

"No. I want to talk about it now," Paco demanded. "What do you mean, 'It began as a kernel'? And 'I contributed to the start'? That freakin' screenplay is *all mine!*"

Paco was dumbfounded. He thought, surely, this must be April Fools' Day. At any moment, Peter and Michael would say, "Can't you take a joke, you little pisher? You're a genius, man. We could never have done this without you!"

Instead, Michael said, "I don't think you quite know how things work in Hollywood. No first-time writer—"

"God, what a stupid line. '*First-time writer*'!" Paco shot back. "No writer is a 'first-time writer.' First time published, maybe. Or first time produced. But every writer works years for that so-called *first-time* or *debut* bullshit."

"What I'm trying to tell you," Michael continued, "is that there's a hierarchy. You have to have a track record..."

"Fuck you and your 'track record.' You're not making sense. Are you telling me that a screenplay that I've written can't be sold with my name on it because I don't have a track record? How else do you get a track record other than selling a screenplay, goddamn it?"

Michael answered in a patronizing tone, "A lot of writers start out doing rewrites or doctoring other people's scripts, but the WGA doesn't officially recognize their contributions. It's just how the Guild works."

"This is a very complicated business," Peter added.

Paco snapped, "There's nothing complicated about getting credit where credit is due!"

"There's no use talking to you when you're in this kind of mood," Michael countered.

"Mood? What kind of *mood* am I in? Shouldn't I be in a *fuck me over* mood? It seems you guys have done that extremely well —with my clothes on, for once. I read the trades. Every day there's a story about a so-called 'first-time scribe' getting big bucks for a mere story treatment. I've written the whole damn screenplay. Four others, too! You guys have screwed me, and you're both going to be so sorry. You think I'm some little brainless plaything? You invited the wrong stud to your party."

Peter and Michael abandoned Paco and congregated at the bar. They poured more martinis and talked among themselves about the film.

Paco stood motionless, glued to the floor, looking bewildered and frozen in time. Finally, still dazed, Paco pitched his now-empty martini glass against the framed portrait of Peter above the mantle. Shards of glass exploded onto the wall and hearth, and Paco stormed out of the room. As he departed, Peter and Michael looked up at him, then at each other. Nobody said a word.

Paco grabbed his laptop from the office and the car keys from the Lalique crystal table in the foyer. He stormed out of the house and got into his Ford Fiesta. He turned on the ignition, put the car in gear, and drove down the cobbled driveway. The gates parted when he passed the infrared security sensor, and he angrily drove away from the estate that he'd less-than-affectionately named "Peter's Pit." He was raving mad, confused, and bewildered, like a loyal employee after unexpectedly being fired. He didn't know what to do or where to go. His first urge was to call Bart. But he was too numb to even pick up his cell phone. Somehow, he drove on automatic pilot along

Mulholland, down the Cahuenga Pass and on to Sterling Studios.

Rich was at the gate. When Paco pulled up at the guard kiosk, he acted smug and self-satisfied. "Hey, man," he said, smiling. "Guess you're ready for more action, eh? Meet me over at Stage 21. I can get away in about five."

Paco had already nearly forgotten about their previous tryst and now tried to turn on his charm but was so drained from his altercation with Peter and Michael that he failed. "Rain check, okay, man? I've got a meeting across town and just need to get Bart Caine to sign some papers."

Rich was disappointed. "The cast of *Totally Kewl* returns in two weeks," he said. "Better make some time again before then." It wasn't a polite request. It sounded more like a threat, as if his access to the lot was dependent on another performance on Stage 21. "Don't be a stranger," he finally said as he waved Paco through.

"Yeah. Can't wait," Paco said without a trace of excitement. "Asshole," he added inaudibly with what little breath he had in his lungs and weakened body as he pulled away to find an open space in the parking area.

Paco's trip from the parking lot to the publicity building felt as though he were plodding through one giant, invisible spider-web. When he finally reached the reception area of the publicity building, he approached Audrey, who immediately recognized him and addressed him by name. "Nice to see you again, Mr. Castillo. I mean Paco. I didn't have a chance to say a proper goodbye to you last time. May I tell Bart that you're here?"

"Mind if I just go up and surprise him?"

"Rules are made to be broken, right?" Audrey giggled.

"Thanks, Audrey," he said. "By the way, great earrings."

She blushed as Paco stepped into the elevator. He gave her an insincere wave.

"Fuck!" said perky Audrey under her breath. On the outside, she looked as if she could play hostess to visiting VIPs and dignitaries at Disneyland. Inside, she was a woman whose libido twitched for almost every man under thirty she laid her blue eyes on. The few heterosexual mail-delivery boys swarmed around her like gnats. Then she blinked back to reality and displayed her disingenuous smile for the next man who came up to the receptionist's desk.

Paco stepped off the elevator on the tenth floor and wandered down to Bart's office. As usual, Brian wasn't at his desk, so Paco simply stood in Bart's doorway until he looked up from his computer monitor.

Bart was momentarily startled. Then he smiled. "Hey, man. What's going on? Time flies. Seems like only yesterday that we had lunch," he joked.

Paco looked crestfallen. "Hope you don't mind me coming by. I just needed someone to talk to." He stared almost lifelessly at Bart, who sat behind his desk in a plush leather chair, surrounded by movie posters of his favorite films. Suddenly, tears began to well up in Paco's eyes and roll down his cheeks.

"Hey...! What the...?" Bart declared. He quickly got up from behind his desk and ushered Paco onto the sofa. He closed the door, reached for a box of Kleenex, and handed it to Paco. "What's the matter? What's going on?"

"Oh, nothing," Paco said evasively. "Nothing that either suicide or murder or both won't cure."

"What in the world...?"

"My screenplay. Peter. Michael. Sterling Studios. Stealing my material. The end of my career before it's even begun."

Bart opened his refrigerator and took out a plastic bottle of cold spring water. He handed it to Paco and said, "I'm not following. Start at the beginning."

Paco took a long moment to regain his composure. Then he

described the situation. "They stole my screenplay. Simple as that. Peter's going to co-star. They've fucked up my life."

Bart tried to console Paco. "They can't do that. There has to be a mistake. They can't possibly get away with such a thing. Even if they tried to steal the screenplay, there's a long paper trail dating all the way back to the studio's story analyst."

"You don't understand," Paco countered. "There's nothing left of the original script or even the original story. Well, maybe a little bit, but not enough to prove I did a damned thing on what's now called *Perfect Love.*"

Bart was quiet for a long moment. "What was Dorothy Parker's famous line? 'The only *ism* Hollywood believes in is plagiarism,'" he said, trying to lighten the mood.

"She was dead right. And how many years ago did she say that? It's still standard practice. Peter and Michael have it all worked out. I thought this kind of stuff was over after Paramount settled with Buchwald for Eddie Murphy's *Coming to America.* I've been a complete idiot."

Bart shook his head. "This is too insane. There's got to be a logical explanation and something we can do. Let me call a friend in the legal department to find out if they're even telling you the truth. Maybe we haven't even acquired the script."

Paco sat quietly while Bart spoke to Jeffrey in legal clearances. Bart made up a story saying he'd been asked to start a press release announcing a new film called *Perfect Love*, and what could Jeffrey tell him about it?

"God, there really are no secrets in this town." Jeffrey laughed, astonished at how short the grapevine was. "There isn't even a contract yet. But, yeah, supposedly that title has been acquired. I've got the file right here."

Bart pressed on. "Just so I can get a head start, can you give me the billing credits?"

"No director yet and no stars attached. But there's a deal memo here that's been prepared for Ben Wishaw."

"I've heard Peter Jacks signed," Bart interrupted.

"That old closet case. It's possible, I guess. There's a Michael Stone set as producer."

"Screenplay credit?" Bart asked.

"Same as the producer, Michael Stone. And somebody named Troy Everett. Oh, this is interesting. It does say, 'Additional dialogue by Peter Jacks.' Hmmm. I don't see that kind of credit very often. Peter Jacks. I thought that dude was through after that video went viral. As long as I've worked in this biz, I'm still surprised at what goes on. Bet there was a lot of gang-bangin' to get him on this film." Jeffrey laughed, thinking of Peter's reputation.

Bart thanked Jeffrey and asked to be kept advised of new developments—casting and the start of production date and anything else pertinent to a press release. He hung up the phone and looked across the desk at Paco. "Seems to be true. You're not listed as a screenwriter. But hold on, these things often go into arbitration."

"How can I arbitrate if I don't even belong to the fucking WGA?" Paco said.

"You've said that Peter is one of the co-stars? There's no one listed yet—except the possibility of Ben Wishaw."

"That was my idea too! I wrote it with him in mind!"

"There is some strange 'additional dialogue by' credit for Peter. What if Michael is screwing Peter over for writing credit? Think that's possible?"

"After what I've seen of this town, anything's possible—and probable," Paco said. "I want 'em both screwed—for life. They're gonna pay."

"Trust me, we'll work this out," Bart said, trying to reassure

Paco. "Come on. I'll leave the office now. Let's go have a drink and talk."

Bart wrote a note for Brian, whom he could never find when he needed him, and posted the message on his computer monitor.

"Are you okay to drive?" Bart asked Paco. "We can take my car if you want."

"No, I can drive myself. Maybe I'll get to die in a horrible car crash on the way. I'll meet you at Ricky's over on Santa Monica."

"I'll call Ryan to let him know where I'll be. Maybe he can join us. Actually, he'd be a great one for you to talk to about this. He's more analytical than I am. Maybe he can come up with some ideas."

"Whatever, man. I just want a drink and maybe a gun to blow my brains out with. And I never want to see Peter Jacks as long as I live. Can I hang at your place for a while?"

"Sure, we can turn the study into a bedroom for a couple of nights." With Paco feeling so low, Bart couldn't say no to his staying with him for a while.

Paco had been thinking of a longer-term arrangement, but he was too physically and emotionally spent to discuss it any further at the moment. He didn't even acknowledge Bart's support. "See you at Ricky's."

Bart telephoned Ryan from the car and asked if he was available to meet with him and Paco. Ryan was nearly finished with a client, and he suggested that Bart pick him up on his way over the hill.

Ryan actually liked the idea that Bart wanted him to be part of helping Paco. Not that Ryan felt the least bit of jealousy about Paco, but it would be nice to finally meet the only other man who, at another time, would have been his competition for Bart's love and affection.

When Bart and Ryan walked into the seedy, dimly lit Ricky's

bar, which even at 5:45 was alive with loud music and a collection of some of West Hollywood's most disreputable-looking people, they found Paco at a table, turning away a guy in blue jeans ripped at the left butt cheek. The guy was wearing a black leather vest exposing his hairy, muscled torso and nipple rings connected by a silver chain. He was holding a bottle of beer and slinked away when Bart and Ryan showed up.

"I may not command respect for my writing," Paco said, "but as long as I have my looks, the world's certainly interested in hiring me for other things. Maybe I should stick to where my true talent lies."

Bart made the introductions. "Paco, I'd like you to meet my boyfriend, Ryan."

Ryan held out his hand to shake Paco's. Paco, however, didn't bother to look up, brushing Ryan off, as he'd brushed off the suitor who had approached him a moment before. "I hear you're *nice*," Paco said sarcastically. "Bart says you're *nice*. Isn't that *nice*?"

"Nice to meet you, too," Ryan said, ignoring Paco's lack of manners and ill disposition. "Bart has told me about you, too."

"No way he said I was *nice*."

"As a matter of fact, the word *asshole* came up the most," Ryan said, smiling.

Paco chuckled involuntarily, caught off guard by the quick comeback.

Although such unattractive language was foreign to Ryan's everyday vocabulary, he was adept at holding his own with almost any type of individual. He was accomplished at dishing out to others what they doled out to him.

Paco finally looked up at Ryan and smiled, realizing the man was no pushover and was smart enough to know how to level the playing field when it came to interacting with difficult people. "Sorry," Paco said. "It's nice to meet you. And I actually mean that. It's just been one of those days."

Bart and Ryan sat down and signaled for the server to take their drinks order. When he arrived, wearing short shorts and a tank top, showing off his assets, both asked for red wine.

"Are you sure you wouldn't prefer beers," the young man with too many facial piercings said. Leaning in conspiratorially, in an exaggerated stage whisper he said, "Confidentially, the wine here comes in a box. I call it 'Château du Poo-Poo Chien.' And there's an expiration date and a skull and crossbones, with a warning from the surgeon general."

Ryan and Bart laughed. "Thanks for the alarm bells," Ryan said. He looked at Bart for approval, then amended the order to two beers. "Heineken, if you have it."

"*Ja. Das ist gut!*" The server spoke with an affected German pronunciation, then pranced away.

"So," Ryan said to Paco, "one of those days, eh? What's the scoop? I mean, I don't have more than a slight clue about the reason for our being here, exactly. Something about you getting screwed out of a screenplay you wrote?"

Paco reiterated the story for Ryan's benefit. "It sucks," was his concluding remark.

Ryan was reaching into his pocket to hand the returning server a ten-dollar bill to pay for their drinks. "Perhaps you'd better run a tab," he said, giving him an ample tip.

"Your wish is my desire."

"I just don't know what to do now," Paco said, nearly in tears again. "This is the worst thing that's ever happened to me. Worse than the time I had to have sex with that Republican senator, what's-his-face..."

～

By the time Bart and Ryan were together again in Ryan's king-size bed, they were still talking about the day's events. They agreed that given the mix of Paco and Stephanie and Peter and Michael and Cy, no one—not even Paco—was a truly reliable character. Each had an agenda, and each seemed to be more than competent at seducing their way into getting whatever they wanted.

"I don't have to tell you to be careful of them all," Ryan warned. "We've both been around these types often enough to know that where money and power are involved, nothing is ever as it seems. Everybody is your friend until there's a payday of some sort involved. Then it can turn into a bloodbath."

"But out of that whole bunch, don't you think that perhaps Paco's at least the most vulnerable?"

"Aren't you?" Ryan queried.

"I don't follow."

"Paco hurt you. Stephanie hurt you. She and Cy are close to destroying your career. It could be argued that even *I'm* using you—in a sense—to help my old friend Owen."

Bart lay cradled in his lover's arms. He looked up at the mural-covered ceiling—a reproduction of Michelangelo's *Last Judgment* frescoes in the Sistine Chapel—but depicting a menagerie of pets instead of apostles, prophets, and martyrs. "'Using' is when you're doing something nefarious to someone else," said Bart. "That's definitely just not in your nature. I guess we could turn it all around and say I'm *using* you to help ruin Stephanie and maybe to get back at Paco for the way he nearly destroyed me."

Ryan rolled over on top of Bart and began passionately kissing his lips, neck, and nipples. "Oh, yeah, use me, baby." Ryan laughed as his hands gamboled all over Bart's body, tickling him.

Bart giggled and screamed out, "No! No! Stop!" in mock

torment as Ryan put aside their conversation for the time being in favor of ravaging Bart. Then, suddenly, the bedroom door burst open. Ryan and Bart both exploded with laughter as three dogs raced to the bed, barking. Their "kids" leaped onto the bed for a snuggle.

19

"Paco can be such a shit," Bart complained to Ryan a few weeks later as they lounged together on Ryan's living room sofa, enjoying a bottle of Pinot Noir, petting the dogs, and listening to Michael Bublé on the music system. "Here I am, playing Lady Bountiful, letting him camp out in my home, and he repays me by sexually teasing me, for crying out loud."

"You're seldom home," Ryan reminded him, dismissing the notion that Paco was harassing Bart. "You're with me five nights a week. The rest of the time you're at the office until all hours. It's not like he doesn't know we're a couple. You don't think he respects the boundaries?"

"I don't think he respects anything or anybody other than Paco Castillo and his libido. When I *am* home, all he does is play Peter's homemade porn tapes over and over, saying he's going to someday force Peter into those same scenarios, but for real... no safe words. Paco's actually got quite a stash of those videos. He stole them from Peter's vault. Says he's keeping 'em as leverage, in case Peter actually ever gets a shot at being in the movie."

"My poor baby," Ryan teased. "Does it hurt to see the most

beautifully constructed man on the planet walking around your apartment without a stitch?" Ryan set down his glass and tried to coax a smile out of a pouting child. "Is the sight of Paco's silky brown, sinewy, muscled body too much of a turn-on for my little darlin'?" Then, playacting, as if he were Shirley Temple making peace between the Yankees and the Confederates, Ryan placed his index fingers in his own honest-to-goodness Shirley Temple dimples and said, "Do you need your cute boyfriend to come over and protect you from the big, bad God of Physical Perfection?"

"Stop!" Bart squealed with laughter. "You don't know how tough it is to go home and see a naked God coming out from the shower, his body glistening from the oil he uses on his skin, for crying out loud. Stop! don't! I'm ticklish!"

Ryan sat back. "Then you'll stop complaining?"

"As best I can," Bart said, opening his arms to express the breadth of his devotion to duty.

"That's my brave and courageous man of steel!"

What Bart didn't tell Ryan was that the mere sight of Paco's body was enough to drive him mad with desire, which was one reason he stayed away from his own apartment as much as possible. However, Sunday nights had always been sacred to Bart, and he spent them in his own apartment. He never went out, even when he began to date Ryan. It was his time to mentally prepare for the coming workweek. "A school night," he called it. He read the *New York Times,* watched *60 Minutes* on television, and reviewed his journal entries covering the past week.

The very next night after he complained to Ryan about Paco and how difficult it was to be in the apartment with him because he was always horny and seemingly just hanging around, hinting that he was up for action, Bart had gone to bed and fallen into a deep sleep. Then, from down in the basement of his unconsciousness, he became vaguely aware that the door to his room was being opened. It wasn't long before he was wide-awake. Paco had slipped into bed beside him.

"What the...?" Bart had said, feeling Paco's naked body against his own bare skin.

"Shhh." Paco placed his mouth over Bart's and rolled on top of him. Although shocked and dumbfounded, the scent and feel of his body brought back a million exciting images of the nights they had been together. Everything collided into one huge, passionate, deep kiss.

Thoughts of Ryan and how much he loved him rushed in, but Bart's memories of Paco's sensuous body deflected all rationalization. He hated himself for giving in to desire, but Paco was so passionate and demanding, there was no way to not fall completely in lust with him all over again. A part of Bart tried to convince himself that this was not premeditated, and Ryan would never know about the encounter. Anyway, whatever Paco and Bart did together was not the same kind of passion he shared with Ryan. It was completely different and therefore should not be an issue. He could rationalize forever. The truth was he was so engulfed in the conflagration of lust, for the moment he didn't care about the consequences.

"Bart! Oh, Christ, Bart!" Paco groaned. "I am *so* fucking hard for you! *Please,* Bart! I've got to fuck you! You want me too, don't you? Yeah, you remember how great it was. You want me! Say you want me! Say it, Bart! Say it! Please say you want me!"

"I want you, Ryan! Yes, Ryan! Please!"

Ryan! Oh, shit, Bart thought to himself as he continued to kiss Paco, pretending the name had not slipped out.

But they'd both heard Ryan's name spoken, in the darkness. Instantly, the spell was broken. Although Paco and Bart continued to hold each other for a time, they slowly drew apart. Soon they lay merely entwined in each other's arms and legs, and their breathing became less heavy, more controlled. Neither spoke, although they stayed wrapped together for a long while.

In the morning, after Bart had showered and was dressed for work, Paco wandered into the kitchen. "I'm *not* sorry I came in there last night, if that's what you're hoping for."

"I'm not sorry either," Bart said, sipping from a mug of coffee as he leaned against the refrigerator. He put his hand out to touch Paco's sculpted chest. "But I'm also not sorry that things didn't go any further—if that's what *you're* hoping for."

"You didn't do anything with me last night that should cause a problem for you and Ryan. Are you going to tell him?"

"What purpose would it serve?"

Paco didn't answer. He guessed it would be stupid to reveal what was essentially two friends enjoying being close together. He hadn't gone all the way with Bart, so it had been relatively benign. Real sex had been aborted. So, indeed, there was nothing to talk about.

Then, in a non sequitur, Paco said, "I want you to read Peter's manuscript. It's not that I didn't trust you before, but to make up for last night... I know you're probably the only one alive who'll keep my secret. I'll give you Peter's whole book. I've highlighted the stuff I intend to use to blackmail the son of a bitch."

Bart was incredulous. "Blackmail? You know that's a federal offense."

"Your point being?"

"I thought you ripped off his videos for that purpose. Is the stuff in the book really worth the price of you possibly going to prison?" Bart asked.

"I didn't steal the videos. I borrowed them and forgot to give them back. As for the content of the book, I don't know. I need you to be the judge of its potential value. All I know is he deserves whatever happens to him."

"We all do," Bart said. "It's called karma. You know, *cause and effect*. Be careful."

"It's also a matter of principle. He's ruined my life. I don't want to have what happened to me happen to some other stud."

"Oh, give me a break," Bart said, placing his coffee mug in the sink. "You just want revenge. You're not trying to save some other poor street hustler from a fate worse than Peter Jacks. And you're not even going about it the right way. Peter's career is already in ashes. Also, you say his body has turned to dough, and he has chronic acne on his butt. I don't know what else you could possibly come up with that would make things worse for him."

"Just read the book." Paco padded out of the kitchen to the office/bedroom.

Bart watched Paco and wished to hell he hadn't allowed a single moment of the night before to occur. He was completely ashamed of his lust for him.

Paco returned moments later with a ream and a half of paper held together with thick rubber bands. He handed it to Bart, who accepted the weighty manuscript and cradled it in his arms.

"A lot of the crap in there is really lame and boring. You can skip right to the stuff I've flagged," Paco said. "It'll make you sorry you ever became associated with Hollywood."

"Like I'm not already?" Bart paused. "I'll read it as soon as I get to the studio, but this is going to take days."

"Then just the parts with the yellow Post-its."

In the car, Bart placed the seven hundred plus pages of double-spaced text on the passenger seat. He looked at it with the dread of knowing he'd have to at least skim the damn thing.

Once at the studio, Bart first made a pot of coffee. Then he listened to his phone messages. Stephanie (angry). Stephanie (livid). The mother of a kid actor (incensed). Stephanie (furious). Ryan (affectionate). Stephanie (petulant).

Then he logged on to his computer to retrieve his emails.

There were twenty-seven postings since the night before. Red flags meant they were urgent. But Bart dismissed them. He'd read his cyber mail when the office officially opened. This was *his* time, although he wasn't in any hurry to begin poring through the voluminous manuscript. He had glanced at the first page while at a stoplight on the way to the studio and immediately noticed long run-on sentences. The book was going to be a chore to wade through; of that he was certain.

Bart hated having to read other people's unpublished work. As the head writer at Sterling and the author of a few short stories here and there and feature articles, novices were constantly after him to read their stuff. They all wanted the same thing: to be told how wonderful their work was and how, with a little more effort, they would be the next Laura Levine or Dorothy Howell.

Finally, with a sigh of resignation, Bart picked up Peter's manuscript. He propped his feet up on the desk and placed the manuscript in his lap. He leaned slightly back in his chair and began to read:

Chapter One

"I cried for forty-eight hours straight!" Peter's memoir began. "When that bitch Meredith Rowland on *Totally Holly-wood* aired a two-part and completely false and slanderous exposé about me, with her doctored video, I was so humiliated, I left the studio in the middle of taping my show, *The Grass is Always Greener*, went to bed, and with my clothes still on, cried myself to sleep! I awoke two days later, ready to fight for the truth! This is why I am writing this book, which is meant as an explanation to all my fans and a vindication of my virtue."

The first chapter was wretched. Bart found himself laughing not only at Peter's lack of writing skills but also his whining about the travails of being a star and how his fame got in the way of having an ordinary life. While most celebrities complained about a lack of privacy, Peter merely griped about sex. He tried to explain how he got caught on video with a gang of prostitutes.

"As I pleaded for my life in what was supposed to be the sanctuary of my guarded estate, I was wrestled to the ground and severely beaten by the gang!" he wrote. "When I eventually regained consciousness, I found myself tied up in my own wine cellar! I was a prisoner in my own home, and I was terrified!" (Peter ended nearly every sentence with an exclamation point.)

"The toughest of the gang members, the one who seemed to be the leader, decided he wanted to video the big, important TV star. I suspected that they wanted to sell the video to the highest bidder—on eBay!"

Bart groaned. It was highly unlikely that prostitutes or hustlers would be hawking celebrity porn on eBay.

"Then, when I finally thought I had found an opportunity to fight back, I was overpowered by the entire horde of thugs! They had their way with me. Then they found a cattle prod that had been used as a gimmick prop on my sitcom, and they decided it would be funny to use it on me for real! It was the darkest moment of my life! I vowed it was the last time I would ever take home a prop that belonged to the show—especially a potentially dangerous one!"

Bart knew better than to buy any of this. First of all, the *Star* or the *National Intruder* tabloid papers would have headlined a story about a burglary and assault at Peter's mansion. They would have immediately detailed the incident if it had been reported to the LAPD. If something as innocuous as George Michael flashing his renowned genitalia in a Beverly Hills public restroom could be "News at Eleven," as well as opening jokes for the late-night television comedians, then surely, they couldn't have kept Peter Jacks off the night sergeant's report.

Second, Peter was well known in various circles for hiring prostitutes. Even his neighbors complained about the types of young men and women who didn't appear to belong in the area coming in and out of Peter's estate. It was the worst-kept secret that Peter had a penchant for being gagged and hog-tied as a prelude to sex.

Third, Bart was unaware of an episode of *The Grass Is Always Greener* in which a cattle prod had been used. The television censors probably wouldn't have allowed it. Although, he remembered that the show did have one highly incendiary episode in which the character of Grammy, played by Sally Sunshine, a third-rate version of comedy legend Betty White, threatened her Neanderthal grandchildren by holding their pet hamster over the open chute of a Cuisinart. Switching the appliance's shiny, scalpel-sharp blades off and on, and with her patented disingenuous smile, the evilly sweet-tempered old-lady had said, "Alrighty, kiddies. Mr. Leonardo DiCaprio here has been awfully depressed lately. Which of you future cocksuckers is going to tell their sweet little ol' grammy where they hid her brand-new bottle of Bombay Safire before Leo decides to commit suicide?"

The slack-jawed kids didn't have to pretend to be mortified. They suspected their TV grandmother was, in real life, quite capable of mixing Leonardo in with the homemade pizza dough she was supposed to be making in that particular scene.

Bart remembered that episode because it was especially hilarious, and the fanatics at PETA had gone more insane than usual and tried to have the episode banned. Their ads in *TV Guide* and *USA Today* only made the ratings soar. Sally even received an Emmy Award nomination for that episode.

Bart decided that, so far, this book was simply too far-fetched to be anything but fiction. It was as silly as Liberace claiming that three times, he'd "come close" to being married (to women).

A few chapters later, Bart found himself rolling his eyes while reading about the failure of Peter's engagement to a woman he called "Jenny." Peter admitted that Jenny wasn't the woman's real name and claimed that he wanted to protect her virtue by using a pseudonym. From all that Bart knew of Peter's sexual proclivities, this Jenny was probably a Jeremy. Or more likely, Diego, considering his penchant for Latinos.

Peter's written reminiscence about hearing the news of his television show's cancellation was another falsehood. He claimed to be completely mystified about the cancellation of the network's #1 sitcom. The truth was, as soon as his infamous video had been leaked to *Totally Hollywood,* he knew the years of rolling sixes or eights had finally hit craps.

Bart's first response to the beginning of the book was to bemoan how poorly the text was written. There didn't seem to be any continuity of thought. Transitions were practically nonexistent. It was like a schizophrenic unable to censor his thoughts. Bart found himself nearly nodding off from boredom a number of times.

Then, suddenly, like the explosion from a firecracker, the book kicked into some kind of warp-speed high gear. It was as though a voice other than the author's had come along and possessed the pages like a demon. The details became startling. It was silent-film star Fatty Arbuckle's scandal magnified to the power of a billion. Only this time it wasn't an obese comic screwing a starlet to death with a Coke bottle, it was the Gen-Z *Father Knows Best* unloading the best of the worst about the nutty, slutty world of Hollywood.

By page 75, Bart was hooked. Until then, Peter had recounted vague incidents of the people he met day in and day out in

Hollywood. He talked of the male casting agents early in his career who insisted that he take off his shirt during meetings under the pretense that the roles most likely to come along were for the daytime dramas, and they required guys with decent builds. This was before the ubiquity of phone cameras, and these so-called agents had often taken snapshots of Peter with their Instamatic or Polaroid cameras. The subsequent years of stardom, with all his drinking, overeating, and indulgence of recreational drugs, had taken their toll. He claimed that when he was starting out, he had an above-average-looking upper torso. (Bart couldn't help but think of his acne bottom.)

Still, Peter couldn't get work. Until the day that the owner of the Comedy Cure caught his act during an open-mike night at the club. Peter retold the oft-quoted story about how she gave him a spot every Monday night for a month. Monday was typically the slowest night of the week for business, so she felt she had nothing to lose and maybe something to gain. She also made a few phone calls to agents and suggested they come around and take a look at this new guy.

Michael Stone was one of those agents.

Over the years many muffin magazines had printed variations on this theme of *discovery*. The only thing new in this book was Peter revealing that Michael, after watching his performance, sensed that a star was about to emerge, and wound up the evening schmoozing and boozing, then snorting coke with the unknown comic to get him to sign an agency contract.

As 9:00 a.m. loomed, Bart couldn't put the manuscript down. On every page he read the names of people he recognized, including some of his colleagues: Stephanie Hough, Cy Lupiano, CEO Dennis Rotenberg, as well as Mare Dickerson, Betty Ford Clinic-regular Britney Austin, tempestuous, tantrum-throwing bully Stan Murray, and so many others.

The pages were peppered with the names of stars and

numerous footnotes about each. They all seemed somehow connected. The *six degrees of separation* link appeared to be long-dead producer Isaac Thomas, whose demise was as poetic as justice comes—one of the biggest assholes in Hollywood, he'd died on the toilet! While Hollywood pretended to grieve and honor the whacked-out druggie with a memorial service on a studio soundstage, practically everybody who ever knew Thomas smiled at the idea that the Wicked Witch of the West was dead—and such an *unforgettable* way to die.

As Bart read along, he decided that truth really is quite often stranger than fiction, but Peter's book was too on-the-nose to be anything but a play-by-play of the people he had to deal with at the studios, as well as guest stars on his show.

The door to Bart's office was closed when Brian arrived at 9:40. His delight at thinking he had, for the first time, come in before his boss was short-lived, however, when he used the spare key and found Bart at his desk. "I'm not in yet," he said. "If anybody asks, I had car trouble. Close the door, please."

Brian was nothing if not happy to be in on something clandestine. He lived to lie. Or, as he called it, "practicing my character study of a sociopath." He closed the door as instructed.

Bart then picked up his cell phone and dialed Paco's private number.

Paco didn't answer. He was probably at the gym. Now that he was out of Peter Jacks's house, he had borrowed enough money from Bart to rejoin his health club and spent at least three hours a day there. His voicemail picked up.

"Paco, it's Bart," he said quietly. "I've read a lot of the book. We have to meet. This is a crazy day for me, but we have to talk. Meet me at the Griffith Park Observatory at 12:30. If you can't make it, call me at noon—not before—on my cell. Got it? See you then, I hope."

After disconnecting, Bart placed the manuscript in his backpack and zipped it closed. He then put the leather bag into the bottom drawer of his filing cabinet and locked the three-drawer unit. Then he opened his office door and acted as though he was ready for a regular day of business.

At noon, having not heard from Paco, Bart reversed the procedure and retrieved his backpack. He left the office and walked with purpose to the parking structure. All along the way, he felt as though he were a drug mule carrying something illegal and probably being trailed by the FBI. He felt conspicuous. For the first time, he paid attention to warning signs posted all around the studio employee parking structure: All cars subject to search. He'd never known anyone whose car had been singled out, but he thought, *I'll probably be the first.* Bart waved to the guard as he drove past the gate and off the studio lot.

Entering the freeway at Riverside Drive, he drove along the 134 to where it split to the 5, taking the off-ramp to Los Feliz, and from there drove up to Griffith Park. On the wide carpets of lawn, families were picnicking, and studs from West Hollywood, wearing practically nothing, were getting a head start on the tanning season.

Bart took the long, serpentine road and followed the signs that directed motorists to the hilltop observatory, which on a clear day could be seen from all over the city, like the Hollywood sign.

Arriving at the observatory, Bart parked his car, grabbed his backpack, and walked around the grounds outside the massive art deco-style building that always made him think of the climactic scene from *Rebel Without a Cause,* which had been shot on this very location. James Dean and Sal Mineo were still both hot young guys all these years after their respective untimely deaths. And with the previously secret details of Dean's gay life now established, Bart could only imagine what must have gone on between him and Mineo.

At 12:30 he saw Paco's Ford Fiesta pull up into the parking area. Dressed in blue jeans and a white tank top that showed off his muscles and his tattoos, Paco looked around until he finally spotted Bart standing by one of the many coin-operated telescopes that allowed a viewer to magnify the city below.

"So, you must've gotten to the part—" Paco began to speak.

"What *is* this?" Bart said, interrupting him. "Do you believe it's true?"

"Pretty amazing shit, eh? Peter wrote it, I think. But he couldn't have done it just over the past few months," Paco said. "I get the impression that he's been working on it—or at least keeping a pretty detailed journal—for years. Maybe that's why the writing got better. Practice."

"Okay. Let me get my bearings straight. Bottom line."

"Bottom line," Paco repeated.

"Stephanie Hough... is... was... I'm totally... by now not really surprised by..."

"*Comprenez-vous?*" Paco asked snidely.

Bart was mute, attempting to fathom what he'd read in Peter's book, and now Paco's confirmation of the truth.

"Wait'll you read the rest."

When Bart returned to the studio from the observatory, he immediately heard that president of publicity Owen Lucas had been fired.

According to the rumors, Owen had been terminated for two reasons: sexual harassment and poor job performance. The gossip further claimed that two unnamed men and a woman from the marketing staff had filed a lawsuit stating that Owen had tried to initiate sex with them. The rumormongers in the office set out like pigs foraging for truffles to discover who the plaintiffs were. Bart was one of the prime suspects.

"You told too many people you thought he was cute," his assistant, Brian, explained when Bart said that he'd overheard a couple of other assistants in the building's stairwell whispering about him. "What else are they going to think at a time like this?"

"But it's not true," Bart protested. "I have to talk to Stephanie." He hurried down the hall, passing the judgmental eyes and shaking heads of several colleagues. When he reached Stephanie's outer office, Mitch looked up with an expression that asked, "You didn't, did you?"

Bart responded before Mitch could utter a word. "Of course it's not true," he insisted. "Trust me, I'm completely innocent. I would never do anything to hurt Owen. I totally adore the guy!"

Mitch nodded. He knew it was impossible that Bart had made any kind of claim against Owen. Even if Owen had come to Bart and he had rejected him, Bart was the type who would have said, "I'm flattered, but you know the old saying, 'Don't get your meat where you get your bread.'"

Mitch gave Bart a smile and cocked his head toward Stephanie's office. "She's in there with Cy. I'll call you when she's free."

But before Mitch could leap up and shield the door with his body, Bart rushed for the handle. As he slammed the tall, solid wooden door behind him and turned the lock, the muted sound of Mitch crying, "No! Wait! Stop! Don't!" followed.

Stephanie looked up from her desk. Cy Lupiano was seated on one of the Barcelona chairs.

"What's this about me suing Owen Lucas for sexual harassment?" Bart declared.

"You can't just fucking barge in here, you little cocksucker," Stephanie cried.

"You guys said you just wanted some ammo in case Owen tried to sack you."

"And like a good boy, that's exactly what you gave us," Stephanie sneered.

"How did I...? What did I...? What's he done to deserve this?"

"You don't know the depth of what's going on, so don't jump to conclusions," Cy said calmly. "You're way over your head. Or Owen's. And I don't mean the one on his shoulders."

Stephanie sniggered at Cy's intentionally sexist remark.

Bart said, "All I know is I'm suddenly a pariah around the office. Everybody thinks I'm one of three responsible for Owen being fired. They think I'm filing a sexual-harassment lawsuit. Which I'm not."

"But you've made so many complaints about him. I have proof," Stephanie said.

"You haven't seemed to care before that the whole studio knows you're a brownnose," Cy said. "So why do you give a shit what else they have to say now?"

Bart blanched at the words brownnose. He felt as if he were back in grammar school, being taunted by bullies on the playground.

Stephanie groaned. "Oh, cut the bullshit, Bart. We know you wanted to sleep with him. Although 'sleep' is hardly the right word."

Bart countered, "All those lies about Owen coming on to me that you had me rehearse, you were setting me up! Oh, it's so clear now. Well, you can fire me if you want, but I'm not suing Owen. Instead, I'll have both of you and Sterling up on charges for harassing me into going along with this charade!"

"Oh, aren't you the high-and-mighty one." Stephanie's voice dripped sarcasm. "We're way ahead of you, mister." She stood up and walked over to Bart. "You're threatening the wrong people, babe," she said, jabbing her index finger into Bart's chest. "The shit we've got on you..." Stephanie stood looking into Bart's eyes and snarling. "As a matter of fact, I'm calling security now to get it over with. You'll be escorted off the lot. You won't even have time to drag that screensaver of your naked Latin lover friend into the trash—where you both belong! Oh, yeah. We know all about him. That's merely a fraction of the evidence we've gathered against you. You know the studio's IT network saves everything. Not only are you a pervert, we've got you on so many other charges, from padding your expense account to using the studio mail room to send personal mail and taking office supplies home. That's called *stealing*."

"You'll never eat lunch in this town again," Cy said. "No other studio will ever have you. We'll make sure of that."

"Can't you come up with anything better than the title of Julia Philips's old Hollywood memoir?" Bart mocked. But he was really completely floored. He couldn't be more shocked. It hadn't really occurred to him that taking a pen or a postage stamp or using the department's copy machine for personal use was stealing. But it actually was. Then he paused, pretending to backtrack. "I can't lose my job. What if I did help you? What about that?"

"Too late." Stephanie smiled evilly.

"What about when this all comes out and I testify and tell the court everything that's happened here?"

"Who's going to believe a disgruntled employee?" Stephanie scoffed. "We've got a file on you complete with complaints and write-ups and poor evaluations. Even got a few letters from celebrities! That lovely director Claudius Parker offered a good one. So did Mare Dickerson. She said, and I quote, 'I find Bart Caine to have a lot of anger in him.' It has only been out of the goodness of our hearts that we kept you here as long as we did. You're a disgrace, Bart! You're a sick, perverted, lazy excuse for a studio staff writer, and nobody's going to argue with that."

Stephanie picked up the telephone and pushed Mitch's extension number on the keypad. "Get security up here now," she demanded.

"You're seriously having me thrown off the lot?" Bart said numbly.

"Yep. I've got a new staff writer starting tomorrow."

Within moments, there was a knock on the door. A master key opened the lock, and two security guards stepped inside the room.

"Gentlemen, this is Bart Caine," Stephanie said. "He's just been terminated. One of you please go lock his office. Then collect his studio ID and throw him off the lot."

Mitch stood in the doorway, shocked at what he was witnessing. Then, furtively, he left quickly and ran to Bart's office. He began to drag Bart's personal files into the computer's trash bin.

"Let me at least get my backpack and jacket," Bart demanded. The security men looked up at Stephanie, who waved them off as if to say, "I suppose that's okay."

As the security contingent, one of whom was Paco's playmate Rich, tried to lead Bart away, he shrugged them off. He turned around and spoke one last time to Stephanie. "Like the lady in the TV commercial says to her boss after she's won the lottery jackpot, 'I can't tell you what a pleasure it's been working for you. Honestly. I can't.'"

"So long, fuckup!" Stephanie spat, then blew Bart a kiss.

As upset as Bart was, he'd made the snap decision not to mention what he knew—or at least had read in Peter's memoir —about a link between producer Isaac Thomas, a prison escapee in Oklahoma, and Stephanie Hough.

Bart passed Mitch in the hallway and smiled sheepishly. Mitch gave him a wink in solidarity. Bart led the security team down to his office, where they watched as he collected his back-pack and jacket.

"Don't touch anything else," one of the security men advised. "Your personal stuff will be packed up and sent to you."

Just as the door was being closed and locked, Brian appeared from wherever he always disappeared to when his boss was away. He looked stunned. "What's going on?"

"Looks like you'll have a new boss tomorrow," Bart said. "He or she probably won't be as understanding of you coming in late each day and leaving early for rehearsals. So you'd better play it safe for a while."

Bart had to wonder how much help Brian had provided to Stephanie, if indeed there was any evidence of him padding his expense reports. He didn't abuse perks as badly as most of his colleagues, some of whom never ate a meal at home. But he knew that Brian resented having to complete the forms and attach receipts from expensive restaurants. "You're a cool liar, Bart," he'd said on more than one occasion. "I can't even afford Denny's for breakfast, and you're taking friends out to the Ivy and Morton's, all on Sterling's dime. Just hope you never get audited by accounting." Bart now wondered if that had been a threat. He would not have been surprised to find that his assistant had been a spy or even an outright traitor. He was jealous of his salary, his car allowance, and of course, the expense account.

"Hey, everybody," Brian announced in his most theatrical voice. "Bart's been sacked! Come say g'bye." The call brought half the Sterling Studios' publicity staff out of their respective offices and cubicles to watch as Bart was led by security to the elevator. Bart looked out at all the faces of the people he had worked with for so many years. Although he was fond of only a few of them, he felt a huge emptiness knowing that this was the end of the line for his career in the motion-picture industry. At least as a publicist for Sterling Studios.

month had passed since Bart's and Owen's terminations, and they'd been busy holding strategy meetings about retaliating against Stephanie, Cy, and Sterling Studios. A core group of trusted conspirators assembled regularly.

Now, seated around the dining room table at Ryan's home were Bart, Owen, Paco, Peter, Mitch, and Hollywood's most celebrated litigator, Gus Fitterman. Ever since Fitterman's triumph in *Neal v. Todman,* the infamous lawsuit in which sex and drug-addicted producer Grey Todman was forced to pay hundreds of millions of dollars to twenty-seven uncredited and unpaid screenwriters who had worked on his hit films over the years, he was both admired and feared.

Two tall silver candelabras, aglow with multiple tapered candles, provided a gentle radiance as music from John Barry's *Movieola* album softly filtered through the speakers. Dinner of a chicken paella was over, and Gus patted his basketball stomach in satisfaction as everyone prepared to get down to the business that had brought them together in the first place.

Bart was the designated leader. He could feel the ricochet of negative protons and electrons leaping around the room like lords in a Christmas song. He took another sip of red wine.

During the brief stopgap, Peter fumed, "I'm still angry with Paco for stealing my manuscript."

"I didn't steal it!" Paco snapped back at Peter. "I just printed out a *copy* to read. Yours is still in the computer. And anyway, I've apologized about a gazillion times," Paco said. "Jeez, you know how to hold a grudge. If it hadn't been for your lousy book—that you thought would bring you millions—I'd have only guessed at what a real prick you were even before we met. You'd do anything to be a star again, eh?"

"Again? I'm *still* a star! You ungrateful prick and *thief*!" Peter bellowed in his best impersonation of an imperious king.

"A prick *and* a thief? My, my, I've moved up a notch." Paco chuckled. "So what if I made a copy of your stupid book? Mr. TV hasn't had a good zap from a cattle prod in a long time, I can tell. Why don't you go gnaw on a frayed electrical cord or lick a fuse box, for Christ's sake!"

"Okay, guys. That's all blood under the bridge," Bart said, his voice raised above the din. "We're soulmates now. We have to be. We have a common purpose."

Mitch piped in: "Bart and Owen would just be two more victims of Stephanie's abuse and her lack of conscience if it weren't for your book, Peter, which I for one am sleepless with desire to read. I hope you included me in one of your more lurid chapters. Just make sure you've spelled my name right. That's Mitch, with a capital W-O-O-D!"

For a moment, Peter was appeased, thinking of his one-nighter with Mitch and feeling like a real author with a real book and a real fan.

"Are we forgetting that I'm about to go to trial for sexual harassment?" Owen cut in.

"And *I'm* being countersued by Sterling for my wrongful-termination suit against them," Bart continued. "They're determined to get away with their lunacy and larceny at our expense. Peter's book could help immeasurably with our claims," Bart said.

Owen smiled. "If Bart's audio recordings and Peter's manuscript can prove my innocence, I'll be buying you each a new BMW."

"I'm still pissed," Peter pouted. "But I guess if I can help blow the whistle on everybody who's done us all wrong, then my efforts won't have been in vain." He was playing the grand dame suffering for the common man.

"And that's what we're here for," Fitterman finally said. Throughout dinner the attorney had explained the complicated scenario of fighting Stephanie and the big Sterling corporation, which was known to be the hardest of legal hitters in town. Fitterman's personality was as dry as the Mojave in summer, and he'd nearly wearied Peter and Mitch with his too-technical dissertation about the law. But he knew precisely what he was talking about. During their appetizers of tamales wrapped in cornhusks, he had recited verbatim the Equal Employment Opportunity Commission's guidelines for sexual harassment.

"Just what is sexual harassment?" he asked the men rhetorically. "Well, it's defined as sex discrimination that is a violation of Title VII of the Civil Rights Act of 1964."

"That was, like, a million years ago," Mitch quipped. "The last century, as a matter of fact!"

Fitterman looked over the rim of his bifocals, irritated by the interruption. He continued, "There are two types of harassment: quid pro quo and hostile environment."

"I love old episodes of *Murder, She Wrote*, and Jessica often says things like 'quid pro quo.' What's it mean... in English?" Mitch asked.

"Quid pro quo means 'this for that' or 'something for something,'" Fitterman answered.

"So, when I have sex for money, I'm doing it quid pro quo?" Paco smiled at the question. "They get *this*"—Paco made a jerk-off motion with his right hand—"and I get ker-ching!" He made the sound of a cash register ringing up a sale.

Bart looked across the table at Paco, who shrugged and added, "A guy's got to make the rent. No one else is keeping me. And no one ever will again." Paco glared evilly at Peter.

"No," Peter said, "that's not quid pro quo. That's quid pro *whore!*"

"It was good enough for you, Mr. Pimple Butt," Paco countered.

"May I continue, gentlemen," Fitterman said. "Did you know that sex as a form of prohibitive discrimination was just tagged on at the end of the Civil Rights Act? The famous Civil Rights Act—yes, from the last century." He looked over at Mitch. "And yes, long before your time. It was originally a race-discrimination bill, but at the last minute they added sex as a category of discrimination."

"That'll come in handy when I'm down to my last lifeline on *Who Wants to be a Millionaire*," Mitch chirped.

Fitterman, not quite getting the reference, eyed him with increasing annoyance. "Hmmm. Yes. Well, in sexual-harassment cases, it means unwelcome sexual advances, requests for sexual favors, and other verbal or physical conduct of a sexual nature where submission to such conduct is made either explicitly or implicitly a term or condition of an individual's employment. Or submission to or rejection of such conduct by an individual is used as the basis for employment decisions affecting such individual."

"*No hablo ingles,*" Peter said, annoyed by the polysyllabic legalese. "*Speekee de ing-gee, por favor?*"

"Then what's 'hostile environment' sexual harassment," Owen asked, ignoring Peter's comment to Fitterman.

Fitterman replied, "It has similar language to quid pro quo but adds 'Sexual harassment when such conduct has the purpose or effect of unreasonably interfering with an individual's work performance or creating an intimidating, hostile, or offensive working environment.'"

"What determines if the harassment is considered hostile?" Ryan asked.

"The court obviously has to look at a number of factors to determine if the environment is hostile," Fitterman continued. "First, they have to ask whether the conduct was verbal or physical or both. Second, how frequently it occurred. Third, whether the conduct was really hostile and patently offensive. Four, whether the alleged harasser was a coworker or supervisor. Then there's whether others joined in perpetrating the harassment and if the harassment was directed at more than one individual. An assessment is made upon the totality of the circumstances."

"I like the one that asks if others joined in perpetrating the harassment," Owen said. "That in itself should sink Stephanie and Cy."

"Not so fast," Fitterman said. "It's *never* been possible to find Sterling legally responsible for harassment by a supervisor. Their legal muscle and their brand-name value make unenlightened jurors sympathetic to the company.

"The US Equal Opportunities Commission says, and I'm quoting one of their releases, 'An employer is always responsible for harassment by a supervisor that culminated in a tangible employment action. If the harassment did not lead to a tangible employment action, the employer is liable unless it proves that it exercised reasonable care to prevent and promptly correct any harassment and the employee unreasonably failed to complain to management or to avoid harm otherwise.' You know full well that Sterling has a zero-tolerance policy."

"In English, *puhl-ese!*" Peter begged again.

"Sorry," Fitterman said. "Simply, an individual qualifies as a 'supervisor' if he has the authority to make decisions affecting the employee or direct the employee's daily work activities."

"That's me, basically," Owen said, dismayed. "*Tangible employment action* means I had the authority to change an employee's status, like hiring, firing, promotions, demotions, and all that, which I did have."

"In our situation it has to do with Owen's—and Stephanie's and Cy's, too—ability to fire or demote a subordinate because he or she makes sexual demands," Fitterman said. "We'll get into all the details about Owen's and Bart's failure to complain about harassment because of legitimate fear of retaliation when we get to trial. But remember, the young men they've got lined up to testify against Owen can use the same excuse—fear—for not going to their supervisor, namely, Stephanie."

Peter said. "Let's get to the good stuff, like how much money Owen and Bart will make when they win."

Fitterman barked, "This is by no stretch of the imagination a win-win situation. How can I make it any clearer that I'll be working extremely hard on behalf of Owen and Bart to bring Stephanie Hough down, along with Cy Lupiano and all of Sterling, Inc. But this is a steep, uphill battle. Sterling has never lost a sexual-harassment case. Ever! They usually settle out of court. This is going to be a complicated procedure. I need each of you to fully cooperate. If you think Stephanie has a hair-trigger temper, wait'll you meet the studio's chief counsel. It's going to be messy.

"However, thanks to the recordings Bart made of his so-called rehearsals with Stephanie, along with the documentation from Peter's notes from when he was in jail in Oklahoma, plus corroboration and testimony from dozens of witnesses, we've amassed a substantial amount of evidence proving Stephanie and Cy are more than gutter-variety Hollywood snakes. But there's a very good chance of losing this trial—and being embarrassed. Your careers and reputations may be destroyed."

"Oh, don't spoil the fun by dashing our dreams for revenge even before the trial begins," Paco pleaded.

"Where's Roy Cohn when you need a dirty, deviant litigator," Mitch said. "No offense, Fitterman. I was just thinking out loud." He then suggested they all adjourn to the living room for tea or coffee.

"There isn't anyone in the legal business better than Gus," Owen said. "He's never lost a case, and he's not going to lose this one either. We've got to be one hundred percent positive that the system will work. Bart and I are completely innocent of all charges and allegations, and Gus is the only man I know who can topple Stephanie and Cy and Sterling Studios. There's no fooling around here, guys. This is the most terrifying thing that's ever happened to me *and* to Bart too. No way are we paying with our careers and reputations—as many before us have done—just because Stephanie and Cy disliked us."

"We're fighting evil here," Bart interrupted. "Those two maggots were afraid of Owen's creativity and intelligence."

"And yours, too," Ryan interjected, looking at Bart.

Peter spoke up in a conciliatory tone. "You're right, and I'm sorry that I've been so self-absorbed. Of course I'll do whatever needs to be done to help you guys. Since I'll be helping myself, too."

"We're with you all the way," Paco said. "I'm sorry, too, that Peter and I keep bickering like two old women. I know how important this trial is. No more animosity." He looked at Peter. "Okay?"

Sheepishly, Peter looked back at Paco. Just feasting his eyes on the sight of this man in his tank-top shirt with his bronzed muscles and gang tattoos gave Peter an immediate ache. "Absolutely."

"Okay, then," Ryan said, relief in his voice. "Who wants coffee? Who wants tea? You all go into the entertainment room. Bart and I will be along."

"Don't forget the after-dinner mints," Mitch chirped.

21

"If no one has any objections, let's begin the evening's entertainment of listening to Bart's recordings," Fitterman said, dropping his ample girth into a love seat in the entertainment room and taking up much of the space. "Ryan," he added, "would you do the honors?"

Ryan finished pouring hot water over a floating bag of peppermint tea in Bart's cup. He set the pot down and picked up a laptop computer from the coffee table. He opened the lid and passed the cursor over a voice-recording app.

"At long last, I'm finally going to hear what's been going on behind Stephanie's closed doors all these years," Mitch said, as if he weren't already a master of eavesdropping, especially on his boss. Most assistants who have been in their positions for long periods of time know more about their boss's personal life than the boss would prefer. That was good for a lot of wives (and the IRS, too) when corroborating facts of a husband's infidelity and getting courts to cough up juicy divorce settlements.

But it wasn't Stephanie's looting the company, such as charging expensive gifts for herself and friends at Tiffany's and expensing the baubles to the overhead accounts of various movies, that mattered to Gus Fitterman. He had his eyes on the bigger things that Mitch could offer. In fact, Mitch had already provided Fitterman with a sworn statement detailing dozens of egregious acts committed by Stephanie.

What the group now heard through the computer's speakers was a less-than-perfectly-clear recording of contemptible things Stephanie had to say to Bart about Owen. The audio was muffled at times because Bart's digital recorder had to be hidden in his pocket. But Stephanie's voice was clear: "That Bart bitch is here. Yeah. We're going over the lines. Not to worry..." The recorder had picked up the end of a phone conversation Stephanie was having with Cy Lupiano. An hour later, after it was many times absolutely obvious that Stephanie and Cy had committed fraud by planning to falsely accuse Owen of sexual indiscretions, the group took a break.

After visits to the bar or bathroom, they reconvened to hear Fitterman reading excerpts from Peter's tell-all book. Fitterman waddled to the center of the room, and in his best legal-eagle-sounding voice, began his performance. "Mind you, this is abridged material. The full text will be used, if necessary, when Stephanie takes the stand at Owen's trial. The hoped-for result is that it will so damage her credibility that Owen will be exonerated, and Bart's lawsuit will not be contested by Sterling. This is just a sample, but here goes. This is from chapters seven through twelve."

Peter was all smiles as his audience listened to Fitterman, who exposed one hell of a shocker:

"'Back in the early 1970s, this cocky, mean-spirited, truly terrible guy named Isaac Thomas was incarcerated in the same jail in Oklahoma where I was serving several months of hell. I was only in for making a soft-porn film. The obscenity laws in

Oklahoma are pretty archaic; you can even get in trouble for posing nude for an artist. Isaac's charge: attempted murder. You might have guessed it; this is the same future-Hollywood-bad-boy Isaac Thomas mogul who made such films as *Enough is Never Enough, Gym Games,* and *Follow the Money.*

"'Then along came a tough, equally cocky and mean-spirited little guy named Garry Dumont. He was charged with the attempted murder of his boyfriend. I mention *his* boyfriend not as any kind of judgment, but because it's completely pertinent to the story.

"'There aren't any secrets in prison, let me tell you. And it was well known—and I saw the evidence—that Garry was halfway through a gender reassignment. His boyfriend on the outside was a total thug and loser. One day, he'd decided life was too dull with a fey Oklahoma grocery-store clerk, which Garry was at the time. So he found himself a husky—not the breed of dog but a beer-chugging redneck—and kicked Garry's sorry ass out of the one-room aluminum-shell hellhole of a traveling house they shared. That wasn't the upsetting part. The boyfriend creep had also reneged on his promise to pay for the final operation that would make Garry the lady she always knew he was inside.

"'Garry was emotionally destroyed. In a premeditated attack, he tried to kill his beer-bellied ex. A long story short, while in prison, Isaac Thomas, who had adopted me the day I arrived, decided he liked the new boy, Garry, better. Isaac made Garry his new steady. Although in the beginning they hated each other, they were cut from the same cloth. They may have been oil and water, but each came to respect the other's devious natures. As I said earlier, Isaac was a common barnyard pig. Slop was slop. And those two were both USDA-certified swill.

"'Isaac had promised Garry he'd eventually get him all the

right anatomical equipment that he had dreamed about. I'll say this about Isaac, although you couldn't turn your back and trust him not to fuck you—literally and figuratively—when he decided to come through for a friend, he did. He had a small capacity for generosity.

"'Isaac and Garry became inseparable, and one day, a second-unit Hollywood film crew came to Oklahoma to shoot exteriors for a remake of *Oklahoma Oil.* Isaac, Garry, and I had been on our best behavior in prison, so they loaned us out to the film shoot, and we were assigned as "atmosphere" on the set. Nothing more than extras, really, our job was to hang around, pretending to be walking past the local turn-of-the-century bank or the grocery store or the courthouse.

"'Then, after a week of befriending the film's transportation coordinator and the first assistant director, Isaac and Garry slipped out of town with the crew as soon as the last frame of film was shot. Those bastards deserted me. Eventually they ended up where most of the world's cons end up: if not in Washington, then in Hollywood. I promised myself I'd get even for being left behind and having my parole revoked because the warden thought I was in on their escape plans.'"

Peter's text went on to detail that it wasn't long before Isaac moved to LA, and he began his meteoric rise in the film industry. He had bullied his way into the studio system. He knew a guy who knew a guy who knew a guy, and in practically no time he became what all schoolyard thugs become: US senators or senior executives at a movie studio. In this case, Isaac Thomas landed at Paramount Pictures. Fitterman continued reading from Peter's manuscript:

"'His real talent was for humiliating assistants and prostitutes, which was practically an oxymoron in his office, and taking credit for everybody's good ideas. The whole town—not just the studio—was petrified of Isaac. He loved the power.

"'Isaac Thomas was a dichotomy. On the one hand, he was devoted to the gods of money, power, Thorazine, Vicodin, lithium, cocaine, and scotch whisky.'"

"Say that again ten times fast," Mitch blurted out, interrupting the hanging-on-every-word spell that Fitterman was weaving.

Fitterman cleared his throat and continued reading:

"'But he also had a soft spot for his old prison alumnus. The drug-induced, self-indulgent, all-black-jeans-wearing fatso tyrant kept his promise and paid for his cellmate's final operation.'"

"So," Fitterman said, taking off his eyeglasses and continuing extemporaneously, "the old Garry Dumont debuted as a new but not necessarily improved... guess who?" Fitterman cleared his throat. "First name rhymes with leprosy. Second name rhymes with evil incarnate."

Mitch, having a ball playing twenty questions, enthusiastically erupted, "Is it Barry? Carrie? Stephanie? Kerry?"

The answer hit everyone simultaneously—except Mitch, who continued with: "Brevity. Mentally. Embassy..."

"Jesus Christ," Peter snapped. "*Stephanie,* for god's sake!"

Everyone was absolutely speechless as Fitterman continued reading, "The testosterone and estrogen levels in Stephanie's body apparently couldn't be balanced."

"Maybe that explains the hairy mole on her breast and the wispy mustache," Bart said. "Instead of becoming the soft and radiant lady that she knew she was inside, she morphed into someone who could easily take down Mike Tyson."

"Garry, er, Stephanie, was a hard-boiled bastard to begin with," Peter said. "A leopard doesn't change its spots. It's all in my book. When we both got to Hollywood, I followed her career. Isaac got her a job as a skateboarding mail girl over at Millennium Pictures; then she started working for the head of feature-film publicity there. Finally, one afternoon she got the call she'd been waiting breathlessly for. One of Isaac's old chums, Cy Lupiano, had just signed a contract at Sterling Studios, and Isaac said he thought that Stephanie would be able to whip the publicity department into shape. He made her the new executive vice president of PR.

"Stephanie practically ran the studio, and when I became a household name, she became afraid that some snooping journalist would eventually put two plus two together and discover the big secret—that she was a prison escapee. It wasn't the sex-reassignment revelation that worried her—everybody's doing that these days—it was that she was an escaped convict and could be sent back to Oklahoma if anybody found out. That's when she sent me a beautiful birthday present: a hustler—already unwrapped and ready to play. The present and I took some videos, and then he stole the recording. He was Helen of Troy's prettier brother! Stephanie got the recording and had it aired on *Totally Hollywood.* To keep her past a secret, she was making sure I disappeared and never worked again. She knew that, like her, I was petrified of Hollywood discovering my criminal past, and wouldn't jeopardize my reputation. But now, I have no career worth saving, so I'm ready to spill the beans."

At last, the evening ended. Bart and Ryan said goodbye to their guests. "And then there were none," Ryan said, embracing Bart and telling him not to worry about the outcome of the trial.

Bart began unbuttoning Ryan's shirt and nestled his face into his lover's chest and inhaled the scent of his warm skin. "Let's clean this stuff up in the morning," he suggested, looking around the room. "I just want to be in bed with you right now and forget about this day."

Ryan grinned.

"Get yourself ready. I'll lock up and put the kids to bed," Bart said. Ryan quickly completed his ablutions and took off his clothes. By the time he turned off the bathroom light, Bart was already in bed, covered only to his waist in a sheet.

22

Sterling Studios' chief counsel, Richard Ward, and his horde of Tweedledee and Tweedledum deputies flanked Stephanie and Cy as they entered courtroom number 340 of the courthouse on Flower Street in Burbank. Stephanie and Richard sat down at the table next to Owen Lucas and Gus Fitterman's. Her arrogance wafted around her as palpably as the Samsara perfume she'd spritzed herself with in the car on the way from the studio. Wearing a beige suit, accented with a silk Donna Karan scarf and a ladybug lapel pin from Cartier, she looked over at the plaintiff's table and gave Owen a slight smirk, as if she were Alex Trebek holding a card with the correct question on *Double Jeopardy*. Owen stared at Stephanie with dead eyes and did not return the smile. Soon she looked away, unable to maintain eye contact.

Feeling completely at ease in what to anyone else would have been an intimidating environment, Stephanie looked over at the jury box and summed up the eight men and four women who were the first to be impaneled as possible jurors. They reeked of the lower classes. Not a jury of *my* peers, she sneered to herself. "*NOCD—not our class, dear,*" she said under her breath, looking down her nose at each of them.

Stephanie's composure was still unruffled when she examined the others in the room. She wasn't surprised to see Bart Caine seated in the back of the courtroom. When their eyes met, Stephanie blew him a kiss of contempt—a reminder of the day she'd fired Bart. Then she smiled. Stephanie also spied Mitch—who was supposed to be minding the office—Peter Jacks, and that stud she'd met once, what was his name? Oh, right, Paco. They were all seated together. *Birds of a feather*, Stephanie thought. They gave her a collective glare, which did not achieve the desired effect of eroding her confidence. In fact, their solidarity seemed to backfire, as Stephanie became as icy as Judge Judy.

When the bailiff announced, "All rise. The Honorable Judge Jonathan Carter is presiding, and court is now in session," Stephanie turned to face the bench.

The entire room became silent, though not just because of the solemnity of the proceedings and the mandatory respect that was due the judicial system. No, they were more than a little surprised by the man entering the court and taking his place behind the bench. Judge Carter was not only extremely young—whatever the minimum age was for a judge—but inordinately handsome, too. Judge Carter was also a formidable-looking man who exuded authority.

Paco imagined Judge Carter in black leather chaps and a vest showing off his endowments. Mitch imagined him wearing Western drag and doing line dancing at the Rawhide Club. Peter felt excitement thinking of Judge Carter coming to his wine cellar wearing his robe and sentencing him to a lashing by Hispanic prison guards. Even the court reporter, a cute, skinny young man with a diamond stud in his left earlobe, could hardly keep his eyes on the keys of his stenographic machine. They all imagined what would be revealed if this hunk of judge were to remove his robe. "I'll wager he's got a gym in his chambers," Mitch whispered to Bart. "Check out those shoulders!"

Having taken his seat, Judge Carter addressed the plaintiff and defendant and their respective counsel. He glared at Owen and Fitterman, then at Stephanie and her Sterling Studios legal team. Bart and Ryan looked at each other, both registering the judge's stern look at Owen. They nonverbally agreed there was something ominous in the way the judge observed Owen that was different from the way he looked at everybody else. Perhaps he was homophobic.

"Was it my imagination," Mitch said to Bart, "but did you notice that flesh-and-blood incarnation of Michelangelo's *David* give Owen a nasty look?"

"No different than the others," Bart said, trying to convince himself that justice was indeed blind. "I'm sure he's a total professional. He won't let the fact that he may think that Owen is guilty interfere with the trial."

"Can you picture him naked?" Mitch asked as an aside, to which Bart laughed just loudly enough for the judge to look down from his bench and scan the room. "Any person who feels this is a court where levity is tolerated may leave immediately," he barked.

Bart slumped down in his seat, trying to disappear.

In what otherwise would have been the most boring part of the trial—the act of the judge reading the case and giving instructions to the potential jurors—all eyes and ears were attentive to His Honor: handsome heartthrob Judge Carter.

"Ladies and gentlemen," Judge Carter began, "this case has been randomly assigned to this court."

"See? No bias," Bart said, this time in a whisper.

"The case that will be tried here is a bit exceptional." Carter looked over at Owen. This time he held his gaze. "Would the plaintiff and defendant please rise and face the jury box. This is a case that includes same-sex sexual harassment. In some jurisdictions same-sex sexual harassment is not actionable. However, in California, both on the federal and state levels, it is, most certainly. California is also one of the few states that has sexual-orientation laws. Therefore, this is an extremely important case. I implore those of you who will be selected to serve on this jury to pay close attention to all the evidence presented by both sides. You will hear often graphic evidence presented by counsel for Sterling Studios, who have the burden to prove that the plaintiff was removed from his position as president of motion-picture marketing when it was alleged that he was engaged in sexual misconduct—harassment—of female and male employees."

A murmur went through the courtroom, and Judge Carter cracked his gavel again.

"On the other hand, the plaintiff alleges that he was unlawfully terminated from employment on the basis of false accusations of said illegal conduct. It is also alleged that soon after commencing his employment at Sterling Studios, the defendant began asking a senior publicist at Sterling if he would like to have a sexual relationship with him. He allegedly said no. However, it is alleged that Mr. Lucas persisted in asking for a sexual relationship as a requirement of his job.

"You may be seated, Mr. Lucas. Ms. Hough."

Judge Carter folded his hands and peered first at those in the jury box, then out into the gallery and to fifty or so other prospective jurors. He had one more comment to make before the selection of those who would sit in judgment of Owen Lucas and Sterling Studios.

"Living in the Los Angeles area, as all of you do, perhaps

you're familiar with the case of *Shermansky v. Gold Productions.* I would ask that if any of you are related to, or friendly with, anyone associated with that case, that you advise the court of this when the voir dire process begins.

"*Shermansky v. Goldmine* is a relatively recent case in which one of the employees at the management level at Goldmine Productions allegedly required as a condition of employment that male assistants stay with him in his hotel room when he traveled and made them watch X-rated films with him. An employee brought a claim of sexual harassment, and the court agreed there was a viable theory of same-sex sexual harassment.

"The court rejected the defendant's argument that upholding this theory would violate the defendant's First Amendment rights, saying that if same-sex sexual harassment was recognized by law, then every employer would have to inquire into the sexual orientation of all its employees. The court did not agree with that argument, because employers are not supposed to inquire into whether their employees are heterosexual. Please keep in mind that the Civil Rights Act of 1964, the antidiscrimination law, does not include a requirement that the victim and harasser be of opposite genders."

After Judge Carter provided the details of the case, the tiresome process of selecting the jury began. Stephanie was bored. She would much rather have been getting her pedicure than sitting on the hard wooden chair listening to the long list of prospective jurors go through voir dire when all of them seemed for one reason or another to want to be excused from service.

"I'm a Christian woman, I am," announced the first prospective juror, a heavyset woman wearing a floral-print dress that accentuated the rolls of flesh beneath the flimsy fabric. Her Charles Laughton face was garnished with almond-shaped eyeglasses in a blue plastic frame covered in rhinestones. When asked if she could render an unbiased verdict, she replied, "I ain't the type to judge another of God's children, no, sir, Your Honor. But if that-there man was fired for being a pervert, then he deserved what he got."

Judge Carter quickly interrupted her and without a moment's hesitation announced, "You may be excused."

"I 'spect he'll be punished in hell when he gets there, too," the woman continued, speaking more to herself than to anyone in particular as she waddled out of the jury box.

"All prospective jurors are cautioned to disregard comments that are not testimony," Judge Carter implored, and brought down his gavel with a thundering clap. He was already irritated, and the trial had not yet begun.

The bailiff called another name from the jury box. This prospective juror wore a baseball cap backward on his head and a wrinkled T-shirt with a boldly written slogan: *I Love My Country. But I Fear My Government.* Annoyed, Judge Carter demanded that the man show respect for the court and remove his hat. The man complied, albeit reluctantly.

Asked if he thought he could render a fair verdict based on the evidence, the man thought for a moment, then delivered a non sequitur. "I think there's a def'nite trend toward sex and violence in Sterling Studios' films today," he said. "This makes me against that studio, and so I guess also against anyone associated with that place."

Judge Carter asked if the potential juror would not be able to put his displeasure with Sterling Studios aside, give equal weight to all the evidence he would hear, and help deliver a verdict.

"I rather doubt that, Your Eminence," he replied. "You see, my ch'ren watch their animated videos practic'ly ev'ry day of their lives..." This response made the entire room erupt with a roar of laughter.

Judge Carter was not amused and pounded his gavel to

demand silence. "Sir, you find the product from Sterling Studios to be offensive, yet you allow your children to watch their movies as a matter of daily routine?"

"Oh, kids'll be kids, Yer Highness, sir. Can't keep my eye on 'em twenty-four seven. They 'specially like the li'l rat in the White House." The man smiled. Again, the room exploded with laughter, which made the man disconcerted, but he continued. Judge Carter tried to interrupt him again, but he kept talking over Carter's objections. "I'm afraid these movies today ain't like they were when we was growin' up. Don't you agree?" he asked.

Judge Carter brought down his gavel and startled the man into silence. "As you know, if you were paying any attention to my earlier admonition, this trial is not about the movies created by Sterling Studios. This is a very serious case. A senior executive with a highly visible position was terminated from his employment at Sterling for allegedly perpetrating an act of sexual harassment on another employee or employees. He's suing for wrongful termination. This case has nothing whatsoever to do with rats in the White House (another chortle from the gallery) or flying carpets or stories about little orphaned girls who become princesses," Judge Carter admonished. He then reiterated his question about whether or not the man could make a determination based on factual evidence and help to render a verdict of guilt or innocence of the defendant.

"Oh, if you put it that way, I s'pose I could try to be fair. But deviant sex is immoral and belongs at home, not in the workplace."

Again, the gallery thundered with laughter. The brainless man turned bright red, not quite comprehending what it was he said that had brought on such a burst of glee. By the time Fitterman and the attorneys for Sterling had asked a few more questions of this man, he, too, was dismissed.

And on it went for the next four hours. Every conceivable

reason for not wanting to serve on this jury was heard. But finally, twelve jurors and two alternates were deemed reasonably acceptable to all the lawyers. As it was nearly four o'clock, Judge Carter decided they would begin proceedings at nine the next morning. He adjourned his court until the following day.

23

J une gloom and the so-called "marine layer" of clouds and fog seeped in from the ocean, all the way into Hollywood and over the hills into Burbank and the San Fernando Valley. When Bart and Owen arrived in court for the first day of testimony, their early euphoria at the prospect of retaliation against Stephanie and Sterling Studios for the crimes against them had withered.

Bart was the first witness called by the defense. Seated at the center of attention, he looked across from the witness stand and saw Stephanie's imperious face. Sterling's chief counsel, Richard Ward, approached and asked Bart to explain the details of Owen Stone's sexual harassment of him.

"The only harassment I've ever received at Sterling is from Stephanie Hough," Bart declared.

There ensued a lot of coughing and harumphing from Ward as well as those at the defendant's table and the jury box.

"Objection" after sustained "objection" came from Fitterman, who accused Ward of badgering the witness by asking such questions as "Mr. Caine, do you mean to sit before this court and refute your previous testimony?"

"I have never testified before," Bart reminded Mr. Ward.

"Is that so?" Ward asked in sarcastic mock surprise. At this point, Ward brought out an audio player and a CD. "Your Honor, I'd like to offer this CD as exhibit A. The evidence will prove beyond any doubt that the witness is perjuring himself."

Judge Carter accepted the plastic jewel box from Ward and examined it for a moment. It was neatly shrink-wrapped. A title had been professionally printed on the inside of the transparent casing:

BART CAINE / STEPHANIE HOUGH / FEBRUARY 9
INTERVIEW

"Nicely presented," Judge Carter said suspiciously. "Why the fresh-from-farm-to-table look?"

"Er, a proper exhibition for the court," Ward said, sounding somewhat unsure.

Carter returned the CD jewel box to Ward. "Just get on with it."

"Indeed, Your Honor." Ward returned to Bart. "Listen carefully to this audio, Mr. Caine," he said in a threatening tone. "You will tell the court, under oath, whether this is or is *not* a conversation you had with Stephanie Hough in which you accuse Mr. Lucas of sexual harassment."

Ward had a moment of trouble peeling off the tightly wrapped cellophane from the CD box, but finally inserted the CD into the machine and pressed the PLAY button. A few minutes of the audio was heard. Bart's and Stephanie's voices:

"He was standing there with his shirt unbuttoned, the president of marketing... his hairy chest. For a moment he just leaned against the doorframe. 'Why don't you blow it off?' he said. Then he asked me if I'd like something to eat.

"Dinner?

"I said I'd grab something on the way home. Then he put his hands in his pockets and started moving them around, like he was feeling for his change or something... said he always made it a practice at all the studios where he'd worked before to have a special employee that he found attractive... and since I was so cute... he said he didn't want to hurt me or create an unpleasant working environment. That's when he asked how much I liked my job and what did I think of him as a man. And what I'd be willing to do to stay on as head writer... told me he wanted sex every now and again... he'd make me happy in return."

Ward stopped the machine in mid-conversation, intending to save the best for later. Smugly, he approached the witness box.

"I ask you, Mr. Caine, did you or did you not have this conversation with Ms. Hough."

"I had *a* conversation."

"Yes or no, Mr. Caine. It's a simple question."

"This conversation?"

"What other conversation are we discussing?"

"My answer would be no."

"Oh, come on, Mr. Caine. You're an intelligent man. Do you deny that one of the voices heard on this recording is yours?"

"Yes. No. Yes."

"Do you deny that the other voice on the recording is Ms. Hough's?"

"No."

"Then how in the name of Pinocchio, if I may use a Hollywood reference, can you sit there and mock this court by lying—under oath—and insist this is not your conversation? Your nose is growing, sir."

"Objection! Harassment!"

"Sustained."

"I'm *not* lying!" Bart said. "With all due respect to the court, I assure you that specific conversation never took place." Bart looked up at Judge Carter.

"I wonder what else you don't recall," Ward asked in his powerful, intimidating tone. "Do you recall what year you graduated college?"

Bart stalled for a moment. "I didn't graduate," he said softly.

"Oh?" Ward pretended to be surprised. "That's interesting. I have a copy of your application for employment at Sterling Studios, along with your original résumé." He removed the documents from a file, first handing them to Judge Carter to examine before passing them to Bart. "Would you please read for the court the academic achievements you listed on the Sterling Studios job application?"

Bart again stalled as he silently reviewed the material. Then, in a small voice, "Education: BS Journalism, University of Southern California at Los Angeles."

"Please speak up and read that statement again," Ward demanded. Bart repeated in a louder voice what appeared on the old application.

"That's rather curious because UCLA has no record of your matriculation from their journalism program, Mr. Caine. Are you suggesting that perhaps their dog ate your transcripts?"

Members of the jury laughed.

Bart appeared defeated. He glanced over at Ryan and Owen with a look that said, *I blew it. I'm a liar. I've demolished the case. I'm so sorry.*

"Why did you blatantly lie on your employment application? Didn't you read the fine print at the bottom just below your signature—this is your signature, isn't it, Mr. Caine? It states that you affirm that all answers given are true and correct and that you may be subject to legal action if they are found to be inaccurate?"

"I put that on my application because I was embarrassed. I left UCLA in my junior year."

"Embarrassed, Mr. Caine? Embarrassed the way you were when Mr. Lucas harassed you in your office? Embarrassed as you must be right now, lying again about not speaking to Ms. Hough about Mr. Lucas's provocations?"

"Objection," Fitterman shouted.

"Establishing character, Your Honor," Ward declared.

Stephanie sat arrogantly behind her table, her arms folded across her chest. She looked straight at Bart with a smug smile frozen on her face.

"Please answer the question, Mr. Caine," Judge Carter said.

"Mr. Lucas never harassed me; that's a fact," Bart stated adamantly. "That audio is a forgery or something."

"Oh, give us all a break, Mr. Caine!" Ward bellowed. "We all have ears. We all heard *your* voice whining to Ms. Hough about harassment. You've lied before, and you're lying now. Am I not correct?"

"You are *not* correct!" Bart turned to Judge Carter. "Your Honor, I, too, recorded meetings between Stephanie Hough and myself."

Stephanie suddenly sat up and flashed an angry look first at Bart, then to her attorneys.

"Do you have audio proof?" Judge Carter asked in a compassionate tone.

"My attorney, Mr. Fitterman, has three CDs from my digital recorder, Your Honor."

Judge Carter looked at the larger-than-life Gus Fitterman. "Do you have evidence to refute opposing counsel's?"

Fitterman nodded. "Indeed, I do, Your Honor. May I approach the bench?"

"Objection!" shouted Richard Ward a split second before the entire contingent of Sterling lawyers agreed in unison. They all deferred to Ward, who argued that they had not been notified of this evidence and would therefore require time to evaluate the authenticity of the recording.

"Everybody, sit down," Judge Carter said. "Bailiff, allow the court to hear the rest of the defendant's recording as well as the plaintiff's."

As the recording presented by Richard Ward continued, Bart's voice could be distinctly heard saying, "Stephanie. This is the most difficult situation I've ever been in. I don't know what to do, so I'm coming to you for advice. Owen Lucas has been harassing me."

"What do you mean by 'harassing'?" Stephanie asked.

"He's come to my office a couple of times when I was working late. His shirt was unbuttoned. He stood next to my desk with his fly unzipped and asked me to give him oral sex."

"Are you sure? And have you gone along with him?"

"I've had no choice. He says he'll fire me if I don't do what he wants."

When the audio ended, it didn't end with any sort of heart-to-heart from Stephanie, any promise to look into the matter or to file a grievance with human resources. It was clear to Bart that this was simply a "Best of the Best" compilation.

Judge Carter ordered the bailiff to remove that CD and to play the one from Bart's attorney.

"How many times do I have to explain this to you, moron? Do it again!" It was Stephanie's voice.

"Okay. Umm. This is the most difficult situation I've ever been in," Bart said. "Umm, I don't know what to do, and since you're the only one I can trust, I'm coming to you for help and advice."

"Go on. Owen Lucas... hitting on you..."

"Right. Owen Lucas has been hitting on me."

"Don't just leave it at that, you simpleton. Tell me what you mean by 'hitting on you.'"

"Er, when I'm working, he comes into my office..."

"No! When you're working late at night..."

"Right. Late at night he comes to my office when I'm working late. His shirt is unbuttoned."

"What else?"

"Oh. Well, he stands next to my desk."

"His pants! His pants! What about his pants, for Christ's sake!"

"Ah, they're unzipped."

"Now is where you say he wants you to give him a blow job."

"That's kind of vulgar, isn't it?" Bart was heard questioning Stephanie. "That's not what I would say. I'm no angel, but nobody would believe those words came from me."

"You're such a little pussy! Just say he stands with his fly unzipped, and he asks for oral sex. Can you say 'sex,' or is that too offensive to you?"

"No, 'sex' is good."

"Are you sure?"

"*Very* sure."

"No, stupid. I mean, does it happen every night when you're here late? You're supposed to say it does."

"It happens every night."

Stephanie had slumped down in her chair, her arms folded in a display of loathing for Bart, the peon publicist who had the audacity to surreptitiously record their meetings.

The audio continued. "And have you gone along with him?" Stephanie's voice asked.

"I've had no choice. He says he'll fire me if I don't do what he asks."

"Anything else?"

"I got to spend every weekend for the past two months at his house having sex."

"'*Got* to spend every weekend...! '*Got to*'... *Pu-leese!* Anybody who heard that would think you're enjoying yourself."

"Nobody's going to hear about this," Bart interjected. "You said we were just practicing because Owen was threatening to fire you, and you might someday need my help."

"Objection, Your Honor!" Ward screamed.

"Grounds?"

"This is detrimental to my client!"

"It's evidence, you twit. Sit down." Carter hammered his gavel.

The audio continued. "Don't worry your cute little ass," Stephanie's voice continued. "You won't ever have to say these things in court. Owen'll be long gone and won't make a peep."

"You can't be serious about being afraid of Owen. He's the first human being to ever occupy that office," Bart said. "As a matter of fact, I wish he *would* proposition me. But he's such a doll, I'd probably have to take a number and wait in line for about twenty years."

At that Stephanie exploded. "You think he's so great. Let me tell you something about that arrogant, self-important snake. He's plotting to have me sacked! Me! It's no secret that he hates me. He was seen having dinner with his old executive VP of publicity from Universal. And he'll sack you, too! Just wait and see!"

"Maybe you're being paranoid," Bart said. "The colleague from Universal might just be a friend from working together."

"You're so naïve. You don't know how it works in Hollywood. Now, get your ass out of my office... and don't say a word about this to anyone. Ya hear!?"

"Who would I tell? I don't have time for a social life. You keep me too damned busy."

"Then get busy. I want that Mare Dickerson press release on my desk before I get in tomorrow."

Then came the sound of Bart closing the door to Stephanie's office. But the audio continued. Bart had stopped for a moment to say good night to Mitch in the outer office.

"You're not the only one she's running lines with about sexual harassment from Owen," said Mitch. "That bleach-blond dweeb, Josh, from promotions, is all in for going along with whatever Stephanie and Cy dictate. They've promised him a promotion if he agrees to file a sexual-harassment claim. He's run out of brain matter, so he'll do whatever he thinks he's got to do to get ahead and—"

The bailiff turned off the audio player.

The entire courtroom was slack-jawed. Judge Carter cleared his throat and in a civil tone instructed counsel for both the plaintiff and defendant to approach the bench. Immediately. The sound of wooden chairs scraping the floor filled the room as the attorneys and the court reporter filed up to the judge's bench. Carter turned off his microphone.

Stephanie looked over at Bart with an expression of repugnance that in previous times would have made tears come to his eyes. Without words, Bart knew what Stephanie was thinking, that she'd find a way to get even with him. Judge Carter looked sternly at Richard Ward and his lackeys. "What, gentlemen—and I use the word loosely—are you trying to pull in my courtroom?"

"Your Honor?" Ward started to speak, but like a kid caught red-handed with a stolen cookie, he decided to keep his mouth shut.

"I'm referring to exhibit A," Carter explained. "Pretty packaging. Professional. No stumbles or stammers on the recording. It's perfect. Exhibit B, on the other hand, is something from a David Mamet play. What gives? I'm just a teeny bit curious."

"Your Honor," Ward stammered, "given the sophisticated audio technology available at Sterling, it shouldn't be at all surprising that their audio sounds vastly superior to the amateur's."

"Considering the technology at Ms. Hough's disposal, it's also not difficult to erase glitches and to edit and create a conversation from bits and pieces of others," the judge countered. "Do I have to call in an expert to examine the two recordings? It's no problem, really. Just a phone call away. I'm happy to help you out." His sarcasm was not lost on everyone in the room.

"Your Honor, I have no idea what you're getting at." Ward tried to sound insulted by the judge's insinuation that there had been any tampering with the evidence.

"Well, then, you're a pussy," Judge Carter said with a derisive smile. "You know, it might even be reasonable for some people" —he paused for a moment—"some people like me for instance, to infer that spoilation of evidence suggests that someone might be guilty of something. It's called *perverting the course of justice*. Get my drift, Counselor?"

Richard Ward wasn't the kind of man who was easily rankled. In fact, he was usually the antagonist in any room. However, Judge Carter's suggestion of him abetting a felony made his face turn red.

"Your Honor," Gus Fitterman said, "I've heard of flushing drugs down the toilet, and deleting incriminating emails, and even lighting a computer's hard drive on fire. In my day we called it 'covering your ass.' But if exhibit A is an intended manipulation of my client's words, then this is a crime—a felony, actually—*within* a crime!"

Judge Carter looked up at the clock above the doors on the far wall and drew in a deep breath. His exhale of irritability could be heard throughout the courtroom. Then he rubbed his hand over his face and said, "I'm tired. But I'm always up for entertainment. I'm actually curious to see just how low and despicable things can get here in the land of Hollywood. Amuse me with your litigation talents, gentlemen."

Richard Ward sighed and looked with contempt at Fitterman. They returned to their respective seats as Judge Carter pronounced, "Mr. Fitterman, you may cross-examine," and the room's attention was directed back to Bart in the witness box.

"Mr. Caine," Fitterman began, "you were fired from Sterling Studios. Why?"

"Objection, Your Honor!" Richard Ward bellowed. "No relevance."

"No relevance?" Fitterman bawled. "Indeed, Mr. Caine was fired for *no relevance*. But his termination *is* relevant to the case against Mr. Lucas."

"Objection, Your Honor!" Ward cried again. "Hearsay and speculative!"

"What's speculative about the fact that Mr. Caine was sacked?" Fitterman countered.

"All your objections are overruled, Mr. Ward," Judge Carter said. "Continue, Mr. Fitterman."

"So tell us, Mr. Caine, why were you terminated?"

"Because I refused to go along with fraudulent actions that were being concocted by executive vice president Stephanie Hough and motion-picture chairman Cy Lupiano, accusing president of marketing Owen Lucas of sexual harassment."

"Is that the reason that was given for your termination?"

"No. I was told that my work performance was unsatisfactory."

"But you have many citations and commendations for your work," Fitterman said, holding up a sheaf of papers with embossed letterhead stationery from well-known actors.

"The Lord giveth and the Lord taketh away," Bart said.

The jury sniggered.

"Tell us, Mr. Caine, what is a typical day in the life of a Hollywood film publicist?"

"To be honest, sir, I was only a publicist by title. I didn't pitch stories to newspapers or magazines, and I didn't interact with the press much at all. I was basically a staff writer. I just wrote all day, all of the studio's publicity materials. Press kits, cast and filmmakers bios, photo captions, press releases, speeches, responses to complaint letters, film synopses, and special assignments, such as feature articles about the actors in our films. I wrote letters on behalf of various stars or producers to the Hollywood Foreign Press Association—the HFPA—as it's known. Basically, everything written about our films came from me."

"So you had nothing to do with that cute little rat in the White House?"

Again, the gallery chuckled at the joke.

"No, sir." Bart smiled. "I handled, or used to handle, writing about film stars and the directors, producers, cinematographers, editors, composers, costume designers, etc."

"Sounds like quite a job," Fitterman said. "Did you enjoy your work?"

"Yes, sir."

"Did you like the people you worked with."

"I like most people."

"Did you like your boss?"

"I admired Stephanie Hough, to a degree," Bart answered. "She has a tough job to do, and she's very successful at it. I totally respect that. There are aspects of her character that I envy. She's definitely not weak. But..." Bart hesitated and looked past Fitterman to Stephanie sitting at the defendant's table, sipping a glass of water.

"You're not working under her now," Fitterman prompted. "You can speak your mind."

"On the whole she is a cruel, devious, vicious human being

who takes enormous pleasure in being despicably malicious toward others," Bart stated.

"Can you be specific?"

"Objection!" Richard Ward complained. "Your Honor, Ms. Hough's personal management style is not on trial here!"

"I seem to recall that you were allowed to establish *Mr. Caine's* character earlier," Judge Carter said patiently. "I think it's only fair to let Mr. Caine establish Ms. Hough's? I'll allow the witness to answer."

Bart again looked at Stephanie, then took a sip of water. "Okay. For instance, there's this one TV star she particularly hates. She doesn't think I know why she hates him, but I do. And it's not just because he's getting fat and losing his looks, which is a sin in her eyes. She's Miss Perfect, with the exercise equipment in her office and the personal fitness trainer and the protein diet and the Mr. Rudolph's of Beverly Hills hairstyle. She devised a scheme to entrap this actor in a salacious scandal in order to ruin his career. She had me research this actor's background and pull newspaper clippings of him being arrested twenty years ago and serving time in an Oklahoma jail for making a soft-porn film. She got hold of some of the videos he did and started a smear campaign. She first forced all of her senior staff to view the tapes. Then she had her friends at the *Los Angeles Times, Daily Variety,* the *Hollywood Reporter,* and *Totally Hollywood* come in to see what this guy had done. He was starring in a family sitcom on television, and she instigated getting him fired. He'd served his time in jail, so his debt to society was paid. But she brought it back into the news to wreck his career."

"Why do you think that is?"

"Because she has a secret that she doesn't want anyone to know about."

Stephanie gave a vigorous nudge to Richard Ward, who

immediately stood up. "Objection! Your Honor, where is this leading?"

"I'm sure I don't know," Judge Carter said in his most condescending tone.

Stephanie leaned over to Ward and whispered something, frantically gesturing with her hands and giving a hard punch to his arm. "You pisser! You promised my personal life would never come up in this trial. You promised, you son of a bitch! Settle this thing!"

Ward stood up and addressed Judge Carter. "Your Honor, may we have a sidebar?"

"For crying out loud! I'll give you a sidebar you'll never forget if this keeps up, Counselor!"

Fitterman looked at Owen. Owen looked at Bart. Bart looked to the back of the room, where Peter and Mitch and Ryan were sitting on the edge of their seats. They simultaneously smiled at one another.

Judge Carter caught the exchange and hammered his gavel. "What's so amusing, Mr. Caine? Would you care to share whatever you think is so funny with the rest of the class?"

Bart's face turned bright red. "No, Your Honor. It's nothing. I apologize to the court, Your Honor."

Again, the attorneys and the court reporter proceeded to the judge's bench. Judge Carter poured himself a glass of water from a stainless-steel pitcher, and after several long swallows, he nodded to Richard Ward.

"Your Honor, I have just been notified by my client that she does not wish to continue with the case. I have the authority to end this on behalf of Sterling Studios."

"Why the change of heart, Mr. Ward?" Judge Carter asked.

"I'm not sure, Your Honor, but my client is vehement that we resolve the case before it goes any further."

"Mr. Ward," Judge Carter said wearily, "we are in the middle of a trial. Why the hell didn't you all settle this case out of court in the first place? Sterling is famous for doing just that. Now you're wasting taxpayers' money and the court's time, which is *my* time! Go back and try this case!"

"But Your Honor," Ward whined.

"Go, for Christ's sake! And call your next witness," Judge Carter demanded.

"I call Ms. Stephanie Hough."

Stephanie rose imperiously from her seat and walked with purpose to the witness box. The bailiff asked her to raise her right hand and to swear to tell the truth, the whole truth, and nothing but the truth. "Hmmm," she responded.

"I know it's a bore," said Judge Carter in mock indulgence, "but would you please answer in the affirmative or negative, Ms. Hough? We sort of need it for the record."

"Yes!" Stephanie said.

"That's a good girl."

"Woman! I'm a *woman*, not a *girl*," Stephanie protested.

"Just recite your name and address, please, and don't yell at me in my own courtroom," Carter said. "It's the one place where I ever get to call the shots."

Mr. Ward's opening questions revolved around her length of service as executive vice president of Sterling Studios, and her association with Owen Lucas, and the number of people who had come to her with allegations of the president of marketing's alleged inappropriate sexual behavior.

"Many people came to me to complain that they were being sexually harassed by Mr. Lucas," Stephanie said. "I taped their conversations as evidence for our human resources department."

"What were the complaints about Mr. Lucas?" Ward asked.

"You heard what was on my audio recording. He demanded sexual favors in exchange for his employees getting raises, promotions, and in the case of Mr. Caine, keeping his job."

"Mr. Lucas was your superior, the next in the chain of command, so to speak. Correct?"

"Yes."

"Therefore, you were his subordinate, correct?"

"Mm-hmm. Yes."

"And Sterling has a strictly enforced zero-tolerance sexual-harassment policy, correct?"

"Yes. That's why I took the matter to the next-highest level."

"Mr. Cy Lupiano?"

"Yes. He and I both determined it was in the best interest of the company to terminate Mr. Lucas."

"But that wasn't your call, now, was it, Ms. Hough?" Ward asked.

"No. It was at the discretion of Mr. Lupiano, the chairman of the motion-picture division."

"And, of course, this was done with the full cooperation of human resources?"

"Objection," Fitterman stated. "Counsel is leading the witness."

"Overruled," Judge Owen called.

Stephanie answered, "Of course. In fact, they had quite a file filled with complaints about Mr. Lucas. Mr. Lupiano didn't require anybody's authorization to do what he felt was in the best interest of his company. He is the final authority."

Mr. Ward held up a large manila file folder and asked her to read the name printed on a tab.

"LUCAS, OWEN."

"May it please the court, we wish to enter this file and its contents into the record as exhibit C. It contains numerous complaints from a variety of sources regarding Mr. Lucas's sexual behavior in the workplace. I have nothing further for Ms. Hough."

"Mr. Fitterman, please proceed," Judge Carter said.

Stephanie remained calm and confident to the point of being defiant.

Waddling to the witness stand, Gus Fitterman was all smiles as Stephanie sat stone-faced, completely disgusted by the man's girth, age, and disingenuous demeanor.

"Why was Mr. Lucas terminated, Ms. Hough?"

Mr. Ward stood up. "Objection, Your Honor. The witness has already testified as to cause!"

"Sustained. Please ask another question."

"I'm sorry, Your Honor." Fitterman smiled. "Ms. Hough, you testified that you made audio recordings of those who complained about sexual harassment. May we hear the other recordings as well?"

"I didn't make other recordings."

Fitterman smiled apologetically. "Guess I've got to have my hearing checked," he said, chuckling. "I was pretty sure that you previously testified that you taped conversations—plural—with employees who made allegations about Mr. Lucas's alleged indiscretions. For HR, I thought I heard you say. My apology."

Stephanie smiled. Self-satisfied.

Fitterman was about to ask another question when he interrupted himself. Scratching his forehead, he turned to the judge and said, "I'm sorry, Your Honor. Would you indulge this old, soon-to-be-retired man and ask the court reporter to read back Ms. Hough's previous testimony. Just at the very beginning, after she was sworn in?"

Judge Carter nodded, and the court reporter worked his way back on his machine. He found the correct place and read in a monotone voice: "Many people came to me to complain that they were being sexually harassed by Mr. Lucas. I taped their conversations as evidence for our human resources department."

"That's the part. That's good," Fitterman said appreciatively. "Thank you. I honestly thought for a moment I might be having a *senior moment* or the imaginings of a man who should have retired when the moment the kids left home. Phew!" Fitterman pretended to be relieved. "My hearing seems to be fine after all. But your memory, Ms. Hough... you previously testified that you made audio recordings—plural—of employees who brought charges of harassment, and now you deny that testimony. Would you please explain?"

"Yes, I recorded other conversations. I misunderstood you."

"Where are those recordings, Ms. Hough?"

"The hell if I know. I think human resources lost them or something."

"Or *something*. Yes. I see. Well, let's move on," Fitterman continued. "Why do you think your CD and the CD produced by Mr. Caine are so different?"

"I'm sure I don't know."

"Can you speculate, because I'm as confused about this as you appear to be," Fitterman said in his best Perry Mason impression.

"Mr. Caine has based his career on lies, as his record proves," Stephanie said.

"Isn't that a publicist's job?" Fitterman smiled.

"Objection!" Richard Ward shouted.

"I apologize, Your Honor," Fitterman said. "A small Hollywood joke."

"Very small," Judge Carter snarled.

Returning his attention to Stephanie, he said, "One of my big dilemmas is that the date on the audiotape you provided—and by the way, it's very pretty and was beautifully packaged—is that it says February ninth. That was a Saturday, wasn't it?"

"I don't remember."

"Trust me, it was a Saturday. Here's a calendar," Fitterman said, walking back to his desk and picking up a daily planner. "You don't remember working on a Saturday?"

"I work seven days a week. One day is the same as another."

"How about Mr. Caine?" Fitterman continued his line of questioning.

"He often works weekends, too."

"But this was also the day of the big bash at Peter Jacks's home. Mr. Caine did not work that Saturday."

"I don't keep his time sheet," Stephanie said, sounding bored with the barrage of questions.

"Another thing I keep scratching my head over is I don't understand why it appears you're giving stage direction on the recording that Mr. Caine provided. It sounds like you were setting him up as a pawn in a plan to terminate Mr. Lucas. Am I correct?"

"Objection, Your Honor!" Ward pounced. "Counsel is giving witness's testimony!"

"Overruled. I'm as curious as Mr. Fitterman."

"Of course not!" Stephanie spat. "Are you now calling *me* a liar?" She gave him a look that would have sent Evander Holyfield crying for his mama.

"I haven't called you a liar. I haven't called you anything other than 'Ms. Hough.' It is *Ms.* Hough, isn't it?"

Richard Ward leaped from his seat. "What is going on here, Your Honor? The defendant has stated her name and address for the record. Mr. Fitterman is just bullying her!"

Judge Carter looked at Ward. "Don't wet yourself," he said. Then he addressed Gus Fitterman. "Mr. Fitterman, please make your point. I'm getting hungry for lunch."

Stephanie recognized something in the wheels that were turning behind the eyes of Gus Fitterman. For the first time, she began to lose her composure. She picked up a water glass from the flat railing of the witness box. It was empty.

"Please allow me," Fitterman said as Stephanie held out her glass. She took her time but swallowed the entire glass of water.

"Are you ready to continue?"

Stephanie simply raised her eyebrows, then looked at Bart and at Owen with the same contempt she offered Fitterman.

"Ms. Hough. And forgive me if I use the feminine pronoun loosely."

Once again Ward erupted from his seat. "Objection! Mr. Fitterman is being unbelievably abusive and offensive!"

"Your Honor," Fitterman interjected, "I don't wish to be rude or indelicate or to cause the witness undue distress. However, I have this newspaper clipping from the *El Reno Oklahoma Gazette*—"

"Counsel for both sides approach the bench immediately," Judge Carter ordered, and turned off his microphone. He grabbed the document from Fitterman and examined it thoroughly. Then he looked at Stephanie before handing the page to Richard Ward and his army, all of whom looked at each other, then looked over at Stephanie. She sat motionless, staring straight ahead at the double doors at the entrance to the courtroom.

Ward and his minions made another plea for a meeting in chambers. Judge Carter turned his microphone back on and asked for the jury's patience while he and counsel stepped away for a few moments. The representatives for Sterling Studios were followed by Fitterman and the court reporter, all of whom disappeared into the room behind the judge's bench. Stephanie continued to sit stone-faced. For the first time, she had the sinking feeling that something ominous was about to unfold.

Although the walls between the judge's chambers and the courtroom were as thick as a fortified castle, the jury and those in the gallery could hear muffled shouting. Words could not be distinguished, but the murmur from the volatile conversation seeped into the outer room.

"I have really had enough of you guys *and* Hollywood," Judge Carter roared at Ward and his cohorts. "And you, Mr. Fitterman, you're no better, surprising opposing counsel with this evidence. You should have made this material available to them during discovery!"

"I'm sorry, Your Honor, I was just provided with these documents a very short while ago," Fitterman lied.

"The defendant's counsel has the right to a postponement to review this material," Judge Carter said.

"I move for a dismissal," Ward stated.

"I'm considering that," Carter said. He turned to Fitterman. "What do you have to say in the matter?"

"A dismissal?" Fitterman asked, giving an indication that it was possible to resolve the legal action pronto. "Although... I sincerely doubt that Sterling Studios has enough cash in their vaults to provide the kind of settlement we'd seek afterward," Fitterman scoffed.

"Forget it!" Ward spat. "Your clients will be paying Sterling and Ms. Hough when this farce is over!"

Fitterman nodded and offered a patronizing smile. "Perhaps you're right," he said. "Perhaps..."

24

"All rise," the bailiff demanded as Judge Carter, Sterling's attorneys, Fitterman, and the stenographer returned to the courtroom.

After a moment, Judge Carter spoke wearily. "Continue, Mr. Fitterman," he said with a sigh.

Stephanie shot a long look of loathing at Ward that said, *Why didn't you settle this? For Christ's sake, I told you to settle!*

Gus Fitterman went to his table and picked up several documents. Then he walked slowly over to Stephanie, who was beginning to look like a lost lamb.

"Ms. Hough," he said, "would you please look at this document and state for the record what it reveals?" He handed her a screenshot copy of the Sterling Studios website page that contained her biography.

This time there was no objection from Sterling's attorneys. Neither of them roared that the witness had already testified, under oath, that she was Stephanie Hough, EVP of marketing at Sterling.

Stephanie took a long moment. Bart watched her and for a moment experienced pity for the woman—a pity reserved for one whose world is instantly and without warning wiped away as if it never existed in the first place.

"For the record, is this a fair and accurate résumé of your background and career, Ms. Hough?" Fitterman prompted. "Including the correct spelling of your name?"

Looking up as defiantly as ever and in a voice that filled the room as if to proclaim a victory, Stephanie said, "Of course! Stephanie Hough. My name is Stephanie Anne Hough! But I don't use my middle name, if that's what you're getting at."

"It's not. But I don't blame you at all for keeping your name simple. And it's a lovely name," he said. "As a matter of fact, I don't use my middle name either. Poindexter? I've never forgiven my parents for that. What the heck kind of cockamamie name is Poindexter, anyway?" The jury and gallery laughed along with his self-deprecation. "But I phrased my question incorrectly, and I apologize," Fitterman patronized. "I'd like you to provide us with the name you used up until about twelve years ago."

"You heard me the first time." Stephanie was fast losing her confidence and arrogance. "And you have a copy of my bio from the studio's website."

Fitterman continued, "Well, let's take a different approach. Do you know Peter Jacks? The television star?"

At the reference to his stardom, Peter beamed.

"I know and work with many stars," Stephanie said, trying to maintain her composure.

"Isn't it true that you knew Mr. Jacks from the time when the two of you were incarcerated in a jail in Oklahoma?"

A loud murmur rippled through the gallery, and Judge Carter brought his gavel down, calling for order. He had to demand silence several times before the crowd quieted down.

Stephanie was flustered and looked with contempt at her team of attorneys. "Stephanie Hough has never been anywhere near a prison."

"Okay. Did you know a man named Isaac Thomas? A film producer?"

"He's dead," Stephanie said with the first trace of sorrow anyone in the court had seen.

"How well did you know Mr. Thomas? How far back did you go as friends?"

Stephanie proceeded cautiously. "When I first started working in Hollywood as an assistant, Mr. Thomas was helpful and encouraging."

"Back to Mr. Peter Jacks for a moment," Fitterman continued. "Where again did you say you met him?"

"I don't think I said."

"Would you tell us now, please? Do you recall where and when?"

"No." Stephanie's facade was practically diaphanous.

"Mr. Jacks has written a fascinating book, the manuscript of which is on my table. Did you know you are heavily featured in his story?"

Suddenly, knowing full well where Fitterman was going with his cross-examination, Stephanie stood up and faced Richard Ward. "Settle, you son of a bitch!" she shouted. "Settle! Settle! You motherfucking bottom-feeder! Settle!"

Judge Carter brought down his gavel, which echoed throughout the courtroom. Before the room could settle down completely and before the judge had an opportunity to render possible sanctions, Fitterman plowed ahead. Holding a document close to Stephanie's face, he said, "This is an affidavit from the Federal Correctional Institution in El Reno, Oklahoma—a medium-security US prison for male inmates. Do you remember encountering Mr. Peter Jacks there? How about Mr. Isaac Thomas?"

Stephanie snarled petulantly. "Stephanie Hough has never visited Oklahoma, let alone El Reno prison. Ever!"

Fitterman nodded. "I apologize to you and to the court," he said, shaking his head. "I keep being imprecise with my language. I *shouldn't* have implied that you visited Messrs. Jacks and Thomas in a federal prison." He chuckled to himself. "What I should have asked is, do you remember befriending those two gentlemen when you yourself were an *inmate* there? Once again, for the record, your legal name, please."

Finally, with no one to back her up, not even the studio's overpaid lawyers, Stephanie stood up in the witness box. With an imperious tone, she proclaimed, "Just tell the world what you already know. My professional bio is missing one small fact about me. My name used to be Garry Dumont! *Mr.* Garry Charles Dumont Junior!"

The gallery was silent as Fitterman completed his assault by stating, "Yes. And this affidavit identifies you as convict number 29282," he said, holding up another document.

"I suppose I am," Stephanie spat, making no apologies. "And I guess this is the point where I'm supposed to start sobbing with shame for attempting to murder a no-good, lying piece of human swill. Well, that ain't gonna happen, mister!"

In the midst of the turmoil in the courtroom, Judge Carter brought his gavel down one more time and declared the trial over. "I have no alternative but to find in favor of the plaintiff, Mr. Lucas Owen. Ms. Hough, aka Mr. Dumont, will be held in custody until it's determined if extradition to Oklahoma is required." He thanked the jury and apologized to them for not having the opportunity to deliberate the case. Then he looked out at Owen, and while looking into his eyes, he spoke collectively to the attorneys as well. "I want you all back in this courtroom next Thursday at nine a.m. At that time, I will determine the monetary damages from Sterling Studios to be granted to Mr. Lucas and Mr. Caine." Carter's eyes stayed on Owen a beat longer before he rose from the bench and disappeared into his chambers.

Owen rushed over and hugged Bart, who by this time was surrounded by Ryan, Paco, Mitch, and Peter. They all thanked Fitterman, who was putting papers into his briefcase.

Bailiffs had surrounded Stephanie and handcuffed the publicity executive. "You are so fucking gonna get what's coming to you, you fucking little nobody," she screamed at Bart.

With new bravado and knowing that Stephanie was shackled, Bart left his clique and walked over to his old boss. "I learned a lot from you, Stephanie," he said. "I learned that there's real value in writing and rewriting and rewriting press materials—or anything—to ensure substance and clarity. I learned that there's more than one way to spin a story. And I've learned that I'm capable of surviving a lot of emotional pummeling and humiliation, and that I shouldn't take it all so personally and seriously. I also found that hard work doesn't always pay off. You worked me like a slave—just for the pleasure of watching me sweat. But perhaps what you taught me most is how *not* to treat other people. So I should thank you, I guess. And I also want to apologize for being so judgmental of you. I have a better understanding now of why you're so mean. I don't excuse your behavior, but I do have compassion."

At that moment, despite past evidence that Stephanie lacked tear ducts, her eyes became moist and glassy. For the very first time ever, Bart saw his former boss as a vulnerable and defenseless human being. This was something that he never expected to witness in a million years. And rather than feeling triumphant over his boss, he realized that everyone feels pain and fear. This was Stephanie's time to come to terms with the consequences of her actions.

But as the court bailiffs started to lead Stephanie away, she shrugged them off and turned back to Bart. "Ever see *The*

Women with Joan Crawford and Norman Shearer, sweetie? One of my faves. Does 'Jungle Red' mean anything to you?"

Stephanie's vulnerability had vanished, and she was back to being the monster she always had been. "Yes, Stephanie," Bart said. "I've seen that old movie. Jungle Red. I do get the reference. You grew claws and painted them Jungle Red."

"Jungle Red!" Stephanie yelled as she was being escorted from the room. "Jungle Red! Jungle Red! Jungle..." Her voice trailed off behind a solid oak door.

25

"Come back to the house, and we'll have Spago deliver something to celebrate," Peter said in a moment of unusual generosity.

Reaching the parking lot, Bart and his friends split up to find their respective cars. Bart and Ryan walked to Ryan's Jag. Mitch got into his Honda. Owen pushed a button on his key fob and from ten paces away deactivated the alarm system in his BMW. Peter made a great show of polishing away a spot from the hood of his Rolls-Royce. Paco drove away in his Ford Fiesta. And Gus Fitterman just barely squeezed into his Volvo. They left Burbank and headed over Barham Boulevard toward the Cahuenga Pass and up into the Hollywood Hills to Peter's estate.

Knowing all the shortcuts, Peter reached Woodrow Wilson Drive before the others. He parked his car in the circular drive and closed the gate behind him. He raced into the house and quickly poured a double gin martini before the first arrival. Soon thereafter, Paco buzzed from the intercom at the gate, and Peter pushed the button to activate the system that opened the enormous front portal.

When Paco entered the house, he immediately inhaled the

smell of booze and realized that Peter had already downed a drink. "This is the first time I've been back here since the day I found out that you and Michael had screwed me out of my script," Paco said.

"Oh, let's not go into that again, shall we?" Peter pleaded. "We have to celebrate Owen's and Bart's victory. Do open a bottle of bubbly. You know where everything is. Nothing's changed. They'll be here any sec. And get Spago on the phone."

"I'm not your fucking houseboy anymore, Peter. You could ask me politely. Anyway, do it yourself."

"Ever the contrary one, aren't you!" Peter sniffed.

Just then the intercom buzzed. It was Bart and Ryan. "We're here," Ryan announced. "And Gus is a moment behind us, and probably Mitch, too, so keep the gate open."

When the guests had all assembled in the library, Paco decided to help play host after all and poured flutes of champagne for everyone. "You're a doll," Peter said to him in a rare display of appreciation.

Peter had even deigned to call Spago himself to order pizzas. By the time the food arrived, everyone was famished. They had been consuming nothing but champagne and melted Brie for an hour and were starting to reminisce about things that probably should have been kept locked up in the vaults of their respective memories.

"Oh, Paco," Peter lamented. "I was an awful shit to you. I'm truly sorry. You're too sexy to stay angry with. I'm even more sorry that they didn't submit my book as evidence. That would have ensured it becoming a best-seller."

"Your manuscript may still be valuable," Fitterman interjected. "You've documented everything from Stephanie's early days as a skateboarding, microskirt-wearing mail-delivery girl at Millennium Pictures, through her reign of terror as the queen of marketing at Sterling Studios. With all your footnotes and the stuff about her criminal past and illegal behavior toward Peter and his career, there's no way she'll succeed in harming Bart again."

"It'll make a damn good movie," Peter mused aloud. "And I could play myself."

"When I began, all I wanted was to get my screenplay produced," Paco said defensively to Peter. "None of this would have happened if it weren't for you and that prick Michael! By the way, whatever happened to him?"

"I'm shocked at you," Peter said. "You always used to *devour* the trades!"

"I haven't been able to afford a shot of tequila let alone buy *Daily Variety*. What's up with him?"

"Nothing, dear boy, except he's persona non grata in the town he was determined to conquer. He's on an unpaid leave of absence from Actors and Others. It's been a scan-*dal*—with a capital D-I-S-H."

"What happened?" asked Ryan.

"Seems his assistant, Troy, followed him to the Trap one night," Peter said. "Picture this: Michael sauntering into that scumhole of a dive, laying a hundred bucks on the counter to pay for whatever, and the bartender dragging him into the back room. With cell phone camera in hand, Troy photographed Michael—in Armani, no less—forced to his knees, where he became, shall we say, a willing human sacrifice for the bartender. Michael must have been in heaven."

Paco wanted to say it served Michael right for all the evil he'd wrought. Instead, self-absorbed to the core, he merely said, "Now he'll never sell my script."

"As a matter of fact," Ryan said, interrupting, "Troy, his assistant, is one of my clients. Beautiful little shih tzu."

"He's got a cute dog, too," Mitch said, smiling at the old joke.

"He was always hot for your script, even though Michael

rejected it," Ryan continued. "The original script, not the fiftieth draft you subsequently wrote based on Michael's lame suggestions. He told me in the strictest confidence—and I wouldn't ordinarily break a confidence, but since I've had too much to drink, and you deserve as much positive news today as Owen and Bart—he's made it his priority to package it for a new discovery he's made. Some Gwyneth Paltrow-Cate Blanchette-Anne Hathaway combo. He just negotiated a deal for her at—of all places—Sterling Studios. He believes that she's going to be a mega star, and he's calling the shots for her career. So keep your fingers crossed about *Blind as a Bat*. You, too, Peter, because he said the one thing Michael did right was to sign you to the agency, and he agrees that the role of the building super would be ideal for your comeback."

"I never left!" Peter said indignantly before checking his temper and realizing that Ryan was not being insulting.

Owen, meanwhile, quietly sipped champagne and watched the sun go down and the city lights appear below from the floor-to-ceiling windows. Bart and Ryan both noticed how withdrawn Owen seemed. They decided to wander over for a chat. Bart said, "A buck fifty for your thoughts?"

"Inflation, eh?" Owen said. "I was just thinking that I'll never be able to repay you for putting your career on the line for me the way you did. You and Ryan are an amazing couple. I've never been so grateful for anything."

"What'll you do now that the nightmare is over?" Bart asked.

"You don't have to worry about me. I'm a survivor."

Ryan looked at Owen in a manner that suggested *Do you want to tell him, or shall I?*

Owen's nonverbal raised-eyebrow response indicated that he trusted Ryan to do whatever he felt was best.

"Owen's the heir to the Lucas grocery store fortune. He's got more money than Elon Musk."

"Jeez," Bart said. "Why would you want to work at a hellhole like Sterling if you didn't have to?"

"I love Hollywood. I love marketing. It's what I got my degree in. Plus, it was a big challenge. Also, when you don't *have* to work, you don't take all the day-to-day politics and bullshit seriously. You tell yourself, *So what if they fire me? It'll be their loss. What am I gonna do, starve?* Money is freedom. But it's you I'm now worried about, Bart. Even if Judge Carter makes Sterling reinstate you in your old job, you won't go back. What will you do?"

Bart smiled. "What happened in court today gave me the ending to the novel I've been writing..."

Ryan turned to Bart. "I didn't know you were that close to finishing it! That's really great."

"I never talk about works in progress. But it's almost done. I just have to find an agent."

"What's it about?" Owen asked.

"About Stephanie. About Peter. About Paco. About Mare Dickerson. About Sterling Studios and egomaniacal producers like Isaac Thomas. It's a potboiler!"

"What's the title?" Owen asked.

"I'm thinking of calling it *Tricks of the Trade.* But the first thing I plan to do when it's finished is something that Ryan and I have both talked about. I'm kidnapping him, and we're running away to live in England!"

Ryan was beaming. Although it had always been a plan to go back to his favorite place on the planet, until now he hadn't had the motivation to actually make it happen.

"Wonderful!" Owen said, genuinely happy. "When do you leave? How long will you be away."

"We're leaving as soon as both of us can get things together. And we're not coming back—except to visit now and then. Of course, we'll take the kids. I've already got a relocation company checking into cottages and farms for us to rent or buy."

Bart turned to Ryan. "I'm sorry I haven't given you a chance to discuss the details... and we don't have to go, really. But we've talked about living abroad so often, I called up an estate agent, and she has some interesting properties. Listen. We don't even have to live there. We'll just take an extended holiday and see how we like it. They're working everything out. But of course, I'm not going if you're not, so..."

The news couldn't have pleased Ryan more. He put his flute of champagne down on the carpet and placed his hands on Bart's face. He pulled his lover toward his lips, and they embraced in a deep, passionate, long, loving kiss. "I love you, Bart," Ryan said with tears in his eyes.

"And I love you, Ryan, more than I ever imagined it was possible to love another human being. I just want us to be together... in England or Van Nuys or Paris or the Pits."

"In Bellflower, Botswana, Baghdad, Loch Mere—or the moon," Ryan countered. "No matter where we are, as long as I'm with you, I'm alive and in love."

"It's true what they say," Owen interrupted. "Money isn't everything. I'd trade the zillions of bucks that keep pouring in, armored truckload after armored truckload, for just a fraction of what you two have."

"What about Judge Carter?" Bart said with a mischievous grin.

"What about him?" Owen smiled but remained on guard.

"Were you too nervous today to see the way he looked at you?"

"He looked angry."

"Only in the beginning. It was his macho facade," Bart said. "From where I sat... hey, guys!" he called out to the others. "Come over here a sec!"

Peter, Paco, Mitch, and Gus ambled over to the window overlooking the city. "Tell Owen how the judge responded today when he got a look at the hot guy sitting in his courtroom," Bart said.

"You mean Stephanie Hough?" Mitch deadpanned.

"You little twit. No. When he first saw Owen... and throughout the trial."

"It was obvious to me that there was something sexual going through his brain," Paco said. "And I can read men as easily as the menu at Starbucks."

Fitterman practically gushed, "Hell, I'm straight, but I have eyes. I can see how handsome he is and how he looked at you."

"Gee," Mitch teased, "most *straight* men don't admit they recognize when another guy is hot," as if to imply that Fitterman was concealing an ambivalent sexuality.

The inference went over Fitterman's head. "And I know for a fact he's available. Not married. Not seriously dating anyone."

"Really?" Owen said, becoming more intrigued.

"One of my legal aides is best friends with the court reporter," Fitterman continued. "She was interested in the judge for herself until... Well, let's just say she found out that while justice may be blind, Judge Carter's scale tips your way."

Owen beamed at the suggestion that Judge Carter might have found him attractive. "I could tell by his posture that under his robe was probably the body of a guy who played quarterback for Harvard. Not that I'd know if he went to Harvard, but he was certainly smart and completely understood the letter of the law."

"Isn't that adorable?" Mitch mocked. He pinched Owen's chest, aiming for where he thought his nipple might be. "We point out the obvious to you, and suddenly you're smitten."

"Am not!" Owen laughed. "Maybe... slightly curious."

Mitch rolled his eyes and poured another flute of champagne for himself and refilled Owen's glass as well. "Here, this will muddle your mind further." Then to the group, he appealed, "Why are there guys like this one who have the looks of Bradley Cooper, the brains of... of... of... well anybody who's smart, and has more money than Jeff Bezos, but they don't think they're worth dating?"

"I *know* I'm worth dating," Owen countered, "but I don't go around thinking everyone wants me. Especially someone as hunky as Judge Carter. But now that you mention it..." Owen had a distant look in his eyes. "I *do* remember sitting at the table and feeling kind of light-headed when the bailiff called, 'All rise.' I mean, am I wrong, but wasn't he just sooo damn good-looking?"

"*YES!*" the entire room exploded in unison.

"I'll place odds that after next week's court date, he'll call you," Bart predicted. "Or you'll just have to call him."

"Like I would even dare presume he found me interesting!"

"Don't presume anything," Bart said. "But if we have to get a summons and haul his studly ass into a restaurant for a date with you, we will." The other men ad-libbed, "Absolutely! Right on! You've got to give him a try. You're a catch. He's a catch."

"Well, this has been some day," Owen finally said. He was basking in both his triumph in the courtroom and the general verdict of his friends that *Love Finds Andy Hardy*. Well, if not Mickey and Judy, maybe Doris and Rock.

"Speaking of love," Ryan interrupted, "Bart and I are going to mosey on down the hill. We've got some celebrating of our own to do."

Bart smiled. He looked first at Fitterman, then to the other men. "This has been one heck of a great day. I can't thank you all enough for everything that each of you did for me and for Owen. You guys are my family. My friends."

At that moment, Paco turned away and went to the bar,

clearly ignoring Bart's departure speech. His cold shoulder was so obvious that the other men all looked at each other and shrugged as if to say, "Somebody needs their diaper changed."

"Give me a sec," Bart said to Ryan. He walked to the bar, where Paco was knocking back another flute of champagne. "What's up, man?" he asked.

"Nothing." Paco poured another champagne. "Why do you assume something's up?"

"Well, for one thing, you've been in great spirits all evening, and now you're behaving as if you're avoiding me."

"If I were avoiding you, I'd hardly be standing here talking to you, would I?"

"Okay. As long as things are cool."

"Cool?" Paco mocked Bart's concern. "Yeah, it's cool that you're going home with Mr. Perfect. I think maybe I'll get back with Peter. I like living in his house. He's really not all that hideous."

"Not when he's unconscious," Bart quipped.

"No one's perfect," Paco said, slurring his words. "Except... I'm going to the bathroom. I'll be a while, so don't wait around." With that, Paco left the room.

Bart, frustrated by Paco's comments, returned to the group. "Peter, it's been a pleasure. We'll see you soon, I hope. Mr. Fitterman, what can I say?"

"You'll be saying a lot when you get my bill." Fitterman laughed. The others joined in despite knowing he was only half-joking.

Bart continued, "Mitch, we'll keep in touch. And Owen, I guess we'll see you next Thursday, if not before."

Owen opened his arms and embraced Bart. "See you at my wedding?" he joked. "Can a judge marry himself? I'll have to look into that." Owen laughed. "Heck, I haven't even had a date with the guy and I'm planning our honeymoon. What a fool!"

"Only fools fall in love," Ryan countered. Then he took Bart by the hand to lead him up the two steps of the sunken living room and into the foyer toward the door.

After Ryan's Jaguar cleared the gates and they moved out onto Woodrow Wilson Drive toward Mulholland, Bart spoke up. "Did you hear what Paco said before we left?"

"We all did. The guy's got some major issues. He's still hung up on you."

"How do you feel about that?"

Ryan reached Mulholland, checked for traffic approaching, and quickly scooted his vehicle across the intersection. He stopped at the light at Laurel Canyon and made a right-hand turn before answering the question. "I trust you to do whatever's right. Plus, I sorta like being envied."

"Mr. Passive-Aggressive." Bart snorted.

"Seriously. I trust you completely, Bart. Really. You totally know I do. Plus, I'm not giving up this possible move to England for anything!"

Both laughed, agreeing there was nothing for either of them to worry about and that any problem Paco had was his alone. Bart leaned over and kissed Ryan on the cheek. "Hurry home, baby," he said. "I need you naked next to me!"

Ryan let the steep, winding road rush them down to Fryman Canyon, where he stepped on the accelerator to avoid a red light at the intersection. Within minutes they were home, in the garage, kissing passionately to the sound of the dogs barking in the house, eager for their share of attention.

26

T hursday arrived, and it was one of those perfect Southern California Chamber of Commerce spring mornings. The sky was as blue as it could ever be in the smog-choked San Fernando Valley, and the air was still filled with the fading scent of night-blooming jasmine. Bart and Ryan met Owen Lucas and Gus Fitterman at the courthouse for Judge Carter's final resolution of their respective cases.

Passing through the metal detector at the building's entrance, the four walked to their assigned courtroom, which was the same one in which their lives had been irrevocably altered the week before. The atmosphere was just as formal as when the jury had been present, but this time, the only occupants of the room were the court reporter, the bailiff, counsel for the defense and the plaintiffs, Bart, Ryan, Owen, and Judge Carter, who entered from his chambers and settled into the black leather chair behind the bench.

Judge Carter began. "Because of the staggering malice as well as reckless and reprehensible indifference to Title VII of the Civil Rights Act perpetrated by Ms. Stephanie Hough, acting for Sterling Studios, who openly and admittedly engaged in discrimination against president of marketing Owen Lucas, I hereby order Sterling Studios to pay compensatory and punitive damages totaling $5.5 million to Mr. Lucas, as well as all legal fees.

"With regard to Bart Caine, who served as senior publicist at Sterling Studios, I decree the studio shall pay compensatory and punitive damages in the amount of $2 million plus all legal fees. Also, if Mr. Caine or Mr. Lucas desire, they are to be reinstated in their respective positions, with compensation doubling the salary they have missed since their wrongful terminations."

Nonverbal sounds of disagreement and disgust issued from Richard Ward, who broke a pencil in half to display his anger.

Smiles and sighs of relief poured from Bart and Owen, with Ryan calmly nodding his head, acknowledging that justice had indeed been served.

"And one more item on my agenda," Judge Carter announced. "I am issuing a formal statement warning the defendants against attempting to practice any type of retaliation against either Mr. Lucas or Mr. Caine. The following note has come to my attention. It was addressed to both Mr. Lucas and Mr. Caine, which leads me to believe someone from Sterling is responsible. The note reads, 'I am warning you to hand over all materials said to be evidence in any case or complaint about Stephanie Hough. You are despicable sneaks and cheats. If you do not comply with this request, you will suffer dire consequences for your abominable, cowardly actions. With deepest contempt, Your Worst Nightmare.'

"This type of behavior will not be tolerated by the law. As an aside, I trust you know that statistical surveys indicate that 50 percent of working women in the workplace and 10 percent of working men have been harassed on the job. I will personally see to it that these two innocent people are also awarded staggering sums of Sterling Studios' money if this case is appealed and Sterling loses. Am I completely clear, gentlemen?"

Richard Ward grudgingly responded, "Yes, Your Honor."

"Then court is adjourned," Judge Carter announced, and brought down his gavel one final time.

Bart and Ryan and Owen rose to their feet. Fitterman shook their hands, offering his congratulations, as Bart and Owen exchanged words of appreciation for all that Fitterman had done for them. The other attorney and the judge left the room in a huff. For a long moment, the three simply looked at each other. They were relieved to be rid of Stephanie and to have the trial over.

Finally, Owen said to Bart and Ryan, "Once you guys are settled in England, I'm coming to stay with you for six months. Maybe I'll buy myself a castle. Or maybe the entire country. But I'm definitely getting away from Hollywood for a while. Who needs the drama?"

"Of course. You're always welcome." Bart smiled, and Ryan eagerly agreed. Just as they were about to leave the room, the court reporter interrupted the trio. "Excuse me," he said, pushing his eyeglass frames up the bridge of his nose. "Judge Carter asked if you wouldn't mind meeting with him for just a moment in his chambers."

They looked at each other, not completely surprised. "Sure," Bart said. "Lead the way."

"*Entrez vous,*" an affable voice responded in answer to their knock on the chamber's door. Feeling a bit like Dorothy venturing into the Great Hall ruled by the Wizard of Oz, they opened the portal and stepped inside. Just as Mitch had predicted when he first saw Judge Carter, there was indeed a bench press, a Peloton treadmill, and an exercise bike next to his desk. The office was also decorated with floor-to-ceiling shelves of law books. And there, removing his robe to reveal a pec-pumped Adonis in faded blue jeans, stood Judge Carter, every inch the hard-bodied specimen they had lustfully imagined.

"The robe gets too hot," Judge Carter whined, explaining why he wasn't wearing a shirt under the cloak. He pulled a tank top from a gym bag lying next to the treadmill and dragged it over his head.

"Quite a case, wasn't it, guys? I just love it when I get to make all that loud noise with my gavel," the judge gushed. "It's my favorite part of the whole job." He had completely metamorphosed from the tough authority figure who administered the law. "That and prying out all sorts of secrets from witnesses on the stand. The stuff you guys came up with about that Stephanie person was just too much fun! What a caution she is! How on earth did you stand to work for the bitch?"

Bart uttered, "Well, Your Honor—"

"Oh, don't 'Your Honor' me when I'm off duty. I'm Jonathan, and I'm happy to finally meet you guys under more congenial circumstances." He held out his hand for Bart, Ryan, and Owen. It was a perfunctory greeting until he shook Owen's hand, which he held for a moment longer than necessary. "Especially nice to meet you, Owen," Jonathan said.

"Same here," Owen responded. "By the way, we're going over to Morton's for a celebratory dinner tonight. Care to come and join us."

"Really?" Judge Carter looked as if he were a child being invited to Disneyland.

"Absolutely," Ryan chimed in.

"I'm there!" the judge accepted. "What time?"

"Seven-*ish*," Owen said. "Andre, the maître d', will hold a table if you're busy and want to make it later."

"How posh is that, knowing the maître d' at Morton's," Jonathan teased. "I'll be there promptly at seven-*ish*."

Bart, Ryan, and Owen left the room, trying to appear dignified. However, once outside the court building, they broke into smiles and nonverbal squeals of laughter. "Now do you believe that Judge... er, *Jonathan*... is interested in you?" Bart chided Owen.

"And did you get a look at those arms and his chest." Owen smiled. "He should never wear robes!"

"Something tells me we'll have to put a king-size bed in the guest room at the farm," Ryan said to Bart. "Something big—to play in."

Owen pretended to protest. "Oh, stop! We don't even know each other." He started to sing an old Dusty Springfield song, *Wishin' and hopin' and thinkin' and prayin', plannin' and dreamin' each night of his charms...*

The banner headline in *Daily Variety* announced, "Hough Hangs at Galaxy." The story that followed revealed that after being released from her contract at Sterling, and the state of Oklahoma not caring about a long-ago escaped criminal, Stephanie Hough had landed a job at Galaxy Studios. The press release from which the story was taken sounded a lot like something Bart Caine would have written:

FOR IMMEDIATE RELEASE

Stephanie Hough, former EVP at Sterling Studios, has been appointed to the position of president, worldwide marketing and promotions, for Galaxy Pictures, it was announced today by Bert Heinz, chairman of Galaxy Studios. Hough will report directly to Heinz.
Commenting on the announcement, Heinz said, "Stephanie Hough is an outstanding motion-picture executive. She has

done extraordinary work throughout her career, and we are delighted that she has chosen to accept this position at Galaxy. We know she will play a vital role in helping us meet our expanded production slate and maintain the high standards of quality that have been a hallmark of her career and our studio. She is tops in her field and will be a tremendous asset to our team."

The articles that appeared in *Daily Variety* and the *Hollywood Reporter* only briefly touched upon her recent dismissal from Sterling. There was no reference to the sexual-harassment trial or reports from the media about her previous incarceration. Her clout in Hollywood was still so strong that there wasn't any negative publicity. She simply and blissfully continued her upward spiral as a power-hungry studio executive.

"She's an itchy bitch today." Mitch Wood whispered the warning to Galaxy Studios' staff writer Jim Waters, who had just been summoned to Stephanie's office to rewrite a press release he'd been rewriting all day.

Jim, in his late twenties, was a rising star in the Galaxy Studios publicity department, where he'd been the staff writer for five years. His awards for excellence from the Publicists Guild of America made him an easy choice when other studios needed a qualified writer for their marketing divisions. But he turned down every offer, fully expecting to one day retire from Galaxy, which he considered the preeminent studio in Hollywood. He loved his job. He loved Galaxy. He loved his colleagues. Until Stephanie Hough came aboard.

It took Jim only one introductory meeting with Stephanie for him to know his days at Galaxy were numbered. Stephanie had practically told him as much. "You've got a great reputation in town, Jim. I've only heard good reports. So why do I already not like you and think you might be happier over at Warner or Universal or Disney?"

Jim teetered out of that first meeting. He knew right away that nothing he ever did from that moment on would please his new boss. He was right. TOO MANY BIG WORDS! POOR SENTENCE STRUCTURE. I COULDN'T FINISH READING THIS CRAP! was scrawled across his written publicity materials and press releases. Now he wished he'd accepted that last offer from DreamWorks. At least their marketing department was known to be run by intelligent human beings.

Now Jim looked at Mitch and swallowed hard as he prepared to enter Stephanie's office for her to review the press release she'd made him rewrite five times.

"God, you're slow," Stephanie sneered.

Jim had nothing to say in response.

"Don't give me the silent treatment, mister."

"I was only—"

"Whoever said you could write, for Christ's sake?"

Mitch, listening to the repartee, was experiencing déjà vu.

Although Mitch Wood had betrayed Stephanie, she was incapable of doing her job without him. She had the *balls*, but he had the *brains* and ability to anticipate potential publicity landmines before they detonated. (He had tried to warn her about *WACS in the White House*, to no avail.) As is the case with most Hollywood executives, they're not too bright when it comes to the fine details of running an office, and they need their underpaid assistants, who, if they had to, could probably perform most of their boss's duties.

A mere few hours after Mitch had read about Stephanie's new job in the trades, his phone had rung. With a kinky version of ESP that was equal to his gaydar, Mitch didn't even need to look at his caller ID before he answered. "Look here, missy," he hissed, intuiting that it was Stephanie, "I want half your yearly bonus and a car allowance. I come in at 9:00 and leave at 6:00. I don't play sentinel while you're fucking on studio property, and I don't massage your feet or trim your toenails."

"You little shit," Stephanie bellowed her salutation, "I wouldn't have you back if—"

"I want all the terms *in writing*. And notarized. And maybe I'll remember not to ever *accidentally on purpose* call you... *Garry.*"

"Have your skinny ass at the desk tomorrow!"

"Monday. This is only Wednesday, and I'm expecting a UPS delivery at any moment. Oh, and a platinum parking sticker so I can park in the reserved spaces," Mitch added.

"Gold. It's still subterranean."

"Platinum."

"Gold, I said! You little fucker!"

"Platinum."

Stephanie paused. "Platinum."

"Oh, and—"

"Fuck you, Judas," Stephanie screamed and hung up on him.

Mitch was actually thrilled to be getting back to work, and at a new studio. While still holding his cell phone, he thought, *New office. Fresh meat. And the guys at Galaxy are reputed to be just as cute as the ones at Sterling or Disney.*

EPILOGUE

"**Q**uiet on the set!" screamed the first assistant director. "*Blind as a Bat!* Scene twenty-seven! Take ten!"

"Action," roared the director, Paco Castillo, as he watched the monitor on which was projected each frame that his cinematographer was shooting. It was the movie's big dramatic moment. The two main characters, a nefarious slumlord and wealthy tenant played by Lance Rawlings and Peter Jacks, respectively, argue about the squalid conditions in a dilapidated brownstone in Chelsea. As the actors began their altercation for the umpteenth time, the tension on the soundstage kept the entire crew silently transfixed on the scene.

Just a few moments into their dialogue, director Castillo called, "Cut!" He left his chair beside the monitor and walked slowly toward the set, which was a precise replication of an apartment near Greenwich Village in New York.

"Peter, Peter, Peter," Paco exploded at Peter Jacks. "Why do you keep disappointing me? Who ever said you could act? Where's the subtext for your character?" Peter was shaken, but that was the exact response Paco wanted to achieve. "We had two weeks of rehearsal! How many times do I have to tell you, this is where you pour out all your bitterness and anger at the inequity of not getting what you want from this scummy slum-lord. How's this for a reference? Just think of the animosity you had when your freakin' *The Grass Is Always Greener* sitcom was so unceremoniously canceled. Remember that, Peter, baby? Or maybe just dig down and find the hostility you felt for your old agent, Michael. I don't care what you have to do to find the emotion, just *do it!* We're behind schedule!"

Paco turned to the star, Lance Rawlings. "By the way, Lance, you're doing a great job, as always." Paco's voice was honeyed, which he hoped would irritate Peter. "Okay, guys, one more time, please! Do me proud!"

It took another five takes before Paco was satisfied with the scene and called, "Cut!" for the last time that day. It was Friday, and the first assistant director yelled for everyone to check their call sheets for the time they were expected back on set Monday morning and also to bone up on what scenes were scheduled to be shot.

Peter walked off to the makeup trailer to get the gunk off his face and have his hair washed.

Paco separated himself from a conversation with the script supervisor when Troy Everett, who was producing the film, came up to him. "Hey, Paco, I've been watching the dailies. I knew you were the right guy for the job."

Paco nodded his head in agreement, indicating he never had a doubt that he could direct his own screenplay; nothing to it. "At last, I finally have that fucking Peter Jacks right where I want him... under *my* thumb." Paco chuckled evilly. "What goes around comes around, eh? I'm making a public asshole of him in front of the entire crew. I humiliate him, and he hates me. He should have heeded that famous warning 'Be nice to the people you meet on the way up.'"

"You're getting a damned good performance out of him, and everyone else," Troy countered. "So far he's walking away with the picture."

"It's not Peter's acting, it's the character I wrote," Paco said as they began to walk off the set. "It could even be played by Judge Reinhold."

"Judge...?"

"Forget it. Long before your time."

"Well, the suits are starting to smell a winner," Todd revealed. "I think Hunter Brawly wants you to direct one of his pictures next. At least I've heard talk."

"Ha! That prick couldn't pay me enough!"

Troy hesitated before revealing another piece of news. "There's also talk of another series for Peter."

Paco stopped in his tracks. "Over my dead..." Then, trying to be gracious, he amended, "Whatever. He'll sink or swim. God knows he's no Ray Romano. But maybe this film will give him another shot."

"You're not still angry with him?"

"Nah. Too much waste of time. I'm not into getting even anymore. The way I've been treating Peter on the set, it's really just so he gives value to the words I wrote. This is *my* picture, all the way, and I won't let him fuck it up with a mediocre performance."

Troy smiled. "And that's precisely why I hired you. 'Cause you're one of the most manipulative sons of bitches I've ever known."

By the end of the summer, Bart and Ryan had traded in the idea of living in England for a small farm in the Highlands of Scotland instead. Two horses, as well as twenty-four head of sheep and a border collie, came with the property and joined their own family of golden retriever, Irish setter, and cocker spaniel.

The cozy thatched-roof house was filled with music and books. One of the first items on their agenda was to hire a woman from the village to cook and clean for them. Mrs. MacBurney served a twofold purpose. First, she was a terrific cook. But more importantly to Bart and Ryan, she was a gossip. The two deliberately wanted a cleaner who would take positive impressions of them back to the village.

It had been suggested by their real-estate agent that this was the best way to become accepted by the people around them. Soon they weren't just a pair of rich interlopers from America, but rather the two regular people who were living in Glenlough Cottage. Everyone who met Bart and Ryan agreed they would be hard-pressed to find two more interesting and delightful neighbors. Mrs. MacBurney had only glowing things to say about them, and her chatter at home and in the village shops and church soon made the two less of a curiosity and more of an accepted part of the community.

The area where Bart and Ryan had decided to settle would have seemed miserable to many people. It rained a lot. The cold was as bitter as either had ever experienced. And the wind at night would often rattle the windows of the otherwise sturdy stone house in a way that reminded them of the earthquakes of Los Angeles. But those were the best nights, the nights when, snuggled together in bed beneath a thick down comforter, they found the most peace. While the wind and rain lashed the outside world, inside they felt completely protected, as if they were in a cocoon.

On such nights, as cold air permeated the house—they did not have central heating, and the warmth from the fireplace on the first floor failed miserably to reach the bedrooms upstairs—Bart and Ryan raced into bed. The first biting sting from the cold sheets (even the flannel was icy cold) was soon replaced by the warmth of their two bare bodies entwined. They were the happiest people on the planet.

The dogs were delighted, too.

THE END

ABOUT THE AUTHOR

RICHARD TYLER JORDAN is a novelist and nonfiction writer. His books include the cozy mysteries *A Corpse in the Castle, Remains to be Scene, Final Curtain, A Talent for Murder, Set Sail for Murder,* and the Christmas novella *Naughty or Nice.* His LGBTQ+ titles include the romcom/mystery *Breakfast at Timothy's,* as well as *Overnight Sensation, Strangers in the Night, Gay Blades* (which was #1 on the InsightOut Book Club Bestsellers List), and *One Night Stand.* He has also contributed novellas to the anthologies *Summer Share* and *All I Want for Christmas* (both of which earned Lambda Literary Award nominations) and *Man of My Dreams.* Jordan is also the author of *But Darling, I'm Your Auntie Mame,* a history of the fictional icon Auntie Mame created by Patrick Dennis. As a senior publicist and staff writer with The Walt Disney Studios for thirty years, Jordan worked on the marketing campaigns of over 500 live-action and animated feature films. Now an expat from America, Richard lives in England in a cozy 16th-century cottage (with his husband and an amiable ghost).

You can contact Richard at **www.Richardtylerjordan.com**.

ALSO BY RICHARD TYLER JORDAN